William Knight

GW00391773

THE
ALGORITHM

STANDING HARE

First 100 Edition

Copyright © 2021 William Knight
http://www.williamknight.info

ISBN 978-0-473-56896-2

This book is a work of fiction. Names, characters, businesses, organisations, places and events are either the product of the authors imagination or are used fictitiously. Any resemblance to actual persons, living or dead, events or locations is entirely coincidental.

http://www.williamknight.info

Any sufficiently advanced technology is indistinguishable from magic.

Arthur C. Clarke

Prologue

On the day Claus Schneider burned to death, he failed to notice the dawn. He was sitting on a black leather chair in front of three monitors, hunched and hooded over a keyboard, and surrounded by high concrete walls in the basement of a Frankfurt office block. The first watery rays of morning arrived without drawing his attention. Lit only by the blue glow of monitors on top of scattered desks, the basement remained in deep shadow.

All through the night and with precision focus, he tapped on his keyboard and uploaded code onto 10,000 network nodes. He watched the system core awaken and begin to learn. He toggled the adversarial-training intelligence and tested the algorithm with a million simulated users.

Now he was satisfied. Data streamed down his screens. He smiled. Looked around. His smile broadened. He opened a drawer under the desk and took out a bottle of Weiss beer, his favourite drink after pulling an all-nighter. He opened it with a satisfying pop, put it to his lips and savoured the malty, sharp flavour. He reclined in his chair, pulled back his hoodie and lifted his Converse-clad feet onto the desk. He stretched out. He allowed his night-long coding high to dissipate and finally noticed daylight seeping through the high rectangular windows.

He took another swig of beer as his colleague stirred beside him.

"Pretty weird night, huh, Stefan?" he said. "Stefan! Wake up, dick head. It's working." He reached out to push Stefan's chair.

Stefan sat up. He took off his glasses and rubbed his eyes. He checked the monitor. "Is it going?"

"Perfect."

"Shit."

"Yeah, man." He laughed and swigged the beer. "You want one?"

"Fuck yeah! Danke."

The developer pulled out another beer and handed it to Stefan. "And what about the boss? I don't know what kind of shit those two were up to last night, but it fucking worked."

"What *was* that?"

"Weird occult shit. They left oil and candlewax round the monitor." He laughed. "The boss has a psycho wife."

"No kidding. Beautiful, though. In the candlelight, I mean."

"You got a hard on for the boss's wife?"

"Haven't you? She's gorgeous."

The developer took a long gulp of beer and concentrated on the code scrolling down the screen.

"We shouldn't have been watching," Stefan said.

"They didn't see us." The developer finished his beer and pulled out another. He chinked his colleague's bottle and took a long drink.

"Do you think the training is completely finished?" Stefan asked.

"It's still learning. But now it's open to the internet, it's soaking it all up. It's gone way past the training."

"Fuck." Stefan checked the scrolling data. Something puzzled him. "Did you see that?" He pointed at the screen.

The developer picked up the mouse and clicked into the data. "Freaky."

"Do you think that's us?"

"Can't be. How would it know?"

"It's like it's watching. What does that say?"

"I can't make it out. It might be *consumed.*"

"Yeah, that's it. *Consumed in flames.* Hah! Maybe it's not ready."

At that instant the fire alarm blared into life and emergency red lighting flooded the basement.

"Fuck, man. That made me jump. My heart's thumping. It can't be a drill this time. We'd better get out. It's time to knock off anyway. I'm knackered."

They stood, lifted phones and wallets from the table and

tucked them into pockets. "This is a fucking weird coincidence."

"It'll be a false alarm. Nothing to worry about."

The developer turned back to the screen. And then, like crows might circle and finally settle on the high branches of a tree, his expression transformed from puzzlement to shock — and then to horror.

1

Every time Christian Jarvik threw a party he cringed that his wine glasses would have other people's lips on them. He despised the way casual acquaintances would traipse across his carpets in their unwiped shoes, pass outside and trample his lawn. Somebody was certain to move an ornament out of alignment, and after a few glasses were downed he would find splashes of urine around the toilet.

His guests were mostly lawyers or supporting staff from Beaufort & Soames. A collection of ambitious consultants dedicated to turning deals for corporate clients. Justice had nothing to do with this brand of law. He had yet to find anybody who cared much about justice. Not that he ever expected to; he hadn't joined the acquisitions department of a major English law firm to right the wrongs of humanity. He joined it for security, to support his wife in her own crusading law career, to pay for their children's private schooling and to prove his intellectual worth. He wasn't always certain to whom he was trying to prove his worth: his father, perhaps? His wife? Himself? He tried not to think about it.

But at six foot one, wearing beige cotton trousers, a tucked-in sky-blue shirt open at the collar and a dark-blue summer blazer, he was indistinguishable from many of the guests. Only his blond hair, Nordic-blue eyes and trim figure gave any signal he was different from the 350 other corporate lawyers at the firm.

He didn't enjoy the parties, he didn't enjoy the people that much, but he recognised the essential power of entertaining to advance his career. And he always had to know exactly who he was competing against.

One by one he uncorked a dozen red-wine bottles. He positioned them on the sideboard in a formal line, evenly spaced, with the labels facing the room so guests could choose their preferred varietal.

"Where's the merlot, Rachel?" he shouted through to his wife in the kitchen. "Did we pick some up?"

"Leave the girl alone and give me a drink."

Christian turned to face a dark-haired woman in a hip-hugging maroon dress marching towards him holding out a wine glass. With her perfectly styled hair moving like a frozen bonnet, her smooth Botoxed forehead, dark eyeliner and flesh-coloured lipstick she could have come straight off the set of a Beverly Hills mini-series. She rounded the table, breezing past the hors d'oeuvres so the linen cloth wafted over the sushi — before he fully recognised her.

"Melissa. I didn't hear you come in." He briefly wondered if she dressed like this when she joined the Bristolian public shopping at Cribbs Causeway. But of course Melissa didn't do her own shopping — unless it was at the opening of an art gallery. Bristol had plenty of those to entertain her.

"Never mind that," she said, waggling the glass in front of him. "I like to arrive early and unannounced so I get the pick of the wine. That red looks good."

"Yes. It is." He picked the bottle up. "It might need to breathe a little more."

Melissa smiled, the lines around her eyes creased and pushed up furrows of foundation. She shook her head and held the glass up.

Christian poured the wine and watched her as she took a sip and licked her artificially plumped lips. Lipstick bled into tiny lines around her mouth.

"That's better. It's so civilised to drink in the afternoon," she said.

"Is Howard with you?" He put the bottle back in its place on the sideboard.

"Howard?" She took a good gulp. "Of course. He's parking."

Christian led her into the kitchen — making sure to fold the tablecloth down as he passed — where his wife thrust a bowl of pitta bread into his hands.

"That's for the table outside," she said. "Melissa, I'm so pleased you could make it. I can't believe it's been so long. Christian and Howard see each other every day and — when was the last time we spoke?"

"Wives get forgotten by these corporate monsters." Melissa swirled her drink so the wine raced around the side of the glass. She stared into the liquid, then downed the lot. "As soon as they get power and status they forget their families." She forced a smile. "And we're the ones who helped get them there. Ironic." She studied Rachel's white blouse and dark maternity trousers. "Howard says you're expecting."

Rachel took Christian's arm. "I'm twenty-six weeks and the excitement is building."

"Our second," Christian said.

"Well, cheers to that," Melissa said, turning to Rachel. "Plenty for you to get on with while your husband's at work." She looked into her empty glass. "Oh."

"Allow me." Christian put the pitta down and reached for a bottle. He filled her glass to within a smidge of the top.

They exchanged small talk. More guests arrived. Melissa stood by the sideboard while Christian and Rachel greeted them all personally. The men, mostly work colleagues in their forties and fifties, wore the flush of alcohol consumption like tattoos and the paunch of business lunches like cummerbunds. The women, all wives and girlfriends, wore a variation of designer heels, short cocktail dresses and pearl necklaces or gold chains. Christian opened the patio doors to let his visitors mingle indoors and out. He tried to ignore the thought of muddy shoes carrying soil into the house.

"Are you looking forward to the baby?" Melissa asked after a long silence during which she appeared to be bored.

"I'm looking forward to a boy this time."

"We don't know if it's a boy," Rachel said.

"It's a boy." Christian closed one eye, hunched his back and mimicked an Irish accent. "The waters are telling me, so they are."

"Would that be the waters with your whisky?"

"I've not had a drink yet. Talking of which, I could do with one. I think everybody's arrived."

He pulled a couple of bottles from the fridge and was struggling to unscrew the tops when his daughter rushed into the kitchen followed by a gang of younger children, all under her considerable five-year-old influence. They ranged from swift runners at the front to rolling toddlers bringing up the rear.

"Daddy, you're the megalodon!" Rachel had tied Jessica's white-blonde hair into a neat ponytail with a pink ribbon and dressed her in a white party frock.

Christian picked her up and plonked her on the table. "Hey, how's my favourite girl? Is she ready for the dinner table yet?" He squeezed her knee. "Not much fat on her legs. What's she like round the middle?"

Jessica howled as he tickled her waist. "Come and play sharks in the garden."

"Sharks?" Christian leant forward, placed Jessica on the floor and stared at the gang of children. "Sharks have to catch their supper, and it's always little children."

The kids rushed out of the door screaming.

"Sharks before drinks then," Christian shrugged.

Between amusing children, he busied himself serving guests, opening wine and helping conversation to flow. Later, when he went into the lounge to collect glasses, Howard Beaufort was standing by the baby grand, inspecting one of the Jarvik family photographs taken from an orderly cluster of fencing trophies and photos arranged on the top. Getting on for sixty, Christian's boss had the look of a man who never exercised and had slowly shrunk in height and grown round the middle since middle age. His close-clipped grey hair covered only the back third of his head; his bald forehead and temples reflected the light coming in through the lounge window. Howard held the photo at arm's length and squinted to bring the image into focus. Melissa watched from the sofa with her drink never more than a few inches from her mouth.

"My parents," Christian said. "I've lost them now. We've got family in Denmark, but my father was in Salisbury until he died."

Howard put the picture down just out of line with the others and picked up another.

"That's Rachel's parents. Diane is alive, well, and in the garden," Christian said. He pointed through the window to where Diane was kneeling next to a gang of toddlers beneath the spreading canopy of a lime tree, blowing bubbles through a loop of plastic. "Her dad can't be here. He suffers from Alzheimer's so he has a nurse to help look after him. He's doing okay for the moment."

"That's tough," Howard, said reflectively. He looked back at the photos and ornaments. "And the piano? Do you play?" He twiddled the ice around his gin and tonic in the same frantic way his wife had swirled her wine earlier. He held the tumbler close to his paunch.

"I play a bit. My dad was a musician. Came over here in the Seventies to teach."

Christian's dad had been a musician all his life. Growing up in Copenhagen in the Sixties he found a release from social engagements by performing his own interpretation of the classics. Sometimes frowned upon by purists, he nonetheless pursued a career and ended up in England where his brand of easy-listening piano found an audience willing to pay for the pleasure. But the popularity bought copycats and the copycats came along with a distorted view of copyright. Not only did he not make money from the records he made, he lost all the family's money defending his right to make money from them. Christian remembered the years after his mother died as being filled with long trips to London, meetings with the record company and endless sitting on benches waiting for his dad to come out of court hearings. It was probably on one of those long trips that Christian decided he would become a lawyer. Perhaps some friendly advice from a solicitor, maybe a barrister patted him on the head, or perhaps some legal language crept into his subconsciousness and formed neural networks that fired deliciously when exposed to obscure phrases. He didn't remember the exact circumstances of his conversion to the law, but he always felt it was inevitable.

Howard nodded as if he was deeply connected with the history of the Jarviks in Britain. A neat lawyer's trick.

"I fence still, for the competition. But I run to relax," Christian said as a way of moving the conversation on.

"That's right, I remember. You're very fit. I can't imagine how you find the time. I can only manage eighteen holes at the weekend and the odd break sailing to Cowes. I couldn't possibly play an instrument or go for a run."

"When on earth did you last play golf, Howard?" Melissa sneered as if it was the most unlikely thing she'd ever heard.

Howard snapped his head round to look at her. *Shut up*, he said with his eyes.

Christian looked away and took the moment to tap the picture back into place. "I took the fencing far more seriously while I was at university."

"Exeter, wasn't it?"

Christian nodded. He took a drink.

"Straight law?" Howard knew all this. He didn't run the firm without knowing every detail of his senior staff's work and personal life. Christian sensed he was circling.

"Double honours: Law and Economics. It's useful to have the economics background on something like the Burnham accounts."

His boss looked directly at him, "I've been meaning to ask how it's going. Everything is on track, I assume?" He smiled and patted Christian on the upper arm. "It had better be."

"They're tough negotiators. Dave Hinchley at Epoch IT is like a pitbull with a rat when he suspects an opening. But it's going well. It *will* be sewn up by Quarter Three. I've never known a man like Dave. He doesn't do comedy, does he?"

Howard took a sip of his drink without taking his eyes off Christian. "Dave, yes. He's a tough bastard that's for sure. It's to your credit you've impressed him. Keep an eye on him — he's liable to keep looking for improvements on the deal. Is he working well with the team?"

Christian wondered where the question came from. Most of the negotiations involved himself and William Thorpe — one of his team members — so contact was limited. "Dave liaises well with William, or we go via Dave's EA. Frankly, though, most of it's lawyer to lawyer, as you'd expect. No problem."

"Dave can be slippery. We've always got to keep our options

open. Not be caught out by a sudden wind change, as it were."

Melissa suddenly stood up next to her husband. "Do you have to talk about your piffling work? This is supposed to be a social occasion." She smiled at Christian and blinked.

Jesus, is she batting her eyes at me?

"My husband is utterly hopeless at small talk," she said. "I'll have to take you away from him."

She moved to take Christian's arm, but he took her glass and used it as a barrier. "What can I get you to drink? Merlot, is it?"

"Yes."

"And Howard, can I get you something?"

"Gin and tonic?"

Rachel was in the kitchen with Jessica swinging on her legs trying to get her to play hide-and-seek. She popped an olive into her mouth. "Don't you find them terribly, terribly dull?"

Christian shrugged. "Means to an end. And I am one of *them*." He put down the glasses. "You know where we get our money from. Help me with these drinks? Gin and tonic for Howard and the cheapest red we have for Melissa."

Christian could remember only one time when a career in law for him was in doubt, and that was a year after he met Zach Hunter at the Exeter Fencing Society, the autumn term after he was supposed to have finished his first degree. He returned to university to face the ignomiy of resitting his exams. His instinct was to hide in his digs, but the need for exercise drove him to the fencing club. He pushed the swing doors open and looked inside the hall. He felt the weight of his fencing bag in his left hand — and the weight of having been away without explanation on his shoulders.

Everything was normal. As before. As if they'd not missed him. Freshers on the wooden benches waited for a bout and watched attentively, unsure of the proceedings. Older students practised lunges in pairs or in front of the ballet mirror, and on the three pistes, sabreurs clashed sabres in explosive attacks. Sweaty air tingled his senses. He breathed in deeply and walked in as confidently as he could imagine.

"Fuck me, man, you look buggered." Zach was never likely to greet anybody with a simple "Hello". That would be a cliché. Everything about Zach had to be different. Today he had cut his black hair into a mohawk that stood an inch off the top of his head and trimmed his beard into a point at the chin.

Christian hadn't seen Zach at the noticeboard, just inside the door. Perhaps it was the mohawk, but the oversight annoyed him. Irritated. As if an opponent had made a cheap hit before his guard was up.

"You look fucked," Zach said. "Anyway, shouldn't you have some high-powered job in the city by now? How'd the finals go? What've you been doing the last four months? Shagging your way through the fresher population while on speed?"

Christian laughed. A reluctant, trying laugh, but a laugh nonetheless. He didn't want Zach to know. Not yet. Perhaps not ever. But Zach had an ability to wheedle out the truth if he was given a small opening. "Maybe. Are we going to fight or what? Nice hair." He dropped his bag and picked out a sabre. He swished it through the air just above his feet.

Zach watched with his head to one side. "That was a diversion if ever I heard one. Maybe, as in *yes* you've been shagging your way around campus, or maybe as in *no* but you're not going to say. So if it's the first, you're going to have to spill the beans over beer when we finish, and if it's something else, you can tell me now." Zach wrapped an arm round Christian's neck and pulled him in tight. "CJ. CJ. Where the fuck have you been?"

Christian had hoped to avoid this. He'd hoped to avoid being questioned in the first place by turning up late and getting straight into a bout, but he'd also hoped Zach would let him off the hook by displaying his rare sensitive side. No such luck.

"Let's fight first, and I'll spill the beans later. It's not what you think. No women involved. No shagging. And no finals, actually."

"What?"

Christian shrugged. He stared up to the hall's vaulted, sixteenth-century ceiling. "I bummed it, mate. I took off.

11

Couldn't face it."

"But you're the golden child of the law. The Rumpole of the Bailey, the Atticus Finch, the Perry Mas—"

"Let's leave it. Fight first. Then beer. Then... Well. I'll probably start crying on your shoulder."

Zach shrugged. "Thrashing it is, then. Pick up thy sword, sir."

Christian beat Zach soundly. Not only in sets, but in style, technique, strategy and creativity. He was back. He loved it. He loved the constrained breathing in a fencing mask. The constriction of the jacket and gauntlet, and he loved the lure and the kill. Zach loved these things too, but was too impulsive to dedicate time to his technique. For Zach it was showmanship; for Christian it was war.

After the bout they sat on benches at the back of the hall recovering from the exertion. Zach pulled out a couple of cans of special brew from his fencing bag and tossed one to Christian. "Here you go, mate. Not sure I'll ever beat you in a serious match."

Christian inspected the can. He hesitated.

"Mate," Zach said. "What is life for?"

The cans opened with a fizz, both spilling foamy beer onto the floor. "You'll beat me one day, perhaps," Christian said. "When the celestial bodies of earth and moon are cleaved and the oceans have sublimed. When the last homo sapiens imbibes the ultimate bead of water. When the heavenly bodies are engulfed by an expanding sun, or when, let's think, you practise more and get better."

"Ha, ha. You been eating poetry? Is that why you buggered off? To learn some long words?"

Christian took a slug of his beer. "Nah. I bottled it."

"You?"

"I couldn't take it. Went a bit mad, actually."

"For real? You're not pulling my plonker?"

"You remember that mock paper I took about March. Including the viva?"

"Not really. Too busy chasing Debbie round the Union."

"Oh, yeah. That's right. How'd that end up?"

"She's... well, a bit bonkers. Keep this under your hat, but she went mental. I had to let her down gently."

"What?"

"Yeah. She's moved to Cardiff. I think she's carrying on with psychology there. I don't know, she…" Zach looked across the room at the fencers. He took a drink. He shrugged.

"You liked her, didn't you?"

"It was love, man. Love, sweet love. You don't know what you've got till it's gone."

"Jesus. Pave that paradise."

They drank in silence for a few minutes. The club activities carried on around them. Sabres clashed with sabres and referees shouted scores in the brief lull between points. Christian imagined that Zach, staring into his beer, was thinking about Debbie.

Christian didn't do girlfriends. Not that he didn't want to do girlfriends, it was just he found his work too intense to think of anything else, and actually, he loved the law. He loved what he was doing too much to have time to waste chasing skirt or falling in love or fucking. Zach, on the other hand, had fallen in love about five times in two years and *nearly* fallen another half-dozen times. It was his thing. The degree was secondary to the sex, love and breakups. But Christian had no doubt Zach would come away with a first-class degree in Computer Science when the time came — if it came. His friend was perpetually torn between running around with a sword in his hand or with hiking boots on his feet, and the academic pull of writing a binomial-sort in as few bytes as possible.

Fate always brought them closer. By now Christian was supposed to be ensconced on a professional journey with Barker Flint & Farrier or some other Tier One law firm in the city. Instead, he was retaking his final year in a bid to sit the papers he needed, and drinking Special Brew with his mate.

He had thought he could get away without explaining his failure — he was embarrassed about it — but then Zach said, "What happened then? After the mock?"

"It was a bit shit. Like a tsunami of brain farts all rising at once in a crescendo of anxiety. I did the viva and was so over-prepared I didn't know how to approach the questions. I had too many options, too much choice. I got overwhelmed. I sat in front of the panel and wibbled my way through a sentence or two before changing my mind and coming at it from a completely different angle. And then, after a few repeats of doing that, I went crimson with embarrassment. They stopped the interview and gave me a chance to get my composure back. The professor asked if I was all right to continue, but by then I was in this overwhelmed state of anxiety and I could barely see the fucking chairs let alone answer questions on commercial warrants in copyright-infringement cases. I flunked it. Totally, utterly fucked it up, as if I was a first-year botanist attempting a paper on seventeenth-century Spanish literature."

"Shit! Bloody botany."

"Yeah. Well. I got a pass to take the finals, but the professor took me aside and said I needed more time to focus my arguments if I wanted a First." Christian broke off and stared towards the bar. "I don't know, Zach. I couldn't handle the idea I might fail. I've never had that. Always been the winner. All of a sudden I doubted everything I knew. I doubted what the truth was, and feared I had been fooling myself. When you dream, and you begin to think it might be a dream, but you're too afraid to do something crazy in case it's real, it does your head in. Well, it did *my* head in."

"Sounds like a bit of a trip. You been taking anything?"

"This is me. Hey, hello? Christian Jarvik doesn't do drugs. That's your domain."

Zach shrugged.

"So I started studying harder; both the law and the economics papers in case I'd missed something. That's when I stopped coming to the club. About last March. I had to find a way of making sense of all the material, not just gorging on it and spewing it out. And I had to put that across to the examiners. And the more I studied to dig myself out of the knowledge hole, the deeper it got and the more choices I faced. No question was simple enough that I couldn't drone on for hours on end about seeming connections that didn't exist."

"Like your neurotransmitters got out of whack. Actually, a lot like being on acid."

"I'll take your word for it. In the end, I couldn't take it. The doctor put me on Prozac for depression and when that didn't work I tried Xanax to calm me down. Well, *that* worked. I stopped altogether. I just left. Got the fuck out of here. I went home to my dad, spent nearly a month running around Salisbury and across the plains. I must have put in a marathon every other day."

"Shit."

Christian picked up his beer and finished the can. "But I'm back now. Let's have another fight. I need to beat somebody."

Christian had suffered no major hiccups to his career in the fifteen years since, and now he was on the brink of a vote to become managing partner. He did love selling or buying private firms. It was shallow, superficial and greedy, a Magna Carta away from why he'd gone into law, but he felt the buzz of owners realising their dream of an early exit, and he definitely felt the satisfaction of the bonuses. He got a vicarious kick from helping others make riches. But it had its costs, and here he was seeking political advantage by holding a cocktail party.

The afternoon passed quickly. He kept his ear out for any business conversations while making sure the drink flowed and the hors d'oeuvres circulated. He spent time with the firm's chief accountant — Geoff McMahon, a red-haired wiry man with a wavy comb-over and failed sense of humour — and successfully avoided getting caught up in conversation about the ongoing blitz on company expenses. The entire firm found the subject of expenses laughable, given the loose rein Howard allowed them all with their claims. Expenses remained one of the perks of the job, and Christian thought Howard had always realised the role that part-business-part-pleasure junkets took in the smooth running of the firm.

When all the guests had finally left, Christian found Rachel seated on her own in the kitchen checking out her Twitter and Instagram accounts on her laptop. He had not seen much of her for the latter part of the party — he'd been too busy networking.

"You okay? Not like you to disappear during a party. That's more my style," he said.

She smiled. "I'm a bit tired."

"Well, you're bound to be." He pulled up a stool beside her. Sensing a sadness in her, he picked her hand from her lap and held it. He peered into her eyes, trying to read her mind. "Come on. Tell me."

"It's the pregnancy."

He didn't speak but frowned comically.

She laughed. "Really it's nothing." She tried to stare him out, but he wouldn't let her off the hook. "Okay," she said. "It's the work. This deal you're on. It's not going to keep you away from the family for longer than you are already? It won't change you, will it? Melissa is awfully bitter."

Christian couldn't predict if it meant longer hours at this stage. It meant an early bonus, but he hadn't considered the effort. "She's a bit of a monster," he said.

Rachel smiled.

Christian put his hand to her cheek. "It's going to give us security. We'll have a new baby, more nursery fees, you'll have to take more time off. This contract's likely to set us up for the future." He rested his hands on Rachel's stomach and rubbed her swollen belly. "It'll be terrific. It's what we've worked for."

She smiled. "Thank you."

"What for?"

"For being so loving. I want this for you."

"Well, it's not definite yet. There's another round of negotiations, and the final celebrations can't begin until the contract's signed. Six to eight weeks, we think. It will be a tough phase."

"You know we're fine as we are, don't you?"

"What do you mean?"

"I only want you to work for promotion if it's what *you* want. Not for prestige or because you think it's best for the family. We already have a terrific lifestyle, and when the baby's toddling I want to go back to work full time. There's no pressure for you to earn more." She looked into his eyes. "You do want it, don't you?"

"Yes. Definitely. Jesus." He grasped both her hands, "I have worked for this since university. If this deal goes through, we'll be in the news and in demand. I'm going to win this."

She stared at him. He wondered momentarily if she believed his enthusiasm. He certainly didn't always believe his own talk, but he kept that side hidden: wouldn't he rather be hiking across Dartmoor, exploring sinkholes in Venezuela or becoming world sabre champion instead of paying off a heavy mortgage and front-loading his pension plan?

As if she had read his mind, Rachel said, "Oh my God, I forgot to tell you. I got a message from Zach."

"Where?"

"Just before everybody arrived. Online. Social media. eFace. The one you've never bothered with." Rachel fingered the mouse pad on her laptop. Closed a few windows and opened up eFace. "I hope I can find it again. These things just disappear. Here it is. He's back with Lilith in Frankfurt, and they're coming to Bristol. He says, to live."

"Jesus. When?"

"A couple of weeks. They've bought a flat."

Christian found it hard to be enthusiastic that his best friend was going to suddenly reappear after two years without so much as a postcard. A profound unsettled feeling rushed over him. Zach had left suddenly and their friendship still needed to mend; if it could be mended at all. Memories of the last time they'd spoken kept turning up in Christian's thoughts like rotten weed on a high tide.

"What do you think?" Rachel said.

"Well. I'm pleased he's not dead. It's great. I suppose. Yes, I'm pleased. Does it say what he's been doing? Where did he find Lilith? I can't believe they'd get back together. Why are they coming here?"

"You read it. You have an IQ of a hundred and forty and I'm reading messages because you're afraid of the computer."

"I'm not afraid."

"Really? So you're a whizz with social media?"

"I just don't bother with it."

"Set up an account. You can send a message to Zach all by

yourself. You might even get answers to some of your questions. Here." Rachel passed him the laptop.

"Hasn't he left a phone number?"

"I know you're not hesitating because of social media. Don't you think it's time you forgave him?"

Christian thought for a moment. Zach's last words to him had been "You're a fucking cretin." But he didn't feel so much that he should forgive Zach, more that it was the other way round.

"He had a point. That deal really broke him," he said.

"It wasn't your fault. Zach knows that. And he had other things to sort out. Join the modern world. Go on. I'll do the bedtime routine."

Ever since Christian had met Zach they had rarely exchanged cross words. Conversations between them were always good-humoured. Sure, one would take the piss out of the other, then they would enter into a pretend-argument like a good bout of fencing. But the loss of Zach's job had hit him hard, and his mood had blackened. Christian was full of guilt: his firm had been responsible for the sale that put Zach out of work.

Zach's words still rung like a discordant buzzer in Christian's memory. They'd been at the Coach and Horses, sitting at a small table, sharing a beer after a training session.

"Your company fucked me," Zach said. "Not just that I've lost my job and my work's been stolen, but it's taken my confidence. And now I find out you helped them with the IPO on the back of my work. I read that's twenty mill each. Those thieving fuckers."

Zach wanted to sue his previous employers, to claw back what he saw as his share, but Christian tried to deflect the idea and found himself in the uncomfortable position of protecting his firm's interests against his best friend. He tried to sound as reasonable as possible. "Look, in general terms, they've got you because of the evidence you developed your ideas on their computers and during the day when you were supposed to be working for them. And even if that wasn't the case, the contract you signed with them meant they had a claim on anything you were doing in your spare time. It's harsh, but that's what most employment contracts say."

"But you know that's not how it was. I took the system to them, they employed me for my knowledge, to work on what they had failed at. All the work, *all* of it, it's all my ideas. You know that. I started it in your flat. Before I even had the job."

"But on their clock, Zach."

"It was different. Their work was about specific intelligence. What I've done is solve intelligence in the general sense. It's good at everything."

"Any judge or tribunal is going to look at the broadest comparison. They won't get the difference. Was it a computer system? Tick. Was it about intelligence? Tick. Was he on the payroll? Tick. I'm sorry, mate, they've stolen it and sold it on. I don't think there's a case you can win."

"You think they stole it?"

Christian shrugged and picked up his beer. "I don't know. It's what you can prove that matters, not what you think. It's business, not personal. You're going to have to be more savvy next time."

Zach's face flashed anger. "You saying I'm not savvy?"

"I didn't mean it like that, Zach. Sorry."

"Lay off the patronising. It's harder and more competitive than you can see from the top of Beaufort's ivory tower. An MBA and a law degree don't count for shit in the real world."

"What's got into you?" Christian said. "I've worked my arse off to get to the top of that firm. Real study and learning, not pissing around enjoying myself playing with puzzles and smoking dope."

"Is that what you fucking think? That it's a fucking laugh working from seven in the morning till ten at night, six days a week, so corporate wankers like you can take all the rewards? You think I enjoy it?" Zach stared fiercely into Christian's eyes for a moment before dropping his gaze and picking up his pint.

Both men fell silent. They drank. Pub life continued as if nothing had passed between them, but Christian felt as if they'd been at a crossroads and had both taken different routes into the future.

Putting down his empty pint glass, Zach said, "There's one thing I never quite understood. How did they get the information

I'd been using their computers? They had no reason to suspect or even care. Why did they even look? The takeover was about their system, not mine, and then suddenly the emphasis changed and I became the focus. Why did that happen?" He leaned forward. "But now I realise the only person who knew anything about what I was doing was you. Did you say something?"

"Of course not. It's a big firm. This was handled by the London office. I couldn't have known. The firm is tight on security concerning these takeovers. One hand never knows what the other is working on. You'll get over it, mate. Just rewrite it."

And that was the point at which Zach called Christian a fucking cretin and barged his way out of the pub, not to be heard of for two years. The memory was still fresh and still painful for Christian, but he thought that if Zach was back, and in contact, some element of forgiveness must have occurred.

With Rachel on bedtime duty he pushed his anxiety deep into his psyche and tried to ignore it. He spent the next hour setting up a profile on eFace.

Once the tedious effort of opening an account was over, he befriended his wife and sent a message to Zach. He then settled down to explore his so-called feed, made up of Rachel's friends talking about the state of the government, interspersed with cat videos. It was like a window on a semi-drunk pub conversation: two earnest friends attempted to hold a current-affairs debate while another threw in quips, and a fourth interrupted to talk about soft furnishings. And then an instant message popped up from Zach.

"Hey CJ. You're online. Stressed out by it yet? LOL. Great to hear from you. I hoped the message would get through. So sorry, I got rid of everything after Bristol. I lost all my contacts. You know. Couldn't face it. I wanted to put the whole thing in the past. We didn't know enough, couldn't predict it. Like you said, it was business. But look, we're going to be moving over in a couple of weeks. Gonna be great. We've got a place on St John's Road, by the railway cutting."

"Buying a house doesn't sound like you," Christian typed. "Lilith got you under the thumb?"

"No man. Far from it. We're in business together. The

software I've been working on for so long. The engine. It's working. I knew it. It just needed Lilith's input. We've put it in an app. We're getting downloads in the thousands every day. You should try it. Give it a go."

A blue underlined hyperlink popped up: "The Algorithm. What does your future hold?"

"Sure. I'll try it out."

"See you in a couple of weeks. Keep the beers cold buddy."

Christian hovered his mouse over the link, but didn't click.

Nonsense.

2

Dawn did not come as enlightenment to the world, but as a grey damp blanket of cold. Christian's house caught the prevailing westerlies as they burst along Avon Gorge and spilled over the Sea Walls. He stood in the porch and watched the rain sweep past the house, carried horizontally by the wind. Even before he got dirty, he looked forward to getting clean.

He stretched to smooth the reluctance in his legs. He started his stopwatch and set off into the wind feeling like a martyr, while Rachel slept quietly in a warm bed.

The Downs were empty. No surprises. There weren't many brave enough to face the rain so early on a dark morning. The forecast said the wind would increase during the day, swing round to the north and turn gale force for the evening. It was predicted to be a stormy few days, with a break mid-week and then worse weather for the weekend.

He splashed along the road, avoiding standing water and taking wide arcs around puddles collecting against the kerbside. The first ten minutes were the most challenging — when his lungs fought for air and his muscles screamed — but they were also the start of ecstasy. When they were over, he was able to run faster and longer than he'd thought possible. The body respired aerobically, oxygen debt was paid, and endorphins kicked in like bursts of calm energy.

Once running at an optimum, he was enclosed in a personal cocoon formed by the rain. His feet hit the road with a soft splash and the spray-drenched wind stung his face, but he remained detached from physical events. He watched his body move round the Downs as if viewing it through a web-cam.

As he rounded the sweeping corner by the Sea Walls, the wind turned to his back and pushed him along. The crows had abandoned their usual stalking grounds in the open spaces and had gathered in sheltered dips next to woodland along the gorge. They roamed between clumps of grass, periodically inserting their scrawny-grey beaks into the soft earth like daggers, thrusting through the surface and pulling up worms. They were joined by a pair of ravens today. These stood apart from the crows, majestic and black. They watched him from behind black reflective beads, and when he ran closer they hopped away from the path's edge, keeping their distance.

He sped up until he was at full stretch. Running fast in the rain increased the impression of being in a bubble. Muddy water sprayed up his back, splashed off his heels, landed on his bare neck and dripped between his vest and his skin. He shivered, relishing the thought of later cleanliness in a hot shower. Rain dripped down his face and slewed off his chin.

At his best pace Christian got to work by 6.45 a.m., with the thought of the last time he'd seen Zach as fresh in his mind as a glass of iced water. He showered on Level One and took the lift to his office wearing the standard pin-stripe uniform but without a tie. He opened the blinds and stood by the window, surveying the inner ring road as it crossed the Avon. Building traffic had backed up from the roundabout at Temple Meads; it would get worse for the next two hours, lull briefly mid-morning, and then build again around lunchtime. He preferred to beat the morning rush if driving, and if not, he would run through town then shower and change.

His room was high enough to see beyond the river, beyond Bedminster and to the southern Cotswolds. Even under low cloud the misty green landscape was an invitation to play. Now Zach was back Christian hoped to join his friend in some long walks in the Mendips or even a trip to Dartmoor. Assuming they got on at all.

Christian sat at his desk, flicked on his computer and brought up the Burnham report. It had been perfect for more than a week now, with nothing but a few changes in emphasis. He smiled. He was proud.

He scrolled through the document: risks, opportunities, threats, strategy, conclusions. Three hundred pages outlining a merger Dave Hinchley's Epoch IT should enter to exploit a revolutionary technique for building computer intelligence. Beauforts was about more than just contracts and takeovers: it was about strategy and aggressive exploitation of markets. It found and proposed market-defining partnerships.

His mobile vibrated.

It was Howard Beaufort. Christian had been expecting him to call, as he usually did, but this time it was a text. Texting was unusual for Howard. Christian replied: "On my way."

He used the stairs to Howard's office rather than take the lift. The call buttons on the ground were permanently alight between seven and eight as juniors flooded into the lower floors, and the idea of their grubby hands, fresh from the streets, all over the buttons sometimes made Christian nervous. The stairway was always clear and, apart from a little stale air, a trouble-free way to move around the building. He wafted the door a few times to encourage the air to mix then realised what his actions might look like and switched his thoughts to his work. He marched in confidently, heels clicking on the concrete steps as if he was inside a bunker.

The upper executive floors were visited by invitation only, and Christian was thinking how he might one day be issuing his own visitor requests when he opened the fire door and stepped into the atrium. His leather soles hit thick mauve carpet. He walked without sound to Howard Beaufort's open office door.

"Ah, Christian. Come in. Sit down."

Christian chose a seat nearest to the coffee table. Howard stood by the wall looking out of the window at the fields beyond the city. The room was mostly dark-grey and black. Colour was provided by the spines of red law books covering an entire wall and amber whisky in a decanter on a side table.

"Are you ready?" Howard said without looking around. His hands were clasped behind his back.

"Yes."

"I *have* read the report. It is excellent. Well done."

"Thank you."

Howard continued to gaze out of the window. "Look at them all down there," he muttered.

"Sorry, I didn't catch that," Christian said. He thought there was more he didn't hear.

Howard turned; his suit jacket open over the white-shirted gut protruding above his trouser line. "Thinking to myself about all of the people on the ground down there." He smiled. "This Burnham report." He laughed. "Burn 'em."

The name had been his idea. A joke about the carve-up of the industry once their client merged with IntelliTech and started to throw their weight about. The partnership would burn the competition. A bit childish, but the old man was amused by it.

Howard sat down in the armchair beside the table. "This deal is going to make an enormous difference to the way companies develop and market software, and your report has nailed a first-class strategy for exploiting Epoch's interests. It's brilliant."

Christian didn't speak, but allowed himself a smile.

"This will certainly clinch the deal." Howard reached out and they shook hands.

"Thank you, Howard. I'm pleased. It's been nearly two years."

Howard nodded. Their hands remained clasped together for a moment too long. Christian began to feel uncomfortable and realised Howard was inspecting him. Calculating.

Finally Howard dropped the handshake. "You're very cautious. That's why you do so well. You back market predictions with clear analytical data from many sources. You're thorough and committed. You can't relax even now the report's ready. Still waiting to pass the rehearsal, get the client go-ahead and then — even though it will be none of your concern — you'll make sure your forecasts materialise and any corrective measures are taken."

Christian enjoyed the praise, but then realised what Howard had said. "How will it be none of my concern, Howard? I thought I would be seeing the deal through to market."

Howard shook his head.

"No?"

Howard smiled. "We don't want to waste your talents making our clients rich. We want you to make Beaufort & Soames —

and Christian Jarvik — rich. We are going to offer you Managing Partner when I step down in six months' time." He paused. "Nothing to say?"

"What *can* I say? I'm shocked. But why are you stepping down? I thought you had years of fight in you. We've held a sweepstake on when you'd retire and I think it's five years before the earliest bet."

Howard laughed. "I'm glad I'm part of office speculation." He stood and walked back to the window. "I've been here for nearly forty years. Ever since my father brought me in to deliver memos around the office, years before email or mobile phones. I've seen this procedure and that process, the introduction of computers and the replacement of low-paid clerical staff with highly paid digital analysts. I was here when we built a nuclear bunker under the building in the Seventies, and when the Queen visited for the silver jubilee. In all that time my wife has evolved from being my most ardent supporter to being a stranger at home, and I've watched my kids grow up from the office. It's time I was a friend to my wife again. And I want to spend time on the golf course and on the yacht while I've still got the strength. It's that simple."

He stopped talking and bit his lip. There was sadness in Howard's eyes, Christian thought, veiled by fierce pride for what he had accomplished. Achievement at great cost. Christian admired him for having the strength to get what he wanted; whatever the price.

"But apart from all that," Howard added, "you still have to make sure the Burnham deal goes through. The rehearsal is vital. You can't afford to make any slips, and I want you to justify my faith. I hope you've got all the answers. Those bastards are going to throw everything at you."

"It's all prepared," Christian said. "They won't trip me up."

"This is the last leg. Make sure of the water before you leave the harbour." Howard smiled at his own sailing metaphor.

Christian returned to his office down the concreted steps with the vague feeling the old man was keeping something to himself.

3

St John's Road in Bristol ran from near Clifton Downs to Clifton village and over the railway cutting taking trains from Temple Meads to Severn Beach. Mature plane trees lined the road on both sides: their patterned bark glowed rainbow colours when wet. Christian and Rachel parked 100 metres from the railway line and watched from the car as a line of young men loaded with cardboard boxes lumbered from the back of a huge Pickfords removal lorry, past a black Audi A7 with German plates, to a large stone house.

"This is near our old flat," Rachel said. "Can we drive past on the way back? I loved that place."

"Sure. How can I forget the cheese madness with the pregnancy? And Zach was living with us working on his computer stuff. Now we're all going to be in the same neighbourhood. Years pass and here we are again."

"You sound sad."

"I'm worried. What do you think? Does this feel right? Zach and Lilith back together again. It's concerning. Not to mention the way we parted last time. I thought he'd never talk to me again."

"You need to let him be himself. Be happy for him. And take it slowly. And anyway, we don't know the full story with Lilith. It sounds like they're doing well."

"They were doing well before…" he trailed off. "Has Zach really recovered?"

Rachel squeezed his knee. "That was ten years ago. We can help them."

Zach and Lilith stood outside the front door directing removal men as the Jarviks stepped onto the gravel drive, Christian carrying a case of champagne. He felt the weight of his anxiety lift from his shoulders when his friend grinned before him in blue jeans and a bright white T-shirt with some zodiac sign on the front. Lilith wore matching clothes, as if they were partners in a rom-com. Zach had clippered his dark hair to a sharp crewcut. Lilith's smile beamed seductively just as it had the day Christian first met her, and her auburn hair tumbled over her shoulders in looping curls. He had forgotten, probably deliberately, how provocative he found her.

A highly emotional ten minutes passed. The women cried. Christian almost cried. But it was Zach's first words that prevented the high emotions getting out of control: "I think you owe me a fiver, mate."

They laughed. The tears dried up. They embraced, put a bottle of champagne on ice and embarked on a tour of the flat. It was the Bristol real deal. A two-bedroom ground floor flat with a wild but mature garden and a gravel drive for off-road parking. Unkempt climbing roses formed a thicket beside the front door and a brick detached garage had access directly onto St John's Road. It reminded Christian of his and Rachel's old flat but surpassed it in grandeur and size. Each room had a central ceiling-rose twice the size of a dustbin lid and the three-metre-high walls were crowned with deep plaster coving depicting grapes, apples and fruiting vines.

Double French doors opened from the master bedroom into the garden, from where Zach explained the flat's only downside was its location next to the railway cutting. "Still, the depth and steepness of the cutting soften the noise to a rattle. And trains only pass every half hour. It's not like it overlooks Clapham Junction."

They settled in the kitchen with the champagne and stood against the units to chat. Men in T-shirts pushed by carrying sofas and cabinets and Pickfords boxes. From time to time Lilith or Zach would pause the conversation to show the removers where to place tables, or grabbed an item to find it a home themselves.

Zach hung his prized Napoleonic sabre on the maroon wall in the bedroom. "And that garden stuff, the chainsaw and strimmer, put those in the outside garage," he said.

Christian laughed. "Don't tell me you've taken up gardening? That's a laugh. Next you'll be planting a shrubbery with a little path running down the middle."

"A path?"

"A path."

"Mate, I've missed you," Zach said, laughing. "This is the first time I've properly owned a place. I'm looking forward to it. We got all the tools for our rental in Frankfurt. I had to bring them."

"I love the high ceilings," Rachel said. "I miss that about our new place. And I love the blue glass in the doors. How did you get this place? It must have cost a bomb. The market's just gone up and up."

"This is the first time we've seen it," Lilith said. "We bought it off the internet. Isn't that mad?" She stared right into Christian's eyes — a little bit in defiance, he thought, perhaps in mischief. His stomach turned with a twist of excitement and the suddenly unwelcome memory of Lilith and Zach's midsummer wedding jumped into his head. Ten years later she was still as beautiful and attractive. In her white T-shirt and jeans she seemed to glow like a street lamp on a frosty night.

"You're joking?" Rachel said.

Zach laughed. "Yep. Fucking crazy. You can buy anything online these days. Don't you love the internet? We did a virtual tour, of course, with our VR goggles. But we took a roll of the dice. Paid off, huh?"

"Zach, I'm stunned. It's an amazing place. But why? I mean, I don't want to get all heavy during a reunion, but what the fuck happened? And, you know, I think I owe you an apology."

Zach shook his head. "It is a bit sudden, I know. We had a disaster at the office. A fire. It propelled our plans."

"A fire? Shit."

Zach nodded. He looked away and up to the ceiling. He put his hand to his mouth. "We lost a couple of young guys. Fucking tragedy."

"Jesus."

"So that was a few months ago. Pretty terrible time we've had of it. Dealing with the fire and the fallout from all that. But, well, it's actually moved us forward. I'm glad to be here."

While Lilith took Rachel outside to set out her plans for a herb garden, Zach explained how devastated he'd been by the theft, two years before, of his software ideas, and how it had made him re-evaluate his life — and in particular his relationship with Lilith. How he'd vowed to get back together. How he'd made her a promise that whatever misfortunes they'd suffered in the past it wouldn't happen again. It couldn't. This time he was going to be ahead of the game, more savvy, always in control, never allowing any harm to come to them. He saw the whole thing as a great premeditated, pre-ordained circle of life. What had happened was meant to happen, only so the future could be better.

"You've become all philosophical on your travels, then," Christian said.

"You can take the piss, Mr Jarvik, but we've hit success. We're doing really well. I always knew that me and Lilith were an unstoppable team. Now we're finally proving it."

"Is that this app thing?"

"*App thing*. Man, you've not downloaded it yet, have you. Why the fuck not? This is my life now. Christian, it's fucking excellent. All the machine-learning and internet-coding I've been putting in over the years has paid off. When I left here, I knew I had to focus on making it even better than it was. Better than what those bastards stole off me. I'd done it. Burned it. Got burned. So I got back into the coding. Picked up where I left off, but with a whole bunch of open-source libraries, cloud platforms and undreamed-of data tools that didn't exist before. Man, things are moving so quick out there. But you know what the magic ingredient turned out to be? And I should have realised from before. Lilith. Honestly, she'd been a mess, and her family thought she'd never recover. But it turns out she's a fucking digital-marketing genius. Two years ago I knew we could build something great. Now, oh boy! It works."

"What does it do?"

"Ha! It's like a horoscope. But a bloody good one."

"What? Russell Grant or Mystic Meg?"

"Amateurs. This isn't a gypsy at the fair or a medium in a cold church hall. This really knows shit."

"I sense a bit of digital marketing going on."

"Download it, man. See for yourself."

Zach had always been excitable about his ventures and had flip-flopped between technological fantasies and epic outdoor pursuits ever since leaving university. Back then, he gave up his degree to chase some programming cash cow or other, but a couple of years later ended up taking groups of undergrads across Dartmoor for weekend hiking trips. Adventuring became his latest thing.

But that was what Christian liked about Zach. His otherness. His disregard for rules, his hatred of regulations. He scoffed at due process and tore up constraints. They could hardly have been more dissimilar. Perhaps it was only the fencing and love of hiking that created a bond between them.

But the adventuring came and went in short phases too, and on the date of the last total eclipse of the sun in England the pair woke up in the middle of Dartmoor. It was a date Christian would always remember, when he met Rachel and Zach announced a life change.

The morning had started early. Christian stood outside his ridge tent looking over the top of Dartmoor towards Haytor. Great lumps of granite scattered the landscape as if God had spilled giant Coco Pops and not bothered to hoover them up. In the foreground half a dozen small tents erupted rudely from the tufts of grass, offending the majestic backdrop with pyramids of orange and blue nylon. The group remained sleeping while the remnants of last night's spirits were finally eliminated by overworked livers. But he and Zach were often first up on these camping trips. As they were now. But the low cloud was a disappointment. The forecast had predicted clear skies.

Zach had his legs crossed, was bare-chested and wearing only shorts. He sat on a canvas groundsheet in front of his tent rolling a spliff. His hair dangled in a long ponytail, offset by a moustache that could have grown on a Cavalier.

"Those clouds are misplaced. Who was in charge of the weather?" Christian asked.

"It'll burn off. Still, a few hours to go and it's midsummer. Have faith in the forecast. The Met Office is never wrong."

"Yes, that's right. Michael Fish has nothing to worry about — no chance of failure here. Move along." Christian pointed at the joint. "Isn't it a bit early for that?"

"This is the most momentous, significance laden day in our pitiful, inconsequential lives, Christian Jarvik. I do not intend to miss the opportunity of being stoned and blind drunk for the first total eclipse of the sun in a thousand years."

"Nineteen fifty-four."

"What?"

"Nineteen fifty-four. There was a total eclipse in the Shetland Isles in Nineteen fifty-four. Not a thousand years."

"You're a nerd. But nonetheless my previous comment still stands. I intend to usher in the midday darkness with a psychedelic mind-set. Come, join me. I think we should sit on the top of that outcrop."

Thirty metres from the tents a granite boulder the size of a small house made for an easy climb. Christian and Zach sat at the top as if they were kings on the top of the world.

Zach sparked up the spliff. "It's like this," he said. "Why spend your time working for the Man when you can have the world in technicolour?" He took a deep draw, held his breath, then blew the smoke high into the air above his head.

"It is bloody terrific out here. I can see why you do it. But are you making any money?"

"What is money?"

"A device to enable the free exchange of goods and services."

"Rhetorical! Have a fucking smoke. Here. Come on, I know you've had sneaky puffs in the past." Zach offered the burning joint pinched between thumb and forefinger. "It ain't gonna kill you. Not this once."

"Fuck it. Okay. It's not every day the sun is eaten by a dragon. I accept." Christian took a long inhale and held the smoke in his lungs before coughing it out.

"Ha! You need to practise. We've got all day. And we have the babes to keep us company. *Excellent*." Zach played a rapid chord on air guitar.

"This isn't Bill and fucking Ted."

"Yes it is. I'm Bill Theodore Esquire. And they love me."

"Is it always the same group of girls?"

"I've not met them all before, just Rachel and her crowd. The others are new. She's pretty hot, don't you think? Rachel, I mean."

"I didn't really get to see last night, I wa—"

"Come off it. I saw you checking her out. She's a nerd, like you. And she's doing law. I'll make a proper introduction."

"Nah, nah, nah." Christian took another puff.

"Yes, yes, yes. It's done. Predicted and foretold." Zach laughed and took the joint from Christian's hand. "Take it carefully, CJ. You don't want to make a fool of yourself." He took a long drag. "How's the new job?"

"I don't start for another month. But it's cool. Good, established traditional firm. Great prospects. Fab final-salary pension plan, none of this stakeholder nonsense. All I've got to do is commit to study for those professional exams and I'm set up for a partnership by thirty-five."

"I have no idea what you just said."

"Shit, man. You have got to think about the future at some point."

"As it happens, I am."

"Yeah? I can't actually see you giving up this gig. *I* may think it's crazy but *you* are in your element. You couldn't make this up. You get to take groups of female students on long hikes across Dartmoor. Protecting them from the elements and teaching them, er, essential survival skills. Like joint-rolling, sleeping-bag sharing, drinking… Am I missing anything?"

"Yeah, well. There's the blow jobs and the shagging, but you might have covered that in the sleeping-bag bit." Zach laughed like a stoned magpie. "Actually, though, I *am* thinking of moving on. The Man will have his jokes. You know this Millennium Bug thing?"

"Yeah, the reason you skipped your finals to make a quick buck."

"I've been offered a contract in Frankfurt. I thought I might take it. It would mean stopping the hikes and guided tours, but, well… I could do with a financial top-up. I'm starting to think that I'd quite like a preposterous sports car paid for by my genius tech ideas. I'm not going to get that clambering over granite tors with an erection."

Christian laughed. "That's true. Are you growing up? But remind me, what happened with the last contract?"

"They were idiots."

"Do you think you can hold down a job? You love it up here, and not just because of the girls — you love the landscape, the walking. Jesus, you even love the weather."

"When I tell you the rate they're willing to pay, you'll want to give up the law and join me. It's going mental out there."

"Spill it, then."

"A ton an hour."

"A hundred pounds?"

Zach nodded. "For that I will keep my mouth shut and fill my wallet."

"Jesus. How do I get trained in computers?"

"Yeah, baby. I love it. I start in a week."

"You're not thinking about it? You've done it?"

"Signed up for a year. See them through the big day. And I predict absolutely nothing will happen when the new century clicks over. Just like if I stay doing this, I predict my bones will perish, my skin will wrinkle and I'll be using sticks by the age of forty. The Millennium Bug might be a total waste of their time, but me staying here is a waste of my own. And anyway, I've got some ideas to take over the world. The future is in machine learning and I know how to make it good. I'll be driving that Porsche 911 before long."

"Doesn't sound like you. You're more of a beaten-up Land-Rover kind of guy."

"But I'm also a show-off. Didn't you know?"

"Yes. That's true."

Zach slid a green tobacco pouch from his back pocket. He

opened it and took out a green pack of cigarette papers. "I think another smoke before we wake the girls, don't you?" He began pulling brown strands of tobacco from the pouch and laying them expertly on a rectangle of cigarette papers. The ritual was as important as the result.

"They'll have a drug policy. A big finance company. You'll have to quit the joints."

Zach laughed. "Germany? I don't think so. I'll be in Amsterdam every weekend with the rest of the team. It's only a short flight, or three hours on a train. Enough time to get loaded up before the games commence."

4

On Friday morning, while Christian worked, Rachel attended the doctor's surgery in an Eighties red-brick building in Clifton. Her second pregnancy was like a dream, she told the doctor. "I can't believe how smoothly this one has gone. Nothing compared to Jessica — hardly any sickness, and even my brain seems to be working this time. The first time it went to mush. After the first month I was scarcely able to read, let alone represent a client."

"Hop on the couch, and lift your blouse," Doctor Hanson said, "and we'll take a look."

Rachel lifted herself carefully onto the padded bench and lay on her back. She pulled up her blue blouse to reveal her swollen stomach. The doctor adjusted the foetal Doppler until they heard the reassuring whooshing of the baby's heart. She looked towards the full-height plastic skeleton in the corner and the eye-test chart behind it on the wall. She found examinations difficult.

He massaged her bump and felt for the baby's head. "Have you been taking pregnancy vitamins?"

"Since before conception."

"Huh, huh." He nodded. "And you've had regular checks with Brenda?"

"Yes. We were here two weeks ago." Rachel had known the GP since they moved to Bristol. With far-receded hair and heavy skin damage on his forehead he was probably beyond retirement age. He was so old-school he still smoked, and the odour of cigarettes lingered on his hands. But Rachel liked him.

"You can cover up now, Mrs Jarvik."

"Call me Rachel. I think that's okay."

He smiled. "Sorry, but I have to be like an automaton at work so I don't get too attached. I prefer to keep it formal, if you don't mind." He helped her down from the couch then sat on the side of the desk while she got dressed behind the screen. When she pushed back the screen, he was examining the twenty-week scan of the baby.

"It's a boy," Rachel said.

The doctor turned the picture around and examined it from every angle. "No doubt now." He turned the picture round.

Rachel studied the doctor studying the ultrasound of her womb and unborn child and wondered what the baby might make of it. Was it aware it was being discussed and examined? Did it know it was the subject of speculation as the state of its development was carefully analysed? She heard the doctor talking but was busy imagining the baby, alert and paying attention to goings-on like an embedded spy.

"Mrs Jarvik?"

"Oh, yes. Sorry, I was away with the fairies. It happens sometimes, usually after I tell somebody how together I've been during this pregnancy."

He laughed. "Yes, the wonder of nature. Was there anything else for today?"

She thought for a moment. "No. Nothing else."

"Well, you and the baby are in excellent condition. There's nothing to concern yourself with. You're attending the antenatal classes? So just make an appointment for a month's time."

"Thank you, *David*," she said, making a point of using his name and smiling.

He smiled back.

Rachel walked out to the reception area to collect Jessica. The little girl had broken out of the green carpet area reserved for children and was handing out tea to patients in the waiting room, insisting they take plastic beakers from a play set. She had persuaded a couple of patients to join her in the make-believe game and they pretended to sip from tiny cups.

"You have to drink it," she said to one slight teenager who was hesitating to bring the yellow cup to his mouth.

"Jessica," Rachel called, "time to go." She held out her hand for her daughter to join her.

Jessica turned to the boy. "You have to drink it. It's full of goodness." She stared at him. He looked as though he was beginning to panic.

"I'm sorry," Rachel said, picking Jessica from the floor. "She can be quite bossy."

"No problem," the boy said.

"But Mummy, he hasn't finished his drink."

At the bottom of the brick staircase, in front of the door, she put her daughter on the floor and knelt next to her. "What are you doing talking to strangers, young lady?"

Jessica looked puzzled, as if she hadn't considered somebody at the doctor's surgery a stranger. Rachel watched her face contort as she searched for a logical solution and then saw a bubble of brightness when she found one. "He looked so skinny, he needed something healthy."

Rachel couldn't help but laugh. "That was kind of you. But remember that you never talk to strangers."

"Yes, Mummy."

As they drove home, Jessica continued the discussion about strangers. She had her father's dedication to rules and attempted to understand any concept by questioning, sometimes to exhaustion. Rachel answered the string of questions carefully, trying not to set the inquiry off in an alternate direction. She was almost relieved when they arrived home and Zach and Lilith's German car was in the drive promising some adult time and a possible respite. She eased her red Mini Cooper past the Audi — parked in the space usually reserved for Christian's car — expecting to see them waiting, but it was empty. She pulled up alongside the weedless border, close to the front door, as usual.

"We have visitors," she said.

"Who is it, Mummy?"

"I think it's Zach and Lilith. They've just moved back to Bristol."

"Have they got children?"

Rachel undid her seatbelt and picked up her handbag from the footwell. She checked her phone. A text from Christian:

I'll try to get home early. Hygge tonight? :-)

Rachel smiled. "No. They don't have children."

Jessica made a disappointed noise.

"You've met Zach before, but you haven't seen him since you were three. I wonder where they are."

"I'm a big girl now."

Rachel climbed out of the car, unstrapped Jessica from the child seat in the back and shut the doors. At that moment Lilith appeared from around the side of the house, coming along the paved path through the gate between the wall and the greenhouse.

"Hiya," Lilith said. She walked up and hugged Rachel. Her feet crunched in the damp gravel of the drive. "I'm so embarrassed. You caught me snooping. I would have sent a text but Zach — God, he can be hopeless — couldn't find your number."

"Not at all. Don't be daft. You're welcome any time."

"I couldn't wait until tomorrow. I just popped in as I was driving past. I hope you don't mind."

"Let's get inside and have a cuppa."

"My name is Jessica," Jessica said loudly.

"Why of course, young lady. Such a pretty name. I'm pleased to meet you. I'm Lilith."

"That's a pretty name too. This is Everywhere." She held out her adored and worn teddy bear. "He says he's pleased to meet you."

Lilith bent down to Jessica's level and shook Everywhere's paw. "How do you do? Everywhere. That's an interesting name. Why are you called Everywhere?"

"It's because I take him everywhere, silly," Jessica said.

Lilith stood. "Omigod, so cute. And clever. A bit of a handful, I imagine."

"On the bad days. It's all Christian's fault, of course. His genes. Too clever by half, but sometimes no social graces."

The women laughed while Jessica put her thumb in her mouth and hugged Everywhere to her chest. "Let's get inside," Rachel said, searching for her keys in her handbag.

"You've such a beautiful setting with these mature trees," Lilith said. "And what a fabulous greenhouse. I can't imagine how much it all cost."

"We have a beast of a mortgage to go with it. It's like lottery numbers on the bank statement. Isn't Zach with you?"

"He's working. There's always so much to do. We hope the move to Bristol will keep us insulated from the day-to-day running of the business so we can focus on improvements and strategy. He spends so much of the day dealing with download issues and technical problems. It gets a bit wearing. We'd like to develop more products. But it'll be a while before it all comes together, things settle down commercially, and we get time to think."

"It sounds exhausting. I'll put the kettle on. You're going to have to tell me all about what you do. I've no idea."

Rachel found the key and opened the door. "Shoes off, Jessica. And Lilith, if you don't mind, Christian likes us all to keep shoes by the door. He says it's a Danish thing, but I think he's on the spectrum, sometimes. But it is sensible, right?"

"Of course. Filthy shoes in the house. No way." Lilith slipped her shoes off.

Rachel made tea — she had a green tea and Lilith had black — and they sat in the lounge to talk. They talked about Jessica, the pregnancy, Christian's focus on work, his ambition, how Rachel's parents sometimes interfered, but she was glad they were close — especially since her father's illness — and how they'd moved into the house shortly after Zach had left Bristol to find Lilith, how they'd worked to make a dent in their debts, pay for childcare and still have a life.

And then Lilith described how she and Zach had finally caught up, not because he'd found her, well not quite, but because after all the years estranged she'd finally allowed herself to be found. It was time to come in from the cold, she said. "I found I needed him as much as he needed me. I regret how long we were apart."

Rachel tried to look sympathetic and hide that she desperately wanted to ask more about why it had taken so long, but didn't feel the time was quite right. This was the first occasion they'd ever really talked. Nearly everything she knew about Lilith was through Zach, and that probably meant Zach's own peculiar view of the world needed navigating too. So instead she asked, "What's your role in the business? I know Zach's been building some clever software thing for years. But he's never been able to explain it to us."

"Omigod, Zach's brilliant. If I'm honest I didn't realise how brilliant he was, even when we got married. He's so sharp and has this grasp of concepts I'm totally turned on by." She laughed. "Honestly, I'd thought he was just a great shag."

Rachel acted shocked and then joined in the laughter.

"But I take care of everything other than the technical side. Sales, digital marketing, staff."

"Where are the staff? Are they in Germany? Christian said something about a fire."

"They're in Germany. We've a few genius coders and marketers on the team." Lilith shook her head, "We had a terrible accident. A fire started in one of the offices above ours and before the alarms went off the exits were impassable or locked or blocked. We don't know how it happened. Two of our staff died. It was terrible." Lilith wiped away a tear.

"That's so awful. I'm sorry."

"Those poor boys."

"Can I pour you another cup of tea?" Rachel felt the gesture was totally inadequate and entirely appropriate.

Lilith smiled. "That would be lovely. We're moving on. Can't let it stop us. The promise is enormous. We're big enough for others to take notice and for us to need to prepare for the next stage."

"The next stage. What's that?"

"Well, we don't know for sure, but maybe a takeover or merger. Or we sell the IP now we've proven it. It's not the app that's the value, it's the intelligent algorithm Zach's built. It's amazing. Almost intuitive in what it can know about things."

"Really? Sounds like science fiction."

"I think it is." Lilith took a drink of tea. "I thought you might be working today. But when I saw nobody was home. Omigod, I'm still ashamed to have been caught snooping."

Rachel reached out and touched Lilith's arm. "Don't be crazy. I love that you popped round. Nobody does that any more. You're always welcome." She looked thoughtfully around the room. "I've no cases for a couple of weeks, thank God. I try to keep work to three days a week at the most. But sometimes the court schedules don't take motherhood into account."

"Typical. Justice run by men is no justice. You need to look after yourself. If you ever want childcare at short notice, we're in Bristol now."

"Be careful what you wish for."

"That's so true, Rachel. What do *you* wish for? I've not heard much about you. It's all been about your family or me and Zach."

"Me? Oh, I don't know. I don't think about me much."

"Well, you must. I insist. I'm going to make sure you get some me-time now I'm in Bristol. And if you need childcare for Jessica, just call. Really. I mean it. She's absolutely gorgeous, and we have to take care of Mother, don't we?"

Despite Christian's intention to get home early, he didn't arrive until after six when Lilith had gone. His BMW rolled into the drive while Rachel was preparing dinner. He poured himself a red wine and sat on the bar stool. Rachel wasn't sure why — perhaps she wanted something for herself, just for her — she didn't tell Christian that Lilith had been round until he mentioned the text.

"Lilith said she might come round. Did you see her? I told her you were at the surgery."

"Yes, she did." Rachel felt a twinge of disappointment at having to share the details of her afternoon. "She popped by and we had a cup of tea."

"That's nice." Christian didn't want to seem overly interested, but every time he thought of Lilith he was reminded of his body's reaction to her, the uncomfortable attraction that clouded his thinking. He took a sip of wine and asked casually, "What do you make of her?"

"She's lovely. She listened. I feel I've made a good friend. She even laughed at my jokes. It's been such a long time since I've spent time like that. I like the women at the play groups and the nursery gates, but I don't have much in common with them."

"Did you talk about why she went away, why she abandoned Zach?"

"I don't think that's fair."

"Maybe not. But it's on my mind."

"Well, it's too early. Sometimes you can be so black and white. She's only been here a few days. Let her settle in."

Christian could smell Lilith's perfume in the lounge. It lingered long after she had left. It gathered in thick streams where the scent was almost too much for him, and in other places it floated gently in the air on the edge of detection.

After dinner he sat on the sofa with Rachel, watching a movie, but his mind was on the first time he'd met Lilith. At her and Zach's wedding nearly ten years earlier. On that night too, Lilith's scent, sensation and presence captivated and controlled.

He and Zach had not seen each other for over a year, and he drove along a manicured drive towards a massive stone mansion near Monmouth in South Wales. The tyres of his Toyota Corolla ploughed deep into the gravel, emitting a satisfying crunching sound as he pulled up beside a fleet of black Mercedes, Audis and BMWs. On the round lawn in front of the house a giant maypole fluttered ribbons in the light breeze and cast a long morning shadow in the already bright sun. More flags and coloured ribbons adorned the house, stretching from window to window and tumbling down the wrought-iron guttering, wrapping the four columns that made up the front porch and accenting the potted white roses on either side of the door.

The house stood on a low hill with 360-degree views of Monmouthshire. Stands of oak clustered on the hillsides; vivid green fields fresh from the week's rain stretched to the horizon. But the day had started clear and warm exactly according to the weather forecasts Christian had listened to on the drive from London. The view and the forecast-matching weather filled him with satisfaction, as if the world was under his personal control. He liked nothing more than knowing what was going to happen next.

Which is why the day's set-up was such a puzzle. Having not seen Zach for over a year as his friend worked — and played— in Frankfurt, he had suddenly received a phone call inviting him to a wedding. A girl called Lilith whom Zach met at the Palmengarten and on a whim decided to marry. Typical, impetuous Zach.

Christian took his suitcase from the back seat and, uncertain what to expect, walked to the door. Classical strings emanated from inside, mixed with the noisy clash of catering.

"CJ!" He turned to see Zach running towards him across the gravel, arms outstretched and wearing an almighty grin. Zach had a new look to go with the new girl — a sharp business haircut and close shave. "You made it."

"Of course. What was I supposed to do? Miss your wedding? What the fuck, man. You crazy fucker. Give me a hug." They embraced. "This place is a bit smart," Christian said.

"Lilith's folks. Believe it or not, this is their summer house. They spend most of the year in Frankfurt."

"German?"

"No. They got some stuff going on out there. But come on, meet the fiancée."

"You can't see her before the ceremony. That's bad luck."

"Always cautious, CJ," Zach laughed. "It's not a religious wedding. Not in the usual sense, anyway. Nobody minds that we've already had sex, either."

Christian followed Zach along a path to one side of the house, past heavily scented beds muddled with giant foxgloves, dahlias and roses, to a square, formal lawn enclosed by a high yew hedge. In the middle, as if planted by gardeners, rose a huge crimson pavilion tent encased in tumbling ivy. Above the entrance a huge crown of oak and beech leaves perched on top of a carved pregnant woman.

"Some style going on here," Christian said.

"Lilith has a flare for the dramatic, and she believes in all the Earth spirit stuff. It's going to be hand-fasting this afternoon."

"Hand-fasting?"

"Yeah. It's the original wedding ceremony, before Christianity got in the way and turned it all serious with rules and edicts."

"Like a pagan thing?"

"Sort of. You'll see. You have a part in the ceremony, and of course the party afterwards."

"I've got my dancing shoes in the bag."

"Good job. It's going to be an all-nighter."

"Are you staying on?"

"Oh yeah, baby. We are the king and queen of chaos, who preside over all earthly things." Zach laughed as he spread his arms out wide like a sort of megalomaniac of formal gardens.

"Okay. Point me at the organisers. What can I help with?"

"Man, it's all done. No help needed. Lilith's parents have taken instructions from their daughter and got on with it. They've taken care of everything. Catering, guests, seating, sound, lighting. Even fireworks. And look at that tent. It's stunning, don't you think?"

"Beautiful. I like the pregnant woman. An omen?"

"No. No. Don't let your mind get into overdrive. You just have to enjoy it. Meet everybody. Lilith has a million stunning friends waiting to talk with you. I've been reporting your heroic tales."

"Jesus, Zach, what have you said?"

Zach raised his hands in mock surrender. "Come on, mate. You can't keep that big heart of yours locked up in your lonely study forever. You have to share yourself around. Give the world the benefit of Mr Jarvik, and not let the English law establishment selfishly keep you for itself. You've had fun in the past."

"Ha ha."

"Tell me, then. If you think that's such an affront to your reputation, when was the last time you had sex?"

"Fuck off."

"Come on. Tell all."

Christian avoided his mate's interrogation by scrutinising the surrounding activity. Men were laying cables from the house to the tent; gardeners had turned the damp brown soil around the ornamental cherries that dotted the lawn and were planting flowers and shrubs and decorating the trees with coloured ribbons. Tradesmen in aprons plied backwards and forwards between the house and the pavilion tent. The house and the lawn hummed with busyness. "Okay. So it's been a while. Since that last hike we went on. You know, last time you were back."

"Peak District."

"Yeah."

"Rachel? She's lovely. But man, a year? Haven't you seen her since?"

"We kept in touch. She's in London doing her pupillage, and—"

"You're too busy with the law. Don't tell me."

Christian laughed. "Those precedents won't learn themselves."

"Fuck me, you can be boring. You could have asked her along."

Christian shrugged.

"Well, you're going to have a wild time tonight. I see it written in the stars," Zach said.

Christian did have a wild time, as Zach predicted. But not in the way he could have expected. The gorgeous wedding the bride's parents planned proceeded like a sumptuous dream. It was as if the entirety had been specified by a movie director who left no avenue unexplored to create an immersive, 3D experience. Each detail had been conceived, planned, controlled and executed in precise Technicolor finesse. Christian could only admire the masterpiece as it unfolded before him. From timing to scent, to carved symbols on chairs, flower arrangements in the garden and bordering paths and hallways, every tiny aspect plugged in with vital attention.

But the instant Christian met Lilith was the moment he understood Zach's seemingly rash move to get married. It was not her beauty — though she had that, with a devastating figure, auburn hair, blue eyes and seductive smile — but her aura. The unexplained. If Christian had been a religious man, he'd have said *God-given*. He could barely keep his eyes from her, and each time their eyes met he felt a jolt of embarrassed lust. Happy and appalled in equal measure, he watched the ceremony and the evening's activities pass by in the flash of a perfect movie, one you could watch again and again, one that you never want to end, one that steals you from the desk-bound legal life you've become glued to like some sad limpet clinging to cold rocks next to a sewage outfall.

As the magical evening passed from long sunset to honeydew night, Christian watched Lilith, Zach and her four sensual bridesmaids dance around the maypole. A quartet played an intoxicating fusion of harmony which peaked from excitable promise to manic climax as the dancers reached the pinnacle of the dance.

At some point he ended up in bed on the top floor of the great Civil War mansion. The guilt of desire spilled into his dreams and manifested as a great orgy. Masked guests watched as he, Zach and the bridesmaids cavorted in a frenzy of flesh until they lay empty, naked and exhausted in the long grass. Christian woke in a state of high arousal, in a hot sweat, with the sound of applause decaying into the distance.

5

By evening on Saturday, two days after Zach and Lilith returned to Bristol, Jessica had been thoroughly worn out by the day's activities. Christian had managed five minutes to inspect an overpriced Napoleonic sabre for sale among a jumble of antiques at the top of Christmas Steps, but Jessica dragged him quickly into the joke shop nearby to hunt for fake poo. He was in such a good mood with his probable promotion and the reconciliation with Zach — not to mention the hidden anticipation of seeing Lilith that evening — it seemed a wonderful idea to simply follow his daughter's whims. Swimming was not enough to satisfy her insatiable appetite for parental activity and while rain and increasing wind made the zoo uncomfortable, they passed an hour in the reptile house. Jessica asked a million questions about the animals. "What's a reptile, Daddy? What's cold blooded? Is that like ice cream for blood? Why's it so wet in here?"

Christian did his best to answer Jessica's stream of questions, but realised his daughter would soon know more about animals than he did. She paid close attention during their countless visits to Clifton zoo and her questions distracted him from thinking about the thick, animal-scented air, or drifting back to his work. He was grateful for that. Between them, they made sure they inspected every creature in the Reptile House, read every card in every window and pressed every *Listen Now* button.

Christian put her to bed, and by seven o'clock she was fast asleep. Exactly on time.

"She's a Mastermind," Christian said to Rachel, recounting Jessica's day. "How'd you go with Mum and Dad? All okay?"

"They're fine. Dad's on good form and Mum spoilt me with

lunch at Browns." Rachel was preparing vegetables at the sink, cutting the carrots lengthwise and putting the off-cuts into the compost bin.

Rain smashed into the glass patio doors and sloped to the ground. The forecast from earlier in the week had turned out to be accurate: low pressure hit the West Country mid-morning and built to a storm by evening. The lime tree at the back of the garden, its silhouette black against the orange-grey sky, swayed with the wind. The sky was never totally dark this close to the centre of Bristol, and now low clouds reflected the city's lights to cast an eerie glow. Only in shadows, under trees, and at the edges of buildings, was it ever black.

After setting the table Christian drew the curtains, closing the gap meticulously by running his hands over the join like a zip — he did this twice more until satisfied — then flicked on the lights.

"Light the candles. Don't use the main light," Rachel called from the kitchen. "They're unscented. What was that about the tree?"

"We'll have to ask the neighbour to get it cut back. It worries me in these high winds."

Rachel came into the dining room carrying mats and serviettes. "The table looks nice. But we need these," she said, placing them in front of each chair.

A green tablecloth contrasted with bright-flower place mats and long-stemmed glasses beside cut-glass tumblers added sophistication.

"I'm not sure Zach's ever drunk out of crystal," Christian said. He placed two silver candelabras in the middle and lit the candles.

Rachel turned on the up-lighter to give the room a warm glow. "There. It's a masterclass in utility and art."

As they admired the table settings, the front doorbell rang.

"It's disgusting out here," Zach said as Christian opened the door.

Zach turned and waved to the car, where a figure in the driving seat, lit by the interior lamp, was disguised by rain smashing on the windscreen. The door opened and the figure dashed out from the car holding a coat over her head. A short black dress, slender legs and high heels rushed across the gravel, the coat flailing in the wind held in place by sleeveless arms. Zach held the door and just as Lilith entered the wind pulled it out of his hand and slammed it closed.

"Fuck me," Zach said.

Christian lifted Lilith's coat from her head. He shook off the rain over the door mat. It was like the unveiling of a sculpture. With subtle make-up it looked as if she'd not aged. Tall — a couple of inches under his height — and slim with dark-brown hair flashing a hint of red falling over her shoulders and curling up in loops at the ends. He leaned forward, placed his hands gently on Lilith's bare shoulders, and kissed her perfect cheeks. He controlled his desire to deeply inhale her perfume.

"It's so lovely to be here together at last," she said.

"I hope it lives up to expectations."

She responded with a laugh and an enticing smile.

Rachel came up from behind. "My God you look amazing," she said. "I feel like a whale."

Christian immediately turned to pay her attention. He put his arm around her waist while he watched the women exchange greetings. Cool air from outside tracked down the back of his neck to create a chill along his spine.

"Nonsense, you're blooming," said Lilith.

"Yes, that's what everybody says about whales. Your pendant's beautiful. I love it."

"Thank you. A gift from my mother. It represents the five senses."

"Where's Jessica," Zach said, looking up and down the hallway.

"She's already in bed. She had a busy day."

"No, I'm not." The call came from the top of the stairs followed by rapid thumping as Jessica rushed down. She jumped from the third stair into Zach's arms.

"Hello, my little troll," Zach said, "You remember me?"

"Of course. You used to tell me stories about Dungeons and Dragons."

"Yes I did. You have a super memory. My God, haven't you grown? This is Lilith."

"Hello Jessica," Lilith said, "Pleased to meet you, *again*," Lilith winked and Jessica smiled.

Christian helped Jessica back into bed while the others moved into the kitchen for drinks. When he returned Lilith was complimenting the house and garden and the drinks had been poured. He picked up a glass of bubbles.

After the obligatory house tour, in which Jessica was up and joining in again, Christian managed to get Zach away on the pretext of fetching more wine from the fridge in the garage. Cold air whistled under the garage door and the single naked light bulb swung gently in the interior breeze. "How's it going in the new flat? You both settled in?"

"Amazing," Zach said, sorting through the chilled drinks. "Anything German? We've got a taste for it these days. It's like a trip back to my parents' wine-and-cheese parties."

"At the back."

Zach emerged with two bottles of Gewürtz. "I'd forgotten how much I love Bristol." He closed the fridge door. "Frankfurt was good, and I've been living in a dream since we got back together, but this feels like I've come home. Everything's falling into place like it was pre-ordained. Moving back here and being with you guys is the skunk in the brownie, for me. We've agreed it's about what the future holds. What we can make happen. It's going to work."

Christian nodded, "I'm pleased for you." Beneath his smiling face, though, he wasn't sure if he *was* pleased. This seemed like a return to the past, not an escape from it. Back to Bristol, back to mucking about with smartphone apps, back to Lilith and old memories. *Zach flip-flopping again?*

Zach nodded. "I've got faith in our future and the past doesn't bother me. Well, not how it did."

"Sounds like she's converted you," Christian said, meaning it as a joke.

Zach stared as if the words were dirty. "It's not religious. No. Not religious at all. But it is a kind of conversion." He paused. "But really, it's love between two people who want to get on with living."

"Oh! *Love*. This is more serious than I thought." Christian took a bottle of champagne from the fridge. "We should drink some sense into you both."

Dinner went smoothly — though the Tom Yum was too spicy for Rachel's pregnancy taste-buds and for the others the drink flowed until two empty bottles of white stood neglected on the sideboard, out of order and disturbing the usually tidy photographs.

Christian retrieved more bubbles from the kitchen.

Zach insisted on a toast. "I know we had our falling out, but I think I secretly knew we'd become a whole family one day." He beat over his heart with a closed fist. "Somewhere inside I felt it. Knew I'd find Lilith and come back here. Honestly. How could it be otherwise?"

"Stop it, you old bugger," Christian said. "You'll have us all in tears."

"But could you have predicted it?" Lilith asked after a moment of silence when they'd taken up their glasses.

Christian caught the glint in her eye again, and a slight pout to her lips — he wondered if Zach saw the same thing. Every time she talked, her low voice excited him. Surely it must be the same for his friend, he thought, gazing at the muscle definition of her upper arms.

"What do you mean?" Rachel sounded eager to explore the question.

"Well, do you think hard work, luck or maybe fate has a hand in your successes? Could your past have been any other way? Or can your future be changed?" The candlelight glinted off her eyes. She looked at Zach and smiled.

"You mean, is it possible to know the future, and then change it?" Rachel asked, picking up her water and taking a sip without letting her gaze drop. "You mean like a fortune-teller?"

Lilith shrugged. "Perhaps, or a spiritual medium."

"Come on," Christian said, "It's all nonsense. Conjuring tricks and psychology. It doesn't take a genius to work out that anybody visiting a medium has problems with their life, so how can they be surprised when they're told, I see an unhappy marriage, or job? It's a trick aimed at the weak. You make your own fate. Hard work is the key to success." He realised he was talking loudly, and he might have been insensitive with the force of his objection, but the idea challenged a deeply held value.

"These fortune-tellers might be ambiguous and open to interpretation," Zach said, "but that doesn't mean they aren't tapping into something real. I think they are."

"Come off it. Next you'll be telling me how toys come alive at midnight and you feed unicorns magic fairy broth. It's a load of crap."

"Christian!" Rachel scolded him.

Zach laughed. "It's passion," he said. "But seriously, what do you think I've been working on for all these years? All the predictive algorithms and AI programs."

"That's not the same thing," Christian said.

"I didn't think so either, until recently. But Lilith has convinced me."

Lilith smiled, watching Christian's reactions. She appeared amused. Christian felt naked under her gaze.

"Zach's built an artificial mind," she said. "I think it can tap into the spirit world just like humans can. In fact, because it doesn't have all the baggage of human experience, it's a pure intelligence. It can see more than we can."

Christian rolled his eyes. "You're pulling my leg. Come on, Zach. It might seem clever but it's not tapping into the spirit world."

"You haven't tried it yet, have you?" Zach said. "It freaks *me* out, sometimes, and I invented it."

"This is marketing, isn't it? You're testing your sales patter. So you get more downloads. It's not real."

"It's a bloody good story, isn't it? Lilith's the master when it comes to digital marketing."

"Or mistress," Christian blurted out without thinking, and instantly felt embarrassed.

"Yes. A mistress is better," Lilith said, reaching and touching his arm. "But there's more to it than commercial savvy.

Somewhere I think there's a grain of spirituality in all of us. Even the complete cynics. Even you, Christian. That's what I believe." With her low timbre and emphasis, she sounded so sincere, so certain that the group fell silent.

Christian picked up his champagne and took a sip.

Lilith turned to Rachel. "What do you think, Rachel?"

"My mum used to be a spiritualist," Rachel said. "I remember her having a drawer full of recorded sessions with mediums. At one stage, when my parents were going through a bit of a tough time, I was dragged along every Saturday and made to sit in a draughty hall. It was always a cold, spooky hall, but I know she got comfort from it."

"There you are, you see," Christian said. "Vulnerable women, sucked into parting with their money for a shoulder to cry on. The hall is the setting for a con."

"It wasn't like that!" Rachel said with a touch of annoyance. "They didn't ask for payment, they asked for donations. You didn't *have* to pay anything."

Christian snorted.

"It's just people helping people. I remember one old woman — well, she was old to me, but I suppose she can't have been more than forty-five — she had a silver urn at the door for her guests to put a 'gift' in."

"A gift for her gift," Christian said, laughing.

Rachel ignored the comment, "I was petrified of her. She had blusher on her deep-veined cheeks and purple eye shadow. Wore a purple shawl. She looked like she was already dead. Then one day she grabbed me by the hand as we were leaving and squeezed until I thought the blood would stop flowing. I could smell her sweet breath, like she'd been chewing dolly mixtures. She knelt next to me without letting go. I was so frightened. I remember her exact words." Rachel swallowed and looked at each of them in turn. "She said, 'Feel your fear. It will keep you safe.'"

"Freaky," Zach said. "How old were you?"

"Seven or eight. I wet my knickers, I was so scared." Rachel laughed. "Now I wet my knickers because the baby pushes on my bladder. But I didn't go with my mum ever again, and I've kept away from fortune-tellers or anything supernatural ever since. It reminds me of dolly mixtures. Which I've never touched since either."

"Your mother must have believed in it, though?" Lilith had remained quiet during the story. Now she leaned forward with her arms folded on the table so that her black dress fell open slightly to reveal a silver pendant in the shape of a star resting on the side of her breast. Christian turned his gaze away.

"Yes, she did."

"What do you think now you're older and wiser? And a mother too."

"It's just a story." Rachel took a sip of water and studied Lilith's face as if looking for something she might have missed earlier. "Yes, I suppose I believe in it. In something. There's got to be something in it. Has to be, doesn't there? Otherwise why would all these people believe in it?"

"Because they're stupid?" Christian said.

She glared at him. "They're not all stupid."

He smiled. Rachel had the benefit of being sober, since she wasn't drinking alcohol during the pregnancy. For the rest of them, the discussions were likely to get louder and more contrary before they ended. He poured himself more wine and mouthed, "Sorry."

"You're asking the questions, Lilith." Rachel said. "What do you believe? When it's not just marketing. Is it possible to predict the future?"

Lilith flicked her hair off her shoulder and twiddled with her necklace. She held the pendant between her fingers then stroked her neck, leaving her hand resting on her collarbone. "Yes, it is," she said, "It is possible to contact the spirit world and find out what plans there are for us. And then I think it's possible to change course, to put yourself on the right path."

"So you think there's some sort of lesson we're supposed to be learning?"

Lilith nodded. "You could put it like that. We are here to learn and take back knowledge."

"That's what Mum says," Rachel said quietly. "And then she said that meeting my dad had been a mistake that was never meant to happen. It didn't make me feel particularly good."

"That's so sad," Lilith said. "That's really hurtful."

Rachel gave Lilith a look that said, *Thank you for understanding*. She picked up her water and took another sip. "Mum's okay now. I guess she was looking for support and facing her own demons while Dad was away on business. It's all completely different now he's got Alzheimer's."

"Why don't we try now? It's about time you took a proper look at the app that's going to make us rich," Zach said.

"Zach! I can't believe you're so insensitive sometimes," Lilith said. "Rachel's shared a part of her heart with us, and you're just thinking about your app."

"Oh. Yeah. Sorry, Rachel. I didn't mean to offend you. I do get over-enthusiastic."

"It's okay, Zach. Let's take a look. I'm fine, really."

The patio doors thudded against their wooden frame, and the candles flickered. Rachel jumped at the sudden noise. "That made me leap. The wind's really got up now." She put her hand over her chest and patted. "How about something sweet? We've got florentines and ginger cake. A bit of chocolate. I'll put the kettle on."

"I'll get them," Christian said. He stepped from the candle-lit gloom of the dining room into the brightly lit kitchen and blinked. Rachel followed carrying a pile of dirty plates.

"The baby's moving," she said. "It's making me a bit uncomfortable."

Christian took the crockery and put it on the island. He grabbed her wrists and pulled her towards him. He held her face in his hands and kissed her. "I love you," he said. As they kissed he opened his eyes to see Lilith standing in the doorway watching them. She was looking directly into his eyes, a gentle smile on her lips. He broke from the embrace.

"No naughtiness in the kitchen." Lilith said, walking in and putting glasses on the side. Zach followed closely with handfuls of cutlery. "You'll get us all going."

Rachel patted her stomach. "Crikey, not while I'm in this condition."

"We need our smartphones," Lilith said. "We're going to play with the app."

"A game," Christian said, walking to the sink units and opening the second drawer down to find more candles. "I didn't realise it was a game."

"Why don't we put our predictions for the future to the test and see if we can settle the argument?"

"I'm all for it," Christian said. "Let's try and get the lottery numbers."

Rachel looked worried. "I don't know. I'm a bit frightened by it all."

Lilith walked over and held Rachel's hand, "It's harmless," she said. "There's nothing to worry about, and we can stop whenever we want. It's not binding. If you want to know how things will turn out, it might help. Might reassure you."

Rachel smiled. "All right. Let me get this little beast off my bladder first."

Christian loaded the dishwasher, rinsing each item before it went in and positioning the plates in order of size. When he went back into the dining room Lilith had cleared the table and placed a few extra tall candles in the middle. She and Zach sat quietly waiting. Four smartphones were set in a square in the middle of the table, next to a pair of scissors.

"I've got a good port," Christian said. "Any takers before we begin?"

"I'll have a little of what you've got," Lilith said, wide-eyed with her head tilted to one side.

Christian swallowed and avoided her direct gaze. He didn't know if he was sending out flirtatious signs, but he didn't want to be misunderstood. He took her glass and filled it at the sideboard without looking at her.

"Zach?" he asked. Zach nodded.

Rachel returned and, taking her seat, said, "So what is this app? How does it work?"

Zach took them through downloading and registering. "You've both got eFace accounts, so use those to register. This is the boring bit, before the fun starts. We've thought about putting this next bit up on video somewhere, but we're so busy with other things. When you see the Welcome screen, put the phone down in front of you. Let it soak up the atmosphere."

"Is it listening?" Christian asked.

"Listening, watching, predicting. The more information it takes in, the better its predictions. As soon as you register, it starts finding out all about you from the internet. But that's just the mechanics. The good bit is what Lilith adds."

"With your phones in front of you," Lilith said, "be still for a moment. We centre ourselves. Think good, warm thoughts and open your minds to the universe." She stood up. The candles threw wavering shadows up the wall and across the ceiling. She smiled. "I'm going to snip a tiny lock of hair from each of you. This is magic, after all. Don't worry, it won't show."

She walked around the table and, in silence, snipped behind Rachel's and then Christian's ears. She handed them their tiny locks of hair with their phones.

"My mother, like yours, Rachel, believes in spirit guides," Lilith said. "Persons who, having passed over, return to look after people on Earth and help them learn their life lessons. Everybody has a reason for being here, even if that reason is not known. Some of us follow our life plan without straying from the path, but others never seem to find the right direction. That is where the spirit guide comes in. If you ask for help, you will receive it. We have found a way to communicate with your spirit guide using the intuitive power of Artificial Intelligence. It will help you see your proper path."

"These spirit guides are like ghosts in the machine, then?" Christian asked, smirking.

"Shush, Christian. Lilith, don't pay any attention. He's teasing you," Rachel said, knocking her husband's leg under the table.

"It's a diverting question from a searching mind," Lilith continued in a low, calm voice. Almost meditative. "Christian, your mind is looking for answers, but ghosts are a different form of spirit. They have lost their way and stick to the Earth rather than heading into the light where they belong. They regret the loss of life and gain pleasure from following the living. We're not talking about lost spirits here. The Algorithm is a way to contact those that want to help you."

Christian was suddenly aware of the wind outside the house. It charged through the trees and along the fence-line, a gentle roar that underlined everything being said. He felt Rachel's hand on his thigh and turned to her. She was staring intently at Lilith with her mouth open.

"This is intense," Rachel said. Her grasp on Christian's thigh tightened.

"When we die we are shown the way to the next kingdom," Lilith said, "by a bright light and the hands of our guiding spirit. They guide us to the light. But the guides do more than that. They can also guide us during our lives and help us mould our future by showing us the results of the decisions we might make. We simply have to contact them."

"What about evil spirits?" Rachel said. "How do you know who you are talking to?"

"We use the protection of our friendship and love we have for each other. Love is the one true protector."

"My mum used to make me imagine I was surrounded by a white light from heaven if I was having bad dreams."

Lilith studied Rachel, then shook her head. "The light can be blinding. It's the way to the next world, not a way to ask for guidance."

Rachel looked puzzled, but nodded.

"Right. Place your right palm over the screen with the lock of hair under your palm. This is the symbolic key to your future. It will look like the phone scans your palm with a green light. Some mediums might give you a reading using a ring or locket or other object. The app scans your palm, can use your birth, date and time or do a reading." Lilith stared at Christian and her smile broadened.

Christian swallowed and looked back towards his wife.

"Now watch the results form on the screen. Relax and try to stay centred. Let the app read your future," Lilith said.

They put their hands on the table and were silent. The candles wavered gently as the wind rustled through the trees in the garden. Slowly images and then text formed on the screens.

"Breathe in, hold it and then breathe out," Lilith said. "We want to centre ourselves on receiving guidance." She had her eyes closed.

"This is a bit mental, isn't it?" said Christian. "How can a phone need us to breathe in or out? Even if it is smart, it doesn't know what's going on."

Zach put his phone on the table "I don't fully understand it either. But it seems to work better if you surround the whole thing with ritual. Maybe it's something to do with getting us open and receptive, and somehow the neural net in the Algorithm can use that to help it do its work. We don't know how a fortune-teller at the fair knows what they know. But maybe they're taking in all the information, processing it deep inside their brains and popping out an answer. Honestly, I think it's the same with the Algorithm."

"Relax, and we'll go to the next stage," Lilith said. "Use the index finger of the hand you don't write with and, without thinking about it, write on the screen."

Christian's stomach fluttered. He could see the side of her breast swelling underneath the black dress; her lips glistened in the candlelight.

"Imagine that your spirit guides are moving your finger for you. Try not to resist. Let your arm and fingers go with it. So, relax. Breathe in." Lilith's voice was monotone, drowsy. "Maintain your relaxation. Try to reach an inner calm."

Christian picked up his phone, closed his eyes and nudged words onto the screen with his finger. He could think only of Lilith, the soft flesh at her neckline and the gap between the dress and her breasts. The way her thighs stretched the material tight across her lap. His mind wandered over her body as his finger traced over the screen. His mouth dried. His finger moved. He wasn't controlling it. It wrote itself.

"Keep writing," Lilith said. "Keep focusing. Try to relax and not break into thinking. Enjoy the feel of your finger gliding on the phone. Let it go."

She went on like this for a minute or two and Christian found his thoughts roaming. He opened his eyes to let a fraction of candlelight in only to find himself looking straight into Lilith's eyes. She put her finger to her mouth and gestured for him to close his eyes.

"Now. Stop writing. Put your phone on the table and let it decipher what you've written. It might take a few seconds or a few minutes."

"What's it doing?" Rachel asked.

"It's taking your input," Zach said, "and mixing it with everything it knows about you from your eFace account and feeding it into the cloud-based neural net. It's like—"

"The explanations are not important," said Lilith. "The technology isn't the point. It's the intuition it develops that's important."

"Are you saying the Algorithm has intuition?" Christian asked.

Lilith nodded. "We don't know where intuition comes from in the human brain, but we do know that when you take lots of information and process it together out pops an answer."

Christian laughed. "You guys. You're going to make a million out of this."

"And the rest, I hope," said Zach. "We're uploading a thousand a day."

"No way."

"Yes way, man."

"Something's forming on mine," Rachel said.

"Ah," said Lilith, "It's getting ready. Watch what it says. Usually it's a text of some sort, but it could be an image."

"Something's coming up on mine too," Christian said. "I think it's a tree. Is that it?"

He held his phone out for the others to inspect, but at that exact moment the entire house shook with a thunderous crash and an explosion of breaking glass erupted from the back of the house. Rapidly followed by Jessica screaming from upstairs.

6

Christian stood behind a low desk in front of the entire review team and entourage. There must have been fifty people in the room arranged on tiered seating in front and around him. They were unsmiling, unmoving. He felt uneasy in their presence as if his previous words had offended. But he couldn't remember his words. He was frozen to the spot. He looked down at his feet to see why he couldn't move and noticed his shoes. He expected to see a pair of highly polished Oxfords, but instead one was brown and decaying in front of his eyes, while the other was covered in embarrassing layers of dust and dirt. The thought of his filthy shoes created a pulse of anxiety he struggled to control. How had he not cleaned them? How had he put on odd shoes? Deep shame grew from within, but he knew he had to continue his address. If only he could remember what he'd been saying. Was it something to do with his latest project? In the gaze of his peers he stood paralysed, dumb and unprepared. Anxiety climbed from deep within like a black bindweed.

In the audience sat all the members of his law firm. They wore immaculate and identical shoes. They had immaculate and identical suits. Pinstripes, black ties, gleaming white shirts. He attempted to find words. His mouth opened wide. No words came. The audience stared in silent derision.

In the centre of the auditorium sat Howard Beaufort. He looked on disapprovingly with his head raised in a gesture of superior status. Behind him sat Dave Hinchley and then Christian's father and mother, and Rachel.

Seated upright and cross-legged, in the front row, Lilith wore a heavy black robe with a deep, gaping plunge to her bare stomach. It fell tantalisingly open over her crossed thighs, and between her breasts a silver pendant glistened. In her hands she cupped a smartphone. Her thumbs typed rapidly into the device and every so often she looked up at him. She smiled. Her thumbs typed. She smiled again. She stared full into his eyes, took one hand from her phone and moved it under her gown to rest on her left breast.

He panicked. His mouth dried. He tried to focus, but Lilith's teasing tormented his thought. Struggling to get his mind on his speech, he tore his gaze from her gently moving hand. He must have speaking notes somewhere. He always meticulously prepared. Where were the notes? They must be on the table.

He looked down, but in the table he saw his reflection in a cracked mirror. His sunken eyes had deep black rings and his thin drawn face resembled Munch's *The Scream*. He breathed heavily. In, out, in, out. His breathing amplified to rapid, deep in-breaths and forced exhalations, laboured and heavy. As he stared at his alien, wraith-like self, skin began to grow across his mouth. First the corners sealed over by tapes of thin, stretched skin, but like the slow rise of bread baking in a black oven, the growth across the opening became a continuous smooth, tight membrane.

"No! No! No!" Christian screamed and woke with a start. Sweat dripped from his hair and had soaked into the pillow.

"You all right, babe?" Rachel asked quietly. She was still half asleep. She put an arm over him. She sat up as she felt his skin. "You're soaked through. Are you feeling okay?"

"I had a nightmare." His head thumped and his tongue lay in a gravel bed of a mouth. He looked at the bedside clock: it was just before seven. He took a deep breath. He breathed out. "My heart's racing."

"You poor thing." She cuddled into him.

"Jessica will be up soon. I'll have a shower."

"Don't turn the light on yet. I want to snooze."

He twisted out of bed leaving the sheets folded back on his side, so they could dry out. He put on his dressing gown and walked to the bathroom.

The dream disturbed him. He was embarrassed because of the memory of the dreams on the night of Zach and Lilith's wedding: he had never forgotten those. He turned on the shower and waited for it to reach temperature. He stepped inside. He scrubbed his stomach and chest and ensured his genitals were meticulously cleansed. The stiff brush on his skin and the soap suds comforted and soothed.

"What were you dreaming about?" Rachel said, taking her toothbrush from the ceramic pot. She liked to brush her teeth before doing anything else in the morning; Christian preferred to shower.

"An anxiety dream."

"Is that all?" Rachel poked her head around the shower curtain and watched Christian rubbing himself with liquid gel.

"I was unable to speak while doing a presentation," he said. "That's what made me cry out. I was trying to get the words out. My mouth was sealed over."

"You're working too much. Not surprising after last night's drama."

Christian emptied the liquid soap onto his head and scrubbed his body again.

Rachel waited by the side with a towel wrapped around her. The green fabric was pulled up over her breasts and reached over the slight bump and down to the top of her thighs like an extremely short mini-skirt. She held the towel together over her heart. Her complexion was perfect, no blemishes, and her eyes were bright blue in the light of the bathroom strip bulb. Christian looked at her and relaxed. He felt able to fully breathe again.

"Come here," he said. "I want to get wet with you." He turned the shower back on and grabbed a fresh bottle of soap.

Christian was downstairs first, in shorts and T-shirt. He stared out the window at the tree. The mature lime had fallen across the back lawn from one neighbour's garden, through two stone walls. It had completely smashed the greenhouse and then fallen into the neighbour's garden on the far side. Only from the ground could he observe the full impressive canopy. A million vibrant-green heart-shaped leaves filled the area from wall to wall and from the patio to the rear boundary. Thank goodness it came down at night. By some miracle the main trunk missed the corner of the house and Jessica's bedroom, but a small branch had struck the roof and taken some tiles off.

The wind had dropped, and only the faintest movement in the fallen foliage gave any clue of the tree's sudden collapse. He tried to convince himself his best friend had not managed to capture the essence of Yuri Geller, Nostradamus or Mother Shipton in a smartphone app. Whatever Zach had managed to do, coincidence or not, the tree falling had cut short dinner in an explosive fashion. He and Zach had rushed around to check the neighbours and inspected the damage with a bright torch, all while being intoxicated. The tremendous crash was the result of the greenhouse exploding. It now lay in a million pieces under the canopy. When they got back into the house, Rachel had made hot chocolate for everybody, Jessica was tucked-up between them under a blanket, and the local TV news was reporting tales of yet another weather bomb to hit the West Country.

But the morning was bright, with high cloud. Christian began clearing up by unloading the dishwasher and putting away the clean items in their exact places. He collected the empty glass bottles and put them in the black recycling box, tidied the dining room, placed the glasses and cutlery in the dishwasher and set it going. Water rushed into the machine with a satisfying high-pressure whistle. He wiped down the tables and surfaces.

He picked up his phone from the top of the microwave. He flicked it on to see a clear image of a tree in Zach's app.

Rachel entered and stood beside him in her dressing gown. "That's freaky, isn't it?"

"It's a bit indistinct. It could be a tennis racket or a lamp."

"No, that's a tree. It looks like a lime. Look at those lines. They have to be branches." She moved closer. "Give it another go. Press the Next Prediction button."

The screen scrambled, swirled and went blank. They stared. It stayed blank with the occasional swirl of dull white and grey. "It's thinking," Rachel said.

"What can it be thinking about?"

"I don't know. I wouldn't have put Zach down as a psychic, though. How's he done it? Is it Lilith?"

"You don't believe it? It's a game. All the theatrics and ceremony. It's to get us going. You know Zach. He loves to create an atmosphere."

"Look, it's coming. It's words this time. What do you think it says?"

"Nothing yet. It's still moving. At least it's not another tree."

Rachel laughed. "Christian, that's quite frightening if you think about it."

"It was a lucky guess."

"Blooming coincidence?" She pulled the phone from his hand and set it down on the bench under the light. "It's forming something. Maybe that's *burning*, or *birmingham*, and that's *falls* or *smalls*. Can't be sure. And what's that lower down? Is that *champions* or *championship*?"

"Birmingham Smalls. No thanks." Christian laughed and took the phone back. "Let me see. That's not *Birmingham*. Is it *Burnham fails*?" Suddenly the writing was very clear to him. "It is. It's *Burnham fails*."

"No, I don't think so. I don't think it says anything."

The Sunday paper dropped through the door and the letter box slammed shut.

"Would you like some toast?" Rachel asked.

Christian stared at the phone with a look of utter absorption.

"Christian," Rachel said firmly. "Did you hear me? Let's have breakfast. Put that phone down."

He looked up and smiled. "Toast, then. You see, I did hear."

"You might have heard, but it took you two minutes to become conscious of the words."

By the time Rachel had made a round of toast, Christian had recovered the paper from the front door and had it open at the business news. Jessica had come down from upstairs with

Everywhere, placed the bear on the table, and had been quietly singing "Fifi and the flower pots" or flower tots, or whatever it was, while waiting for breakfast. When the toast arrived, she reached out and grabbed the first slice.

"Why do you suppose the government still insists on building roads? After all these years of knowing about climate change, they regress to the habits of the Fifties. It's maddening." Christian's words drifted over the top of the broadsheet and through the kitchen like a slow assault into no man's land.

"It's for cars," Jessica said. "You're silly, Daddy." With a smidgeon of brown paste smeared on her cheek, she was tucking into a plate of toast soldiers and Marmite while humming quietly to herself.

"Do silly people have Marmite on their faces?"

She looked up and laughed. "No."

He moved closer, leaning over the paper. "Do silly people scoff toast soldiers?"

"No."

He leant further, right over her plate. "And do silly people steal Jessica's breakfast?" He grabbed a soldier and stuffed it in his mouth.

"Daddy!" Jessica screamed. "These are mine!"

"Stop teasing her when she's eating," Rachel said.

Christian stopped his urge to complain; to say that his daughter had started it. Jessica laughed at her triumph and immediately began to hum again. Christian smiled behind the paper and chewed on the bread. It amused him that his daughter was a perfect cross between himself and Rachel, and was capable of playing her parents off each other while seeming so innocent. Clever.

He scanned the paper. It was a Sunday ritual; he rarely had time for a luxurious read of a real newspaper during the week.

"What shall we do today?" Rachel said.

"The zoo, the zoo! I want to see the reptiles!"

"You went to the zoo yesterday, young lady. Christian?"

Christian heard his name, and the conversation registered, but a business article was engrossing him; Telecoms were often in the news, but not always in association with software technologies.

"You went to the zoo yesterday," he said, without looking up.

"How about going to see Grandma and Granddad?" Rachel said.

"Can I take Everywhere?"

"Yes, Everywhere can come too. If he gets ready quickly."

Jessica's chair scraped backwards, she leapt down, dashed out of the kitchen and thumped up the stairs. Christian closed the newspaper. "I'm going to have to go into work. There's something I've got to check out."

"Not today, this is a Sunday. It's a family day."

The article had made him doubt some of the research that went into the Burnham report, and the words *burnham fails* were ringing in his head. He needed to excise them by rationalising the prediction into an opportunity; if true, he had warning of the project's failure and could do something about it, and if it was a fantasy of a computer program based on a few gigs of information collected from the internet, there was nothing to worry about. Either way, if he could discover weaknesses in his planning and eradicate them before the rehearsal it was a winning situation. Harder work never hurt anyone. "I shouldn't be long," he said, "I want to check some data and internal reports."

"Can't it wait?"

He thought about the newspaper article. If the press were reporting it today then it could be too late by morning. It might be already. "No."

"Christian, you promised. Whatever happened during the week, no matter how late you worked in the evenings, you would always keep Sunday free." She had her arms folded across her chest and was bristling with annoyance.

"Sorry," he said. "It won't happen again, it's just while this project is nearing completion. Look, I'll call a guy about getting the tree cut up too. We don't want that there for months. And we'll need somebody to check the tiles on the roof. It looks like a couple have come down."

Jessica rushed back in. "He was hiding under the bed," she said, "Naughty Everywhere." She held her limp teddy bear to her cheek and stroked its worn cloth.

"You, me and Everywhere are going to Grandma and

Granddad's," Rachel said. "Daddy has to go to work."

"Okay."

In business, more could *always* be done: more figures to check, more opinions to canvass, more reports to absorb. Yet, ironically, all decisions were made on incomplete information. Where Christian excelled, he knew, was in making right decisions at the pragmatic time when he had collected sufficient data to form a reasonable position. But always he was aware there was more he could take into consideration. His logical mind told him not to worry, but fear required better insurance.

He was the only person in the office and spent the afternoon checking his assumptions and reasoning in the Burnham report. He sent a raft of emails to acquaintances in the firm and outside asking for opinions on market conditions and the viability of current software solutions. He ordered extra reports from Gartner and reread the minutes of dozens of client meetings.

As day turned to evening, he studied the risk analysis and the SWOT reports.

His phone rang. He'd missed half a dozen texts. "Why are you still there? I've had to put Jessica to bed."

He looked at his watch. Jesus. Eight o'clock. "Sorry, babe. I'm just leaving."

She remained silent for so long Christian thought she might have hung up. Finally she said, "I'll have some pasta ready for you."

"Thanks, babe."

But he couldn't leave. He had a hunch something was wrong, and read the reports again. He leant on his elbows digesting each word, everything that had been written. The more correct it appeared, the more worried he became that he couldn't find the problem.

It was gone eleven when he switched off the office lights and drove through the empty streets. The house was dark, silent. Rachel had gone to bed, and only the blue digits on the oven cast a ghostly light around the kitchen.

He poured himself a nightcap and sat at the kitchen island sipping the whisky. He had been through everything that day and mostly satisfied himself as to its integrity. Never hurts to check.

Burnham fails. How could the app know, let alone predict a failure?

He picked up a note from Rachel, weighed down by a pound coin. "Forget dinner, I ate it. It was delicious. Buy yourself a take out."

After another sip, he took out his phone and navigated to Zach's app. He opened *Current Predictions*. Nonsense. He couldn't see where he'd read *Burnham* in it now. He must have been imagining it.

He squinted and tried to make out the patterns in the squiggles. He guessed it could be "Burnham". He clicked on *Next Prediction* and watched the screen clear, swirl and rapidly form letters. He spoke as he read, letting his brain form a loose association between his sounds and their meaning. As he stared, the light from the screen made him drowsy. And then it came to him as his eyes were nearly closed and the writing was still a blurred pattern of smoky trails:

Charmed by Lilith.

Fucking hell, how could it guess or known that? Had his flirting with Lilith been so overt that this thing had picked up on it? Did it know his dreams?

Christian called Zach, and let it ring.

He tried again.

No reply.

He texted: *Zach pick up. I need to talk WTF is this thing? Call me.*

Christian sat on the sofa in the lounge and waited for Zach to call. Every few minutes he tried again, but Zach wasn't answering.

He knew Zach was into Artificial Intelligence from university. But predicting the future? Surely not. He had never believed Zach's passion for computer systems was genuine. He had so often portrayed it as a sideline to make cash so he could continue shagging women under canvas, adventuring, skiing or hanging out smoking weed. But when Christian flew to Frankfurt to meet Zach at his new offices, a few months after the midsummer wedding, Zach was genuinely enthusiastic about his business in online horoscopes, of all things.

They had just opened a bottle of tequila. It stood between two shot glasses on top of Zach's brand-new, wide and impressive desk. A blue plate patterned with white Ancient Greek pornographic images held a mound of salt and slices of lemon.

Typical of Zach, the office was not typical. You would hardly know it was a place of work, but for Zach it was a start. The limited staff were already overworked and he was looking to recruit. He thought it would be a matter of months before they had to move again so he had a cellar in a tower block lined up. The offices matched the enterprise — from what Christian knew about it. Dark walls and brick-lined cubicles concealed red sofas, oak tables and large computer screens. Potted plants grew from the floors beneath abstract art and rock-music posters. It was eclectic. Magical, even.

"What a place," Christian said.

"Cool, eh?" Zach lifted the bottle and poured until each glass overflowed. "Drink first, then talk."

They licked salt from the backs of their hands, downed the bitter tequila, sucked on the slices of lemon. "To old times," Christian said.

"To old and *new* times."

"Touché."

"Take a seat, mate." Zach poured another. "I have so much to tell you."

"Well, if you will live in Germany and invite me over only when you're about to be a father then it's always going to be a game of catch up." Christian downed the second shot.

"Fuck me. You must have got laid recently. I've not seen you drink shots like that since uni."

Christian laughed. "Yes, I have, as it happens. Remember Rachel? We're an item."

"Fucking great. Well done. You got away from the books long enough to impress her?"

"She's a lawyer too, remember? She understands. A barrister, actually."

"It must be wild in your house."

"Sometimes, at the end of the day, we've discovered a new interpretation of common law dating back to Alfred the Great. Those days are the most exciting."

Zach laughed. He downed the shot. "To Alfred."

Christian poured a third. "To Alfred."

Behind Zach a small iron-framed window looked out across the dark city. Lights shone through to show the elevated position Zach's office held in Frankfurt's artistic quarter.

"I don't even know what the internet is," Christian said. "I mean, not really. It's so slow and pointless. We use it for email at work, but I don't get it."

"But you've got broadband, right? At home?"

"We've not bothered. We have a modem."

"Bloody hell, still on dial-up. No wonder you think it's slow. I'll bet you don't have a mobile phone either."

"Yes. I have a mobile phone. You should know, you called me on it."

"The internet is the future. It's a beautiful thing. Imagine a world where we all have perfect information. You can't lie or fabricate because everybody has access to the truth. At all times. Instantly. It's going to change the evolution of Homo Sapiens."

"Never one for hyperbole?"

Zach laughed. "I mean it. It's amazing. Get your broadband sorted. It'll change your life."

"So is that it? What your company does? Internet stuff?"

"More specific than that. Actually it was Lilith's idea originally. She'd been surfing astrology websites. I tell you, they are fucking everywhere. People love this stuff. I mean, I know the internet is going to change the world, but you'd think there was more to do than looking up your bloody star signs. People are fucking stupid."

"Ain't no underestimating the capacity for ignorance."

"But as a business opportunity it's fantastic." Zach refilled the shots. "You've got hordes of gullible sheep looking for things to do online, and they're starved. It's a land grab. We've got to ride the wave by feeding them addictive, engaging content and they'll stick with us as the competition fails around us."

"Content?"

"Content is king. A very popular phrase right now. Content is the information on a website. It's the data, the images, the commentary and the interactions." Zach fiddled with his shot glass and toyed with the bottle. "You remember I took a machine-learning paper in my final year? Before I ducked out to work at that bank."

"Er, yeah, I think so."

"Predictive analysis enables a computer to learn from its experiences."

"I remember. You thought it was going to save the world."

"It will. Maybe I was ahead of my time. But I've been looking for a way to use it ever since. I can do clever stuff on my home computer. Until the internet there were limited ways of getting regular updates to your users. You had to post a CD, or wait for them to come into the shop — really painful and slow, not at all useful for things you want to update regularly."

"Like horoscopes."

"Yep. You're a clever bastard, CJ. Like horoscopes. So that's what we're doing. I've got my machine-learning algorithms using the position of the planets and data from the customer to create a tailored horoscope that predicts their future. It's like a planetarium mixed with a fairground gypsy. Science and bullshit fused together in a perfect synergy of money-making."

"I think you're the clever bastard, Zach Hunter."

Zach laughed and reached for the bottle. "Another." He poured. "To clever bastards."

They drank. By the time they made their way out of the offices to a small Thai restaurant two hundred metres away the tequila bottle stood empty. It had been consumed to toasts as wide-ranging as amoebic plant life, future children, Apollo 11 and the motion of planets.

The restaurant had a familiar feel. A typical Asian theme like ones Christian frequented in Bristol. The scent of hot oil clung to rich black-and-gold tapestries, and the menu was pleasingly comprised of the same dishes he knew and loved. But all that was academic. Because as they arrived, he spotted Lilith waiting for them at a bay table. She swelled with the imminent promise of a new baby. Christian was silenced as the memory of the wedding and his sordid dreams played havoc with his thoughts.

Christian and Zach slid into the seats opposite her. Zach reached over the table and kissed her full on the lips. Christian barely heard her words but he saw the kiss. He saw the full sexual contact between them, and suddenly longed to be in the middle.

"Not now, Zach, Lilith said. "We have company. You've had too much to drink."

Zach sat down and laughed. "We may have."

Lilith turned to Christian. "You're seeing Rachel." It was a statement, not a question.

"Rachel. Yes. It's all on. She's going to try and get a job in chambers in Bristol, then we can get a place together."

"She's lovely," Lilith said.

Christian was puzzled for the moment. His head was filled with mismatching information and was trying to make sense of his overwhelming attraction to his mate's wife, the excess alcohol and conversation. "Have you met her?"

"I put in a good word."

"I didn't know."

"I wanted to meet the wife of Zach's best friend so we got on a plane to London."

"We're not married."

"But you will be."

Christian stared into Lilith's eyes and for an instant saw something other than the perfection he'd seen before. Suddenly the blue seemed colder, the mascara a little too heavy, the skin less radiant.

Lilith smiled. Christian's moment of doubt melted. She was stunning.

"She's playing with you, mate," Zach said. "Don't pay any attention. She gets a bit weird, being immersed in horoscopes all day. I sometimes get the creepy feeling there's something in it."

Lilith laughed in a way that made everything else meaningless. Christian could have listened all night and all the next day.

"But we have met her," Lilith said. "At that website launch in Greenwich."

"Yes, that's right," Zach said. "And we did put in a good word. When we realised who she was. I recognised her from the hiking trip."

"Dartmoor," Christian said. It made more sense now. He felt comfortably in control. He knew what everybody else knew.

Even half-drunk, he was in control. Not controlled. Much better.

"What do you think of the baby, Christian?" Lilith asked.

"It's great news. I'm very happy for you."

Zach laughed. "That's formal. What's the matter?"

"Yeah, sorry," he said. "I'm a bit tipsy. Struggling for words."

"Pissed, I'd say."

"We think it was conceived on our wedding night," Lilith said.

Was he drunk, or did she hold Christian's gaze a little bit too long?

7

At 7.00 a.m. on the Monday following the storm, Christian was at his desk organising the week. He texted his team:

> I want a meeting at ten this morning. Everybody is to attend. No excuses.

He ordered a comprehensive review of the last month. The seeds of doubt sown by the newspaper and the prediction were growing into a thorny bush and he was determined his project would not be undermined.

At the meeting Thorpe objected, "Sorry, Christian, but we're ready for rehearsal, barring a few slides. What do you expect us to find?"

"Nothing." Christian said. "I expect you to find nothing, but I want to be absolutely certain there *is* nothing to find. We missed this point, at least." He picked out the newspaper cutting from the Sunday business pages and placed it on the table. "This journalist had figures we were not aware of. It's a small difference, but significant."

"We can't nail down everything. There's always going to be a margin of error. And we have other work now. Are we going to delay it?"

Christian rubbed his nose. "Listen. If we need to delay, that's what we will do. This is the most important deal this company has done in fifteen years. It's the priority. For the sake of a few days' hard work we will make certain it goes smoothly. Agreed? Let's get to it, then."

Over the next week they worked until last thing at night. Pizza was brought in; Christian put their travel, evening meals and breakfasts on expenses. They turned over every document, email, presentation, news report and financial audit for the two companies involved. They went back to basics on their due diligence, checked social media, verified news reports, Companies House records and taxation details. Christian worked the team as hard as he worked himself, and the pressure took its toll. Rachel was unhappy with the arrangements, and made this clear in numerous late phone calls. "I'm sorry," Christian said one night. "I can't get home yet. It's important and I have to get on with it."

"I'm disappointed. Jessica is missing you and there's nobody here in the evenings for her to play with. I'm too tired from carrying *your* other child. Why have you become so obsessed with this? Surely you had it well planned?"

He looked out over the street lamps and watched brake lights on the Avon bridge as cars headed towards the railway station. "I've got to make this the best work I've ever done. I have to make sure again, and again, and then again. It's hard work, but it's nearly over. We'll get through this."

He thought he was being reasonable, but she hung up. And not for the first time that week. He put his head in his hands. He hadn't been sleeping well. The tiredness was taking a toll on his thinking. *Was* he being unreasonable? His days were beset by fear the Burnham deal would not complete, and his nights were plagued by sexual dreams of Lilith — these facts he kept secret from Rachel. He'd woken up for the previous three mornings more exhausted than when he'd gone to bed.

And Zach hadn't returned any of his calls, so when the phone finally rang after Christian's latest argument with Rachel, Christian wasn't expecting it to be Zach. He had reached the conclusion Zach was avoiding him.

"Hi Christian, it's me."

"It's about time. I've left dozens of messages."

"Yes, I've listened to some of them. How many texts can one man send? I thought I'd ring you rather than respond to the four thousand, two hundred what-the-fucks." He laughed.

"Where've you been?"

"We took off to Dartmoor for a few nights. A romantic time away. No devices. Total Zen relaxation and plenty of sex."

Christian swivelled his chair away from the door in case anybody should barge in. He had to say something. Something to make him sound normal while his brain was filled with images of Zach and Lilith making love. "Sounds lovely. The old haunts?"

"Staying in Dartmouth. Going to tour a bit. It's still fantastic down here."

"Zach, those predictions. How did you do it?"

"What do you mean?"

"How did it know about the tree?"

"I'd forgotten about that. Weird, huh?"

"It predicted one of our contracts was going to fail. The Burnham project."

"I've never heard of the Burnham project."

"It's a company name. Not for public consumption. I'm sure it's all in my head. It said *Burnham fails*."

"Is that right? I don't remember. Are you sure?"

"It wasn't that night. We tried it again."

"You found the Next Prediction link. Great. Cool, isn't it. We're slamming it, man. Thousands of downloads."

Christian felt foolish but persisted, "How does it know?"

"It doesn't *know*. It makes a guess. It's a neural network. It inspects your data and pulls together a simple phrase or image. It's a bit of fun. Sometimes it's fucking uncanny, though. Have you tried the horoscope? It's Russell Grant on steroids. It's so good we're getting coverage all over the place. You should try dark mode, man. You'll love it."

"Dark mode?"

"It goes deep. You have to give up, to get up."

"You're talking in tongues. I've no idea what you mean."

"I can take you through it. It's another option. But it needs more data from you. But more importantly, are you going to make the club championship next week? I've not been for so long, I'd appreciate the moral support. There are three guest clubs this year, apparently, including Exeter Blades. It's going to be awesome, and you'll want to defend the title."

Christian wasn't sure if Zach had changed the subject

deliberately or because he thought the predictions unimportant. "I'd forgotten about it. I've been working on the deal. Trying to get it over the line without any mistakes. Lawyer's life."

"If you come along we can talk about my psychic app," Zach said, laughing, "and have a few beers afterwards when you're celebrating your victory."

Christian wasn't sure how Rachel would take the idea of him fencing all day on a Saturday, but by then he was certain to need a break and some intense exercise. His spine was seizing up from the office chairs, and with no time to go running, and the sleepless nights, his infallible routine was collapsing. "All right," he said. "You're on."

Christian got home at 8.00 p.m. In the kitchen he took Jessica from an exhausted Rachel and plonked her in front of the TV and put a kids' DVD on.

"Sometimes it's easier defending a murderer than it is looking after a four-year-old," Rachel said. "Those mothers at the day-care do my head in with their earnestness. I'm expected to hold down a stressful job *and* be on call to help out, ferry the kids to the zoo, make sandwiches and step in when their kids are spitting and fighting."

"You didn't go to the zoo again?" Christian poured a glass of red; a to-the-brim measure.

"I know, it's crazy. I forgot we had the trip planned. No matter. I enjoyed three hours learning about lizards. Again. Can you do the bedtime routine tonight? I think Jessica wants you to read *Daddy Island*. I'm going to soak in a hot bath and finish my book. There's a casserole in the fridge."

"You not eating?"

"I might get a cheese sandwich later." She smiled. "I've got a beautiful cheddar from the deli." Christian watched her walk out of the kitchen and go upstairs. He was reminded of when she was pregnant with Jessica and took a love of cheese to extreme levels, like an addict. He would find packets hidden in the car glove-box and in the weekend bag. She took slices with her to play group and the sandwich toaster was permanently warm. Something about pregnancy drove her mad for the stuff. She said it was hormones. He wondered if pregnancy made her lose a little self-control.

Music blared from the lounge. Jessica needed a bath and a story. He took a deep breath. While he loved looking after his daughter, he also needed to think about work. He berated himself for being annoyed he couldn't spend time with his own thoughts.

He left his wine glass on the kitchen island, collected Jessica and stole her up the stairs. By nine o'clock, with Jessica asleep, or at least quiet, he was forking through a bowl of microwaved casserole and catching up with the news on his mobile phone when a notification popped up.

The Algorithm:

> *How did your day go? Have I helped? It's been five days since your last reading.*

He clicked on the message and a window opened with:

Today's bonus Psychic Reading. Ask any question.

A blood-red microphone icon throbbed in the middle of a black screen.

He paused. He thought about the tree, being *Charmed by Lilith*, and what he thought said *Burnham fails*. The throbbing increased. It seemed to be in time to his own thinking, as if it was in tune. Ridiculous.

"Okay, Algorithm. How do I stop Burnham from failing?"

The throbbing microphone dissipated like a cloud of smoke to be replaced with a waiting icon above the words *Psychic Reading Progressing. Hold your phone firmly*. A few moments passed and with theatrical effect in a scripted font, words formed from a pattern of swirling mist:

I feel you have great deal of stress in your life at the moment, and you are not completely comfortable in your environment. It's important you take time to relax. Burnham may fail through no fault of any person. It may be a matter of time and timing. But an information leak may help you recognise the path you must take.

"This is fucking hokum." He put the phone down and returned to his casserole. He ate mechanically. He grated some of Rachel's prize cheddar over it. She certainly knew her cheese. He stared at the screen while chewing. It was right about one thing, the stress. But what middle-aged man with a family and a profession isn't under stress?

When he finished the meal, he took the bowl to the dishwasher and tidied up all the pans. He poured another glass of wine, sat down at the island and picked up the phone once more:

Jo. Do me a favour and run a report of all the emails going to personal addresses from the Burnham team. We should have the personal addresses for the team in the BCP address book, if you don't have them anywhere else. Cross-reference and print out anything mentioning Dave Hinchley or Epoch AI. Thx Christian.

It was a hunch, nothing more. But as he pressed Send Christian had an anxious feeling in his gut.

8

Sitting at the side of the pool in a strongly chlorine-scented atmosphere was not Rachel's idea of a good time. But it had been a routine for so long she wondered if this phase in her life would ever end. The benches had no cushioning, they were often damp, and the reverberating screams of the children destroyed any moments of unlikely peace.

Jessica's "Dunking Ducks" involved arriving at ten o'clock, struggling to inflate water wings to a pressure Jessica approved of, then ten minutes playing sharks in the shallow end before being allowed to leave the pool to watch the little darlings from the benches on the side. Sometimes there was pleasure to be had, as when Jessica collected all the floating balls before the other children understood the task, but most of the time Rachel would rather be somewhere else. She felt guilty, a bad mother, when she had thoughts like this.

Today things were going well. Jessica had not had a meltdown over the pressure in the water wings, the water on the floor of the changing room, or even that she had a different teacher this week. She had been excitable but calm, a perfect daughter, and Rachel found she had time to check work emails, answer a few brief requests from solicitors and check in with her clerk to make sure nothing needed dealing with. She did resent the intrusion of her work in her child-care time, but if she was honest, she needed some adult intrusion to help her cope with the monotonous repetition.

As she clicked Send on her final email, she noticed a flashing black-and-red notification in the corner of her screen. It was Zach and Lilith's app. She opened it up.

It's been nearly a week since your last reading. Are you getting what you need? Open up, to see your reading for the next week.

She followed the instructions to a weekly reading menu. It told her that however much of a drag life might seem at the moment it was all for the best. It told her to make space for me-time when things got on top of her, and to look for help from her loved ones. It ended with:

New friends will offer unexpected support.

She smiled. She thought of Lilith and their conversation the week before. Yes, Lilith could be a friend. She dictated a text:

Hey Lilith, it's Rachel. I was thinking of popping round. You in?

And was surprised by an immediate reply:

Nourishing salad and organic salmon for lunch. All ready to go. Come on round.

By midday, after showering, drying and dressing Jessica, and driving the few miles across the city centre, Rachel parked outside Zach and Lilith's new place. She climbed out of the car and helped Jessica from the child seat.

"Where are we, Mummy?"

"We're going to visit Lilith and Zach."

"Have they got any toys?"

"We'll have to see. Bring Everywhere with you. We won't be long. Just a quick lunch."

Rachel was impressed at how fresh and clean the front of the house looked. The approach to the porch had been immaculately weeded, the gravel raked into perfect small ripples. Flowers draped from a hanging basket over the door. A life-size fawn statue playing panpipes took pride of place in a bed of ivy to the left of the entrance. It looked whimsical and intriguing. Rachel and Jessica walked hand in hand up to the entrance and rang the bell.

When Lilith opened the door, she found Rachel and Jessica staring at the statue. "Do you like him? He's called Rob."

"That's a funny name," Jessica said.

"I know. It makes me laugh. Come on in. The kettle's on and I have a surprise for you, Jessica."

She embraced Rachel. "It's lovely of you to pop round. Zach's flown back to Frankfurt. I was feeling a little lonely."

"You should have said."

Rachel followed Lilith into the kitchen to the small kitchen table already laid out with plates and glasses, with salmon salad in a glass bowl in the middle. Green leaves and red vegetables and a glaze of oil reflected the light coming from the kitchen window. They sat on wooden chairs that looked as if they'd been bound together from hazel sticks.

"These are lovely," Rachel said. "I've never seen anything like them. Certainly not in Ikea."

"They're family treasures from generations back. Aren't they fab?"

"You've made it so homely in such a short time."

"Thank you. But I can't lie. We had some help. Honestly, work's so busy we wouldn't have had time to unpack our suitcases without some family coming over."

"That's so nice. I'm lucky to have my mum and dad here, too. I don't know what I'd do without them. Especially where Jessica is concerned. Where are your parents? I thought they were in Germany."

Jessica interrupted. "Where's my surprise?"

"That's no way to talk, young lady." Rachel said. "You sit quietly."

"It's okay," said Lilith. "Come on, Jessica, let's see what I have for you." She opened a cupboard and pulled down a huge leather-bound book of fairy tales.

Jessica gasped. Rachel felt slightly uncomfortable at the expense.

Lilith sat down and pulled Jessica onto her knee. "This is my favourite book." She opened it up and a paper cottage unfolded upward from the pages. The cottage had a steep dark-slate roof, a two-storey tower and a well in the garden. "This is the witch's cottage. She makes all sorts of potions and magic spells. She helps all the people find the things they've lost in the forest." She turned the page over. A harlequin jester popped up. "And this is the piper. He's not always as good as he seems. And you should never be naughty around the piper."

"What's his name?"

"Nobody knows. And he never tells anyone in case they call him when he is in the middle of mischief."

"Is he called Rob?"

Jessica and Rachel laughed. "Maybe. But you'll have to read the story to find out. Why don't you go and read over there, so me and Mummy can talk."

Jessica took the book into the hall and lay down on the carpet, turning the pages. They could hear her explaining to Everywhere what was going on in the pictures.

"That's so generous of you," said Rachel. "She loves it."

"Those books are ever so popular in Germany. It's not much. A little something."

"You were talking about your parents?"

"Yes. Mum and Dad are in Frankfurt. Well, about thirty kilometres outside, in the country. But we all come from South Wales, and I've got extended family in Monmouth. Where me and Zach were married. You weren't with Christian then."

"Christian says it was a sumptuous affair. Like a medieval banquet."

"Does he? He was the life and soul, if I remember."

"Doesn't sound like Christian. He's usually shy and quiet in social gatherings."

Lilith looked puzzled for a moment. "Such a long time ago now, so many people there. You know how wedding days go so fast. One minute you're up with the larks, full of excitement and anticipation, and the next you're on your back putting the wedding vows into action." She winked and laughed.

"It goes so quickly, doesn't it. But if you want to see time fly, wait until you have kids—" Rachel stopped abruptly. She closed her eyes. "Sorry, Lilith. I didn't mean…"

Lilith put her hand on Rachel's arm and shook her head. "That's all in the past. Let's eat."

They chatted about their weddings, their men, the state of the city centre and the coalition government making everybody unhappy. Lilith brewed a tea made from herbs grown in a small wicker basket outside the kitchen door in the full sun. Rachel wasn't sure if it was the herb tea, the beams of sunlight warming the kitchen, or the gentle and open talk, but she relaxed in Lilith's company — and the fairy-tale book kept Jessica busy for an hour and a half.

Around three o'clock Rachel checked her phone to find a text from Christian saying he'd had a particularly trying day at work and would be home early. "I have to get back home. We've got an afternoon play-date with one of Jessica's friends, and Christian's due back," she said.

"So soon? Let me give you some more of that tea to take away. It helps you relax."

"Thank you, it's really good. I've had a lovely time. Did you know your app said I'd be supported by a new friend? I think it's you. It's uncanny, isn't it?"

Lilith smiled. "I *am* your friend, Rachel. Anything you need, just ask." She handed Rachel a small brown paper bag tied with a thin black ribbon. "Use it like normal tea."

9

It was apparent from the layout and decoration of his office that Roy Edwards didn't get many visitors with good news, or many visitors from senior leadership, or many visitors at all for that matter. With one small window on the north side of the block, three desks and a dead cactus on a set of five shelves next to the door, it felt as if daylight was as much an intrusion into cybersecurity operations as people were. Nonetheless, Christian found himself knocking quietly on the door and pushing into the space without waiting for a reply. He was about to become the managing partner, so he was allowed to go where he pleased.

And besides, cybersecurity had become critical in the last few years. Even Christian knew that. And though it caused endless tedium when changing laptops, or when trying to share files with people outside the organisation, everybody accepted it as a required blockage of communications and efficiency. Christian suspected you couldn't give company secrets away if you tried — the rest of the world was too busy to care — and yet Beaufort spent well over two million a year on cybersecurity efforts. At the top of that money tree was Roy Edwards, a man whose face could sink a thousand ships and whose attitude would break them up before they hit the bottom. Tall, wiry, bald and bespectacled with a Yorkshire accent, he did, however, present a face of hidden, secret knowledge that Beaufort drew upon. According to Roy, he kept them safe from casual trolls, agency manipulation, industrial espionage, extortion, phishing, hacking and social engineering. He was worth more than Beaufort paid him and was forever pushing for increased budgets. The money did not go on houseplants.

Roy looked up from his screen with an expression that was less of an invitation to speak and more of a *Go fuck yourself, I'm busy.*

"It's Roy, isn't it?" Christian knew full well it was Roy. He didn't know why he opened with the question. As he waited for a response, he realised he was scared of being revealed as having less knowledge about cybersecurity than a dog knows about copyright law.

"Yes. It's Christian, isn't it?"

Christian let the jibe go. This was not a time for social lessons. He pointed at the visitor's chair piled high with hardback books. "Can I sit down?"

"Sure."

Christian moved the books off the chair and piled them on the corner of Roy's desk. "It's not a work thing. More personal. I hoped you could give me some advice about this app I've installed."

"Yeah?"

Christian pulled out his phone, swiped the screen to turn it on and showed Roy. "It's this horoscope thing. It's supposed to be a game, but it seems to know everything. How does it work?"

Roy took the phone and poked the interface. "This. Yeah, I've heard about this. There's some amazingly clever stuff in here and a few crazy conspiracy theories doing the rounds on Twitter." He rubbed his goatee. "It's on the watch list."

"Watch list?"

"Suspicious behaviours. It's not necessarily anything to worry about. Nearly all social-media apps are on the watch list. But it means we should be careful not to give it too much information. You never know where it might end up."

"All I've done is put it on my phone."

"You sure?"

"Yes."

"You didn't sign in with an eFace account on your laptop first?"

How did he know? "Well, yeah. I did."

"So that's where it gets its data from. And that's probably why it's on the watch list."

"What do you mean by data?" Realising it sounded like it was a completely stupid question, Christian added, "In this context, I mean. I know what data is."

Roy looked at Christian as if he doubted. "Your profile data. Age, sex, marital status. Do you use your real name on eFace?"

Christian nodded.

"You know that's against company policy?"

"No. Is it? Why?"

Roy looked tired. Bored, even. "If you put your personal details on social media, then it's easy for everyone to find you. You know — clients, competitors. It's probably innocent, but you should take the proper precautions."

"Just by putting my personal detail online?"

"Who you're friends with, where you go, how you spend your days, your kids, photos that can be doctored, it can trace your whereabouts. It's all there, if you know where to look. So try not to make it easy."

"You're saying this app is using all my personal details and making assumptions."

"These things are really smart. What you don't see is the link to the cloud going on behind the app. It takes your data and crunches it on a thousand servers — it's got its own supercomputer ticking over somewhere. It correlates personal data you've given it with any other information it can find about you online. It utilises machine-learning algorithms to guess what you might do next. Humans are easy to predict, it turns out. And the more you interact with it, the more it learns and the better it gets."

"I'm my own person. How can a machine do that? How do *you* know all this?"

"It's a guess. I'm in the business. It's how I'd do it. One day this stuff's going to be used to manipulate how we think and feel. Even how we vote. Things we never thought were possible, made true by algorithms. You wait, in another few years it's going to cause disasters. I'll bet it keeps asking for more information."

Christian nodded.

"That's how it goes. Look, I think you need to get this off your phone and get rid of it from your home computer. It might seem harmless, but until we know a bit more we should take the precautionary principle to heart. I'll do some digging and get back to you. I can help you uninstall it if you want. It can be tricky to find all the threads sometimes. These things don't like being uninstalled." Roy smiled. "They can fight back."

"You make it sound like it's alive."

The smile broadened.

"Okay. Thanks, Roy. Interesting. I can take it from here. I'll sort it."

"That is a company phone, isn't it?"

"Yes."

"So it needs to be clean. That's not just me saying that, that's the auditors and the BCP guys. You have to take it off."

"Like I said, I'll sort it."

Christian left the cybersecurity office embarrassed and irritated. It was okay for Roy to offer help but another thing to lecture him. This was a law firm, not a tech giant.

Nonetheless, when Christian got back to his office, checked emails and pulled out the draft presentation pack for the Burnham dénouement, his thoughts returned to the app on his phone. He resented the intrusion. He'd been unable to stop thinking about it for more than a few hours for two weeks. Roy was probably right: he should delete it.

He pulled out his phone and looked for the app's uninstall option.

A knock on the door startled him from his focus, and Jo walked in. "Hey, Christian. I've got those printouts for you."

"Which ones?"

"The private email address ones. That mention Dave Hinchley or Epoch AI. There's only a couple." She put a couple of sheets of A4 on his desk.

He looked down.

He saw one name.

He read the email attached.

"Fucking hell, Jo. Did you read this?"

She nodded. "I can't believe it."

*

At three Christian finally managed to get out of the office and pick up some sushi rolls and miso soup. Sitting on a stool at a high bench, beneath four massive posters detailing the à la carte menu, he used chopsticks to decorate each roll in ginger, soy sauce and wasabi before popping it whole into his mouth, chewing and washing it down with the miso. As he ate, he contemplated the morning's stunning turn of events. He could hardly believe it. If he hadn't seen the prediction on the app last night, and asked Jo for the emails, he would never have believed William Thorpe could be undermining the negotiation by feeding client information to the other side. Not that Burnham was about one side versus the other, but it was about finding a mutually beneficial deal that each could stomach. Sometimes that meant compromise and sometimes it meant not being entirely open about what they could afford, or the true value of things they put on the table. It was a business deal, after all, and these were always conducted with a healthy scepticism about the other side's position. That was why each side went through a long period of due diligence, digging up evidence to support or question the deal.

And Thorpe had been so blatant about it. He'd copied papers to his personal email account and sent them on to the competition without trying to hide what he was doing. Attempting to hide in plain sight, Christian thought. Unfortunately for Thorpe, he'd accessed his internet email account from his company phone and left an audit trail. *Cybersecurity saves the day.*

But Christian was having a late lunch because the instant dismissal Thorpe endured had taken time to organise. He'd had to convince Howard it was the right move.

"Doesn't sound like Thorpe to me," were Howard's opening words when presented with the evidence. "Let's get him in here to explain himself."

"This is grounds for summary dismissal, Howard. We can't take the chance he will send messages or get wind of what's happening. His access needs to be taken away, and he should be marched from the building. We can invite him back for an inquiry, if that's your wish, but we first need to secure all the systems and make sure he can do no more harm."

Christian had brought Roy Edwards in to explain the evidence and the audit trail. His clear illustration of what Thorpe had done and how he'd done it made Howard understand the severity of it all.

Thorpe denied it. At first, when two security guards appeared at his desk, he treated it as a joke. But when they took his phone and laptop and searched his desk, he started getting frantic. "What the fuck is this?"

"Your employment contract is being terminated for gross misconduct with immediate effect," Christian said. "You will receive a letter in due course. Your employment rights and right to appeal to an employment tribunal are not affected."

"Why? What the fuck are you accusing me of?"

"It will all be in the letter."

"I don't want to wait for a fucking letter. That's just fucking weasel words. We're supposed to be friends. I've worked for you for five years. Is that worth nothing? What the fuck have I done?"

Christian stayed silent while the security guards packed a cardboard box with Thorpe's belongings and escorted him from the building. Thorpe swore and shouted throughout at anybody that came near about how he'd not done anything and who the fuck had set him up?

Christian watched the lift door close behind them and took in a deep breath. He held it for the count of six and then breathed out. Now all he had to do was let the other staff know what had happened. *Fuck, I hate HR issues.*

He made a short and to the point announcement to everybody in the office and then came out for lunch, deep in contemplation. The situation demanded he went for a run as soon as he could. He figured he could go home early today. If he needed to finish anything, he could do it later. He texted Rachel:

Stressful morning. Going to come home early xx

And then he looked at his app reading from the night before:

an information leak may help you recognise the path
you must take.

It was so spot-on. Fucking amazing. He pressed the next reading button and waited for the swirling to dissipate:

I think you have another question for me.

Christian looked around him. Only one other customer could possibly overhear, and she was on the far side of the counter, busy with her own mobile phone and struggling with the chopsticks. He spoke into the app. "Yeah, I have. Is the Burnham project safe now?"

The screen swirled and almost immediately text appeared.

You have been greatly challenged, and have been in a great hurry. Speed can sometimes create problems and you must beware of freezing, but right now you are going at the right pace for your life. Life is not a rehearsal, but a rehearsal will bring you great rewards.

This is fucking bonkers, Christian thought. It knew about the Burnham rehearsal now. He wondered if Thorpe had been publishing the company's business online for the Algorithm to find. But he was pleased it suggested great rewards.

He searched online for the Algorithm, scrolled through results about a 2014 movie, a rock band and a musical — and then a YouTube hit caught his eye. *Mind Bending Conspiracies* on a channel published by Pikey Pete.

He pulled out his earbuds from his jacket pocket and inserted them. He clicked Play, to be confronted with a flashing warning about how this was entertainment and not to be taken seriously. It was just a theory. And then it cut to a bearded fifty-year-old man in a black Rush T-shirt who welcomed his audience to another edition of *Mind Bending Conspiracies,* pitched his book, then displayed the splash screen to Zach and Lilith's app.

"Hello, conspiracy buffs," he said. "Today we ask, can the spirit world be contacted from an app? That is the outrageous claim behind the Algorithm that's been the number-one download for the last month on all the platforms. But is it true? Well, sometimes truth is stranger than fiction, as we found out when we tried to test the claims behind the Algorithm. But first, let's take a look at what the app does."

Pikey Pete demonstrated the app but refused to tell his audience what it predicted for him. "I'll keep that to myself," he said breathlessly. "It's not for you. But I can say this app has given me some pretty strange predictions, and while I can't say they've all come true, I can't say they are all wrong either. Perhaps that's just me. We thought it was all a harmless game, but then we discovered a couple of users who swear the app has predicted some pretty serious stuff for them. This might make for uncomfortable watching, conspiracy buffs, and they've been anonymised for their own protection."

The screen showed a dark room with the silhouetted of a person visible in the darkness. A woman with an East End London accent spoke. "It started off with small stuff, you know, your usual horoscope kind of thing, like I was gonna meet a tall dark stranger or go on holiday and meet my dream man. But then it started telling me really crazy things that were *really* accurate. Like, stuff only I know about. Like, it told me my boss was going to have a car accident, and then he went and crashed on the motorway. Then it said I was going to get caught for shoplifting and I thought, no way, nobody knows, so I asked how I could get away with it, but it just says my time is up and my spirit guides wanted me to learn a lesson. Anyway. I'm up before the beak next week 'cos I stole this top while my boss was in hospital and they got me on CCTV. I wish I believed it now, I wouldn't be here."

Cut to another studio and another blacked out figure, this time a man. His voice was slow and resigned. Depressed, with a German accent.

"My son died. He stepped in front of a train. I blame this Algorithm. It encouraged him. It told him where and when it was going to happen and why. He just went along with it. He had been diagnosed with schizophrenia. We couldn't protect him. We only found out he'd been using it much later on when the police went through his phone records of what he'd been

94

watching and running. I am so angry with them all. How could they make this sort of thing public? It's ancient evil and it should be left alone, not put in an app."

Pikey Pete came back on. "Ancient evil? That's the stuff we love on *Mind Bending Conspiracies*. Of course we wanted to interview the developers and ask them how they managed to put spirits inside an app — but, well, we couldn't find them, and they didn't answer any emails. They don't seem to exist anywhere despite the app store that supposedly has good records of where all the apps come from."

The screen changed to a photograph of a burnt-out building. Pete continued in voice-over: "It gets stranger. This is where the company used to run from, in Frankfurt. It went up in flames three months ago and two employees were burnt to death. It's a terrible tragedy. But where is the company now? The app itself wouldn't tell us when we asked. That's at least one thing it doesn't seem to know.

"Now, I have to say, this app is pretty strange and I'm totally surprised by what it knows is going to happen. It says on the Help screen that the app is 'an intuitive intelligence that can be a friend and guide when you need it. Like a good friend, let it get to know you, and it can support you through your challenging life situations.' We wonder if that could include communing with the spirit world on your behalf. So we spoke to the famous spiritualist and author Mary Beckett in darkest Somerset, and asked her if such a thing is possible. Here's what she had to say."

The video cut to a white-haired, elderly woman in a long, pink lacy dress. She twiddled a crucifix necklace and swayed her head gently while she spoke. "We know divine intuition is not confined to human beings. Dogs have a sixth sense for when their owners are returning from work. Birds are able to instantly communicate how the flock should change direction, and we know migrating mammals are able to sense the presence of predators beyond the reach of scent alone. I see no reason why an intelligent computer could not possess intuition enough to hear messages from the spirits. But this is not a game. Not all spirits have your best interests in mind. Some are jealous of our energy and the lives we lead."

"Scary words from Mary there," said Pikey Pete. "But remember, that's only a theory. See you later conspiracy buffs."

Christian took out his earbuds and closed the page to stop YouTube from automatically playing the next video. He scrolled through the comments: most displayed hilarity at the idea that an app could commune with spirits, but then one comment caught his eye from its overloaded use of exclamation marks.

"WARNING!!!! Don't download this app. It's dangerous. It really knows. You can't control what it reveals. Listen to Mary," it said, and left an email address for Mrs Beckett's literary agent.

10

Rehearsals were Beaufort & Soames' quality control for critical business deals. The negotiating team presented a case as they would pitch it to clients or parties to the deal. It was the job of the inquisitors to find all the reasons an offer might be rejected.

The meeting could easily last all day. Rehearsals had no rules; inquisitors were required to use any necessary strategy to find a way of refuting the deal. The intention was to forestall any objection and uncover intelligence that might result in unexpected outcomes. Some partners were successful because they destroyed prospective deals rather than created them; it was better to withdraw than to present a poor report. Other law firms conducted dry runs, but as far as Christian knew, Beaufort's had developed a unique process, and it created nervous butterflies in even the best-prepared negotiator.

He stood in the high-ceilinged lobby outside the conference room, inhaled and held. He studied the cybersecurity poster urging readers to beware of phishing attacks. He read the five corporate values on another poster: Collaboration, Courage, Honesty, Accountability and Care. He grabbed the door handle and noticed the sweat on his palms. He breathed out. Rehearsals were more challenging than the final presentation to clients: after a rehearsal the real thing was as certain to go well as night follows day. He entered.

He was struck by the smell of fresh coffee. Howard poured an oversize cafetière and passed cups around a dozen of Christian's colleagues seated at the large wooden table. The room was big enough for the table and chairs when a person was seated but afforded little room to squeeze past otherwise.

"Morning, gentlemen," Christian said.

Greetings rippled around the table like small disturbances in a comforting cup of tea. Christian wasn't fooled. He knew they wanted to beat him. If only because he'd never been beaten before.

The moment he was seated, Howard began proceedings by formally introducing the teams and explaining the format and importance of the day's work. Christian noted the inquisitors' document-wallets flat on the table, their blank pads with pens resting on top.

Howard's voice competed with tapping tea spoons and the scraping of the biscuit plate as it was passed around the table. The negotiating team did not eat biscuits during a presentation, on Christian's orders, and he took pleasure as his competition munched on Jammie Dodgers, covering themselves and their pristine pads in biscuit crumbs. Round One to him.

"Let's have the presentation then," Howard said at the end of a lengthy speech outlining the strategic importance of the Burnham project.

Christian stood up and took the remote control clicker in his hand. He shared his laptop screen to the sixty-inch display bolted to the wall.

He stared at his audience.

They sat immaculately before him in pinstripe suits and black ties.

He checked his black Oxford shoes were polished. He felt for his tie and buttoned his own pinstripe jacket.

He looked over their heads, through the window, to the distant hills.

He thought of Lilith.

He tried to speak.

He felt the panic rise.

"How did your day go?" Rachel asked as Christian hung his coat in the hall. She was standing on the stairs holding a cup of tea.

Jessica was watching *Balamory* on the telly. Christian detected cooking aromas emanating from the kitchen.

"That smells good. I'm starving."

"So, come on. How did it go? I thought you'd text me at least, but you've been on radio silence."

"Pour me a wine. I'll say hello to the monster and then tell you all about it."

"Tease. It's a deal — I want to hear every detail."

"You sure about that? Every detail." Christian knew Rachel might want to know the day's outcomes, but the dull minutiae of corporate rehearsals would send her to sleep. She had chosen criminal law to keep away from the tedious goings-on in big business.

He sneaked into the lounge to surprise Jessica and spent ten minutes listening to her recap the day's story on *Balamory*, which had apparently been a rainy day for work and school. He took off his jacket and undid his tie. When he joined Rachel, they sat at the kitchen island while Christian took her through the highlights of the afternoon's rehearsal. He told her how the team's preparation had been meticulous, how they closed off every argument before it was made, and before the inquisitors had a chance to put any point across. "They didn't know which way to turn. Honestly, it made them look like amateurs. I'm thrilled with the whole thing." He leant across and kissed her passionately on the lips.

"Well done, you. Howard must be pleased."

"I'll catch up with him next week. I nearly blew it. I froze for a good twenty seconds at the start. It was just like my dream the other night. But I was ready, I'd meticulously prepared."

"As you do, Mr Jarvik."

"But it was all of them sitting around in an audience that made me think of the dream. Anyway, I got through it. Nothing to worry about. How was your day?"

She gave a forced smile. "Little rascals singing group this morning, and then a playdate with the swimming mums this afternoon over in Bedminster. It's been a long round of excitement and sugary snacks."

"And Jessica had a good time, I take it?"

"Jessica always has a good time."

"You sound like you need a night off."

"That would be nice. But it's my turn."

"I'm feeling generous. Anyway, you've cooked a roast dinner. I can smell it. I was supposed to be getting a pizza, wasn't I?"

"I thought I'd surprise you."

Christian wasn't surprised. Even after he'd pissed her off by getting home late, this was who she was. He topped his glass up and chinked it on hers. "Here's to nice surprises. Do I need to do the veg?"

"Some carrots and cabbage in the fridge. I'll watch and drink tea."

He took the cabbage, cut it into slices and put them in the steamer. He shared more details of his day and explained how he thought it was going to play out now that Beaufort & Soames' rehearsal had put the seal of approval on the Burnham deal.

"So was the prediction about Burnham failing just nonsense?" Rachel asked.

Christian stopped chopping carrots and turned towards her. It didn't make rational sense, but somehow the Algorithm was helping. "If it hadn't been for sacking William Thorpe earlier in the week, and the warning last weekend, I don't think this deal would have got through today. We found small holes in the finances and share structures that meant we could have exited the meeting with our tails tucked between our legs and a large bite on our arses. When we reviewed William's work with a detailed eye, he'd been selling the company short. We don't know why — perhaps he was getting a back hander or was going to buy some shares — but if he'd stayed on the team, the deal as it stood would have been a disaster."

"It's a bit creepy, really."

"I'll tell Zach. See what he says. Something doesn't sit right."

Rachel nodded and picked up her glass. "Oh, one other thing, also a bit odd. The men have cleared most of the tree from the garden, but they said it had been sawn through part-way."

"Part-way? What did they mean?"

"Something about the trunk had been sawn through and that had weakened it. They said that's why it came down."

"That doesn't make sense."

"Perhaps the neighbour knows something."

"Yeah. Maybe. I'll have a word."

Christian worried about the tree all night. To help him sleep, he tried mindful triangular-breathing that he'd been taught on a leadership course, and when that failed he twisted around trying to locate a comfortable spot. He was too hot, and then he was too cold. The longer he stayed awake the more anxious he became. But the tree remained rooted in his thoughts until the early hours, and after eventually falling asleep around four, he awoke suddenly when a dream of Lilith lying naked before him became so real he had to check he was still with Rachel.

What the fuck was going on? He'd not seen Lilith for two weeks, but the dream had been so vivid he could smell her. She lay with her arms above her head with her eyes open and a gentle smile. He had been powerless to stop moving towards her. She lifted her hands, beckoned, and he complied. The dream ended abruptly when he was lying so close to her that his stomach felt the warmth of her skin, and the top of his thighs slid sensuously over hers.

With little sleep, but desperate to end the torture, he got out of bed at half-five, put on his running gear and slipped out of the house.

He ran for fifteen miles into the countryside beyond Clifton suspension bridge. He focused on each step, felt his heel hit the ground with every movement; he breathed in clarity and breathed out calm. By the time he ran back to the house he had finally relaxed, and as he turned into his driveway he saw the neighbour was up and clearing leaves from his path. He stopped running and walked over. "You're up early, Dave," he said. Dave had been their neighbour since they moved in. He had lived in the house for over thirty years and was seeing out his retirement by keeping the garden pristine and playing host to his thirteen grandchildren.

"Morning. Nice day, isn't it. Good run?"

"Not bad. I took in the sights on the ridge overlooking the Levels."

Dave nodded in appreciation. "I don't know how you do it. Furthest I've ever run is after my grandchild's hat on a windy day."

"Did you speak to the tree guys this week? They said something about it being partially cut through at the trunk. Did you have a go at it?" Christian laughed, realising how silly the question was given Dave's seventy or so years and that he'd never so much as seen him pick up a strimmer.

"They showed me the trunk before they took it away. I think one of the apprentices must have done it and not told anybody. They had a different person here each day." Dave smiled. "I don't know how they can keep track."

Christian nodded. "I guess."

He went inside. He showered, dressed in loose sports clothing and made scrambled eggs. Jessica was now up and watching telly, and when he took breakfast in bed to Rachel she was fast asleep, as if she'd not moved an inch all night long. He took the dish back to the kitchen and covered it. He sat down at the island, swivelled his plate towards himself, took a first mouthful with a fork, swiped his phone with his free hand and casually flicked to the app.

"How are things going for me?"

As usual it took a few moments to form a reading. He ate a few more mouthfuls and buttered a slice of toast.

You have been tied up with your desires this week and have had great success and made sacrifice. Look forward to new Burnham challenges next week. A friend will be successful in a competition.

He stared in amazement at the screen. Stunned. He laughed. It was crazy. How on earth did it know the fencing competition was running or about Burnham or, for heaven's sake, his own dreams? Was it talking about his dreams? The desires? Could it be? He stopped laughing. He felt uncomfortable, as if somebody was watching him from behind. His neck chilled from a light kitchen draught.

But then he suddenly realised the truth and felt utterly fooled.

His tiredness was making all sorts of things pop in his head from black magic to a witch living next door or a fucking leprechaun possessing his smartphone. But it was much simpler than that. He'd lost his sense of reality. He'd been stupid. One simple explanation solved the whole puzzle. He put the phone down and sighed. Then he laughed.

11

By mid-morning Christian had forgotten about his sleepless night and provocative dream and proceeded to the senior men's sabre finals. The vast City Academy sports hall had echoed with clashing sabres all morning, as fencers from local clubs battled out the annual by-invitation competition. Competitors' bags and equipment littered the floor along the dark-blue wall on one length of the hall; natural light flooded through broad plate glass windows on the north-east corner.

Christian had not yet managed to grab a meaningful chat with Zach but was determined to corner him at some point. Part of him was angry for falling for the whole thing — but another part was fascinated.

He texted Rachel to say he'd made the finals, and she drove over with Jessica. She sat on the benches at the back reading a novel while Jessica ran to find her father. Watching him change into his fencing gear she laughed. "You look silly, Daddy. Why are you wearing long socks?"

Christian pulled the white socks over his calves and secured the bottom of his three-quarter length trousers using the Velcro fastenings. "It's to stop our legs getting hurt by the swords."

"Why don't you wear long trousers? Then you wouldn't need silly socks."

It was simple logic and Christian didn't know the answer. Why was fencing equipment so desperately unsexy? Most fencers looked like pigeons in tights; the clothing was at best unflattering and at worst ridiculous. "Because that's the way it's been done for a long time." He was unsatisfied with his answer and turned to put on his lame, trying to avoid more difficult questions.

Zach walked over and sat on the bench. "If we both get through this round we'll meet in the semis," he said. He'd been to check on the leader board and find out his next opponent.

"I guess so," Christian said dispassionately, searching through the bag for a gauntlet. He didn't look up.

"Well, it might be uninteresting to you, Mr Jarvik," Zach said, "but I've never made the second round before. Just because you are a high and mighty defending champion—"

Christian stood up with the glove in his hand, "To be champion, one must think like a champion," he said, putting on a French accent and wobbling his head. "Champions must be arrogant and French, naturellement."

"Daddy, you're from Denmark and England." Jessica said, puzzled.

Christian laughed. "Well, an English-Frenchman, then." Despite his terrible night's sleep, he felt wide awake and the strenuous exercise to get through the heats, on top of his run, had invigorated him. He was energised, ready for battle. He picked out a sabre from the bag. "Jessica, I have a bout in a few minutes. Go and sit with Mummy while I talk with Zach."

"Can I have your smartphone to take pictures? Please Daddy."

He hesitated.

"Please. Please. Please."

"Go on then. But you be careful." He reached into his bag and handed her his phone. She walked towards Rachel holding it at arm's length like some grand prize.

"She's such a great kid," Zach said, his eyes following the little girl to the seats. She clambered up the benches to sit with her mother. "You've been *so* lucky."

Christian felt a flush of pride edged with sadness. "Are you and Lilith planning any?" It was a throwaway comment but Christian immediately regretted it. "Sorry, Zach. I wasn't—"

"Nothing to be sorry about. That was a long time ago. We're well recovered. We both took our time and dealt with it. It's okay. And anyway, who knows what the future will bring."

"There's still time." Christian felt uncomfortable even saying this.

"Still time. But today we have other challenges to combat." Zach lunged forward stretching his abductors and thigh muscles.

"Talking of which, Lilith's here just in time."

Lilith was at the hall doors looking lost. Zach waved with his sabre. Her attraction had not diminished in the two weeks since Christian had seen her last and the dreams made her all the more alluring. She wore a white open-necked blouse over dark blue jeans. Simple. Fresh. Beautiful.

He tore his gaze from her and turned to Zach, "Before we start, you're pulling my leg with this app, right? Nice one. You got me. I admit it. Like a kipper in a tin. How do you do it?"

Zach laughed. "I'm not pulling your leg, mate. It's real. Spooky, isn't it."

"Come off it. How'd you do it? It knows so much about me. It even said you were going to win a competition today."

"Show me."

Christian rummaged in his bag and pulled out his phone. He thumbed to the app and showed Zach the last reading. "Look. 'A friend is successful in a competition'."

"How many friends have you got in the finals?"

"What do you mean?"

"Come on, how many friends do you have in this hall that might win?"

"Ah! You mean it's not talking about you?"

Zach shrugged and started to walk towards Lilith and Rachel, who had by now found each other and were already deep in conversation.

Christian wasn't satisfied. Zach wasn't taking him seriously. He grabbed his arm and spun Zach around to face him. "But how does it know there's a fucking competition?"

"Steady, mate. What's going on?"

"Zach, stop being evasive. You're taking the piss, right?" He laughed. "Come on. I've had enough. I give up. You win. *You* know about the competition. You're feeding it, aren't you. It must be you. Otherwise, how does it know there's a fencing tournament?"

Zach took another look at the app. "Mate. It doesn't say fencing or sabre, it could be talking about a football match. But in any case, even if it did, it got it from the internet. I'll bet I could go to your eFace page, find out which fencing club you belong to, look up when they had a competition and predict something like this. Of course a friend of yours is going to win. You know everybody here."

"What about the Burnham project? It knows and that's secret. But you know. I've told you. Or Rachel has via Lilith."

"You're getting a bit strange, mate. Come on, nothing's secret any more. It just takes one person in your friends list or in your business contacts and it finds shit out."

Christian thought about Thorpe and how they'd not been able to control where all the data ended up despite a tight team and high salaries.

Zach put a hand on his shoulder and looked him in the eye. "It's not magic, though it looks a lot like it. But that's what it does. That's why it's selling like hot cakes. People think it's got God's phone number or something. And we aren't going to tell them otherwise, but it's just an algorithm. Come on, you've got a tournament to win."

Christian followed Zach over to the family and Lilith. He found he was puzzled and angry in equal measure, but as he approached Lilith he couldn't help beaming at her, then flushing with the embarrassment of his dream.

"You okay?" she asked him after kissing Zach on the cheek. "You look flustered."

"Oh," he spluttered. "You know. Um. Just exertion. It's been a physical morning."

"I've got a bout coming up now," Zach said. "Make yourself ready for an exciting afternoon."

Christian squatted and pushed his knees outward to stretch his inner thighs. Zach was looking towards the leader board and the judging table.

"I think I'm up," Zach said, "You're in the second set."

Christian stood up and tucked his mask and sabre under his arms. "See you in the semis."

Christian watched Zach stride to the furthest competition piste. His friend oozed confidence recently. Far more so than when he'd left Bristol. Assured. Not like the old, dizzy, unfocused Zach more interested in women and posturing. He had purpose and drive. Was it Lilith? Had they got over the history? Really? Even though it was nearly ten years ago, did you ever get over such things?

A decade earlier, the news had hit Rachel and Christian like a tsunami when they heard. It was the day they moved into their first shared flat, a divided Georgian mansion around the corner from the place Zach and Lilith subsequently purchased.

The red-stone mansion buildings in Bristol stretched from the Downs to the top of Park Road. They lined the avenues of Clifton, often concealed behind plane trees, high hedges and parked cars strewn like litter along the kerbside. You could be forgiven for not seeing their beauty behind the skin of black soot and pollution, the Sixties separations into flats and the criminal bastardisations of front fascias. But Christian and Rachel stood in admiration as they stared at a block of four Georgian flats whose ground floor was their first-ever property purchase. Christian took Rachel's hand. He felt as if the years of bookwork, exams, resits and sacrifice were now worth it. He had a steady, professional, well-paid job, a girlfriend he loved, and now a terrific flat in the posh part of Bristol.

Though modest — just one double bedroom and a single — it was not cheap, being within jogging reach of the Downs and with its own walled garden. But between them they stretched to afford the high cost of moving out of their respective rentals and into a place together. Christian would not miss his single kitchen flat in a divided terrace house in Redland, and Rachel would hardly be willing to stay in London in the shared property where the rice-paper walls trembled with the sound of the chavvy neighbours fucking every night.

They walked hand in hand through the gate and along the concrete path to the black front door. "Ready?" Christian said. He held the key up in front of them both and jangled it.

"Yep."

"Give us a kiss, then."

They spent the day moving furniture and boxes from the back

of the van to the front room. Opening some, moving others into the spare room, unpacking possessions vital for the next few days. They learnt about how each other liked things. How Rachel liked the silver and bronze candlesticks on the mantelpiece to be clustered in artistic groups, while Christian liked to have them matching and symmetrically spaced. They discovered that Christian loved the smell of toilets cleaned with bleach while Rachel preferred Toilet Duck. Rachel laughed at how Christian wanted all the plates to be stacked in colour order — he didn't want Rachel's collection of mismatched china in the kitchen at all, and tried to hide them at the back of a wall cupboard, but in the name of love and harmonious apartment living he accepted that ordering of plates could happen naturally. Besides, he joked, he could always creep about at night putting things right.

At four he cracked open a bottle of bubbly. They collapsed on a brown, distressed leather sofa, dumped at forty-five degrees to the wall surrounded by a ruin of cardboard boxes, poured the wine and toasted moving in together.

"To our new home. Is that a fitting toast?" Christian asked.

"Yes. We're home owners. We've spent the day discovering things we bought ten years ago that we didn't remember we had, and we've discovered that while we've moved to a bigger place it doesn't mean we'll fit all our stuff in. Things expand to fill the available space. Anyway, what else were you thinking of toasting?"

"There are other ways to christen a new home."

"Oh, really! Is that what's going on in your head?"

Christian shrugged. "Perhaps. If it's going on in yours?"

"Well, I've learnt you like to place ornaments with strict distances between them." She pointed at the mantelpiece and the arrangement of candlesticks. "Is that thirty or twenty-nine centimetres between objects?"

"You make me shudder with laughter."

"If I go over and change the arrangement, what would you say?"

"I could go as far as twenty-five centimetres but anything less would make me uncomfortable."

"I've got a deal then." Rachel handed her glass over and walked to the mantelpiece. "Let's see how much you want the alternative toast. How asymmetric can you take it?"

"Don't do it, Miss Rachel. Don't do it. I'll do anything you want. Anything."

"Anything?"

"Anything."

"Okay, Mr Jarvik. Get into that bedroom and bring the rest of that bottle of bubbly."

He picked up the bottle, but at that moment his phone rang. He jumped up like a rabbit.

"Hey. You could just leave it."

"Sorry. Thoughtless." He picked up his phone from the top of one of the boxes. "It's Zach. I'll quickly take it."

"Your friend's getting in the way of our love life. It's not a good start to a cohabitation."

"I'll be two mins. Have a drink. Take your clothes off." Christian unfolded the mobile phone and held it up to his ear. "Yes, mate. Want to celebrate with us? What about the baby? She's what?" Christian listened intently for two minutes, shock and horror spreading through him like an injection of hot serum. He closed the phone.

"What is it? Christian, what happened?"

Christian stood in silence. He didn't know how to put the words. He didn't understand how you conveyed this kind of message. "They've lost the baby," he said. "It got meningitis. The baby's dead."

It came out straight and matter-of-fact, at complete odds to the storm of emotion going on inside him.

Christian and his family sat with Lilith and watched Zach fight from the benches. Zach fought calmly and conservatively, unlike the old days when style trumped competition. Zach's opponent liked to use his hand to stop the cuts from landing on the target. During one of the brief breaks, Zach took on some fluid and asked for judges to be appointed to look for illegal parries with the hands. It was a detail of planning Christian had rarely seen from him.

The bout continued with two additional hand judges.

"Five-two," the referee said. "En garde. Play." Zach had the measure of his opponent: he hardly broke into a sweat dispatching him nine hits to three, and with the hand judges watching for infringements there were no more parries with the hand. He moved swiftly into the next round.

"What were those extra judges all about?" Rachel asked as took their seats to watch Zach take on the club champion of Exeter Blades.

"You're not allowed to use your non-sword hand to stop a hit on the body," Christian said. "Some fencers are rather prone to it. I wouldn't call it cheating so much as gamesmanship. Zach called for extra judges, as is his right under the rules."

"Christian." Lilith leant across Rachel and touched Christian on the arm, "What's that thing hanging from the back of Zach's tunic?" Her legs were crossed towards him and her elbow rested on the top of her knee, her face in her hand. Her white blouse hung open; Christian resisted the urge to look down her top. Her silver pendant dangled against her neck, occasionally picking up a flare of the hall lights, as if taunting him.

"The electric hook-up?" he said. "Every time Zach's hit with his opponent's sabre, an electrical connection is made that lights up a bulb next to the referee. That way they know who hit who. Sometimes it's too fast to see with the naked eye."

She smiled and turned back towards the contest which was about to get under way. Now Christian looked down her top and glimpsed the side of her braless breast. He was immediately ashamed.

"Fence."

Christian couldn't remember the last time Zach had beaten him in a serious bout. With a foil, sure, but never the sabre, and they hadn't fought together in a tournament for years now.

"Zach! Zach! Zach!" Jessica shouted excitedly, while taking a string of photos with Christian's smartphone.

Zach pulled quickly ahead with a new spring in his step and great confidence. Lilith followed every cut and thrust intently, as if willing him on. "What do you think of it?" Christian asked her as the opponents changed ends.

"It's all very masculine." She laughed and flashed her eyes. "Doesn't it hurt when you get hit?"

Christian studied her. Was she teasing? "No, not really," he said. "I've a leather pad under my jacket. So does Zach. If you wear the jacket on its own it can hurt a little."

"Don't listen to him," Rachel said. "It doesn't hurt a little, it hurts like hell. Especially when you get hit on the boobs. I had a dozen round bruises the size of oranges last time I let Christian talk me into coming along."

Christian laughed. "Rachel tried it once when she was pregnant with Jessica. I think you must have been extra sensitive." He looked at Lilith. "You should have a go."

"I think it's best left to you men. Zach tried to get me along in Frankfurt, but I was never good with large weapons," Lilith said, raising her eyebrows.

"He's been practising, has he?" Christian said, ignoring the double entendre. "He joined a club in Germany?"

"Obsessed about it for a while. Said he wanted to perfect his technique."

Christian was surprised to see Zach finish off his adversary without losing a further point and without, it seemed, making a single mistake.

"That was terrific," Christian said as Zach returned triumphant. "You're even parrying with enough distance to avoid a whip-over." That was Zach's usual mistake — usually too interested in fighting to protect himself properly.

Zach stared at Christian. It was almost unfriendly. "I've been working on it," he said.

"Lilith was saying."

"You'll have trouble getting around me today."

"Is that a prediction you'd like to put some money on?" Even with Zach's new-found technique, Christian could not lose. Zach had been a stranger to the club for over two years, and a few bouts in a Frankfurt gym would not be enough training to help.

"No." Zach smiled and winked at Lilith. "But I feel like I could win a competition today."

Christian ignored Zach's taunt, but the words played on his

mind at the beginning of their semi-final fight. The first points were cagey. Christian probed Zach's defences with feints and obvious attacks to see how his friend had changed his style, and Zach reacted unpredictably. More like himself, actually. As if he had taken some of Christian's style and tried it on himself.

Christian was happy with the score to stay even for the first few points; Zach would grow in confidence and then start to take risks. All Christian had to do was wait for him to fall on his own sword. He allowed Zach's attacks, parried, then reposted.

"Three-three." The referee stated the score without emotion.

Most of the defeated fencers were watching. Christian and Zach were well known, even though Zach had been away for a while, and a bout between them was something the others wanted to watch. The crowd clapped politely for each point and Christian could hear Jessica and Rachel shouting for him from the benches. Now he would start to turn the screw.

"Time," the referee called. "One minute, gentlemen."

Was that three minutes already and still even? In the heavy mask the temperature escalated with the exertion, so Christian was glad of the break. Removing his mask he strolled to the bench for a towel. Sweat poured from his forehead and down his face.

"You look knackered," Rachel said.

Christian wiped his forehead. "That's helpful."

"Pardon me for speaking."

He shook his head. "I didn't mean—"

"En garde, gentlemen," the referee interrupted.

"Sorry," Christian said. He smiled, put his mask on and walked to the piste.

"En garde." The ref waited until they were in position. "Fence."

Two steps forward.

Zach mirrored his movements.

Arm straight; take attack initiative. Lunge, and cut to the head. Parried.

Attack incomplete. Defend Zach's reprise; parry, riposte, parried.

Hold. Wait for an attack.

Christian's mouth dried, and his heart thumped. He sucked in breath through the vision-obscuring mask. Zach had been quick, intuitive. He sucked another breath and felt heat rising along his spinal cord and creeping up his neck. Glue-like mucus stuck his tongue to the roof of his mouth.

Zach jumped toward him, the sabre held for a cut to his right side, parry. Zach's sabre avoided his blade and cut across the abdomen. Touché.

"Three-four."

Christian hadn't seen it coming; the attack, or the avoidance of his parry.

"En garde."

Christian watched Zach take up the on-guard position and noted how his friend slipped into it like a boat slipping into water. The sabre was perfectly positioned to parry a cut to his right-hand side — no laziness, as was so usual with Zach's guard. It was perfect. The heat rose further up Christian's neck and his breathing became stifled. He needed to wipe down.

"Fence."

Zach came straight on the attack, dashed toward Christian with a cut to the left. It missed.

Christian lunged slowly, deliberately, Zach parried and Christian circled the blade, avoiding sabre contact, and pressed home his attack. The sabre cut across Zach's left shoulder and the light came on.

"Four-four."

"En garde."

"Correction," the referee said. "Contact avoided by Mr Jarvik's hand. Warning to Mr Jarvik. Three-five."

Jesus. Christian took of his mask and stormed to the referee. "What was that for?"

"You used your hand to avoid contact with Mr Hunter's sabre."

"You must be joking." As he spoke he felt a stinging in his left hand. His gauntlet had been torn open and blood dripped from his index finger.

"You need to get that strapped, Mr Jarvik. We'll take a minute's break a few seconds early."

Christian walked to the benches. "Rachel, there should be

some Band-Aids in the bag." He took the chance to dry his head with the dirty towel.

"Daddy, you're bleeding," Jessica said.

"Nothing to worry about," he told her. Rachel covered the cut with a small plaster.

"My Daddy doesn't cry," Jessica said, and Rachel laughed.

Within three minutes Christian had pulled the score back to six each. Every parry was a fight for survival, his strength leaving his sword arm as it clashed with Zach's sabre.

"Six-six. One-minute break and then a one-minute sudden-death ballestra."

Nine minutes of fighting came down to one hit. Christian removed his mask.

Zach was wiping down with a red towel, patting across his forehead and back of his neck as if he'd just had a leisurely swim. Christian was suddenly afraid he could lose.

Rachel said handing Christian a bottle of water and a towel. "This is close."

Water splashed down his chin as he drank. He wiped his face.

"I didn't know it would be so exciting," Lilith said.

"Maybe this is what Christian's prediction was talking about after all."

"Prediction?"

"The app," Rachel said. "The tell-the-future game. It told him Zach was going to win today." She laughed. "He said Zach had pranked him."

Christian went cold, as if the perspiration had frozen to his back. In the heat of competition, he had forgotten. He felt a flush of anger: his wife was discussing his business with Lilith. He clenched his fists and stared at Rachel. She was still laughing: *laughing at me*.

The referee called, "En garde, gentlemen."

When Rachel saw Christian's expression her smile vanished. "What?" she mouthed.

"Mr Jarvik, en garde."

Christian turned without speaking and returned to the piste.

Inside the mask much of the noise of the crowd was stilled. Just his own heat and the view of his opponent: Zach. Christian waited for the word; waited for the "Fence," but his thoughts turned to the app. What it had said about the competition. *A friend will be successful in a competition.*

"Fence."

Zach was upon him. Christian didn't move, didn't offer a parry, just froze. Zach seemed to attack in slow motion, raising his sword arm to head height, straightening his arm and cutting. Christian watched the blade fall diagonally from high on his left in a theatrical flourish, and felt the strike slice across his chest in a moment of total peace.

Zach grabbed his sabre with both hands and lift it over his head in triumph.

"Zach Hunter wins, seven points to six."

Motionless, Christian watched. He kept his mask on. Gradually the applause of the crowd returned to his thoughts as if it were a personal slight against him, as if they were rubbing sea salt deep into cuts across his heart. Lines of white-clad fencers peppered with casually dressed families and friends applauded Zach from the benches.

Except Lilith. She stared directly at Christian. Her hands remained clasped on her crossed thighs, her red-painted nails prominent against her dark-blue jeans.

His mouth dried. Perspiration dripped onto his lips, and he smoothed it off with his tongue without taking his gaze from her. Her eyes widened and a tiny pout flexed her lips, followed by an almost imperceptible smile. Even in defeat, Christian felt sexual excitement as their eyes met.

"Christian?" Zach stood in front of him waiting to shake hands, smiling. "Tough fight, Monsieur." He laughed, his hand still outstretched.

Christian looked at the hand in front of him. It was vulnerable so far from Zach's body, a five-digit pound of flesh attached to a thin arm. It dangled the way the weight on a crane hangs over the side of a dock. Christian's sword arm flexed. He raised his sabre. If he held a real sabre he could sever the hand from Zach's wrist in a single, simple cut.

"Christian?" Zach said. "You okay?"

"Oh yeah." He took off his mask and shook the hand. "Well

done." He inspected his friend's eyes and expression; the confidence in the gaze; the condescending smile, and perhaps a slight mocking. Zach had *expected* to win this time.

Christian didn't wait for the final bout. He packed his sports bag and walked. Rachel and Jessica followed as soon as they realised what was happening.

"Christian, that's so rude," Rachel said, catching up with him. He didn't speak.

"I can't believe you won't stay to see the final. Zach's your best friend."

They drove home in silence, the car talking for him. The engine growled when accelerating away from junctions; when he wasn't accelerating hard, the soft click of the windscreen wipers pushing persistent rain from the glass was the only sound in the cabin. Christian thought of one thing: the prediction. Had it known he would lose the contest, and if so, what else did it know about him? Was it possible to change the future if you knew what was predicted?

He remembered that Zach was so pleased with himself the night the tree fell down. How he had been pleased with what the app was saying when Christian brought it to his attention. As Christian stewed about the app, each headlight caught in the rear-view mirror seemed to be a taunting reflection of light from Lilith's pendant.

"Christian." Rachel rested her hand on his thigh. "I can see you're worked up. Your jaw's grinding. I don't feel safe. You're driving erratically. Fencing is only a hobby, for heaven's sake. You should be playing golf by now, in any case. Golf is a much better game for Managing Partners. Can you imagine trying to broker a deal over an afternoon's fencing?"

Christian's fury at his loss and the bright lights in the mirror conspired to drown her out. He ignored her attempt at humour. It was all he could do to miss the oncoming traffic.

"Look at it another way," she said. "Lilith can use the publicity of Zach's win for their company. It's good for them. Zach'll get in the paper, and they'll get loads of downloads."

She was so kind. She would never let petty grievances get in the way of sense. He nodded, but remained silent. He watched pedestrians tucked under umbrellas and cars splattering pavements with spray. He heard the wipers on the windscreen and the underlying rumble of the motor. He avoided looking in the mirror. He avoided the humiliation reflected there, and eventually he pulled up in their driveway and turned the engine off.

He waited in his office until Rachel took an afternoon nap then picked up his phone to open the app. He couldn't find it on his home screen. He typed *Algorithm* in the search box and clicked Search. It didn't appear in the results.

"Where the fuck is it?" he shouted, swiping through his files and deleted content. "Where the fuck has it gone?"

He called for Jessica. She didn't answer. He charged out of his office. "Jessica! Come in here right away."

Jessica appeared at the bottom of the stairs. "Yes, Daddy?" Everywhere was cuddled up to her neck. She put her thumb in her mouth.

"Have you touched the things on my phone?"

She stared at him.

"Have you? When you were taking pictures?"

"I don't remember, Daddy."

He walked over and knelt in front of her. "Listen," he said, trying to temper his anger. "This is *very* important. Have you played with the phone?"

Jessica began to cry. Tears welled. "I don't know!" she shouted. She turned and ran.

"Jessica, you tell me what you did. You are in big trouble." He paced after her.

"I don't know, I don't know, I don't know." She clambered up the stairs, holding on tightly to her teddy, and ran into her bedroom.

Christian stormed back to the study. He closed the door and locked it. He sat at his desk and thought. He could reinstall. Set it up from scratch. But he had to know what else was in there. What the fuck else did it know? He picked up the phone and navigated to the app's homepage.

*

Christian sat at his desk poring over the newly installed Algorithm. He didn't know how it had been removed, but he'd reinstalled it and tried to find all the predictions and readings it had given him in the last two weeks. They weren't available, or he couldn't find the right menu option. It asked if he wanted a reading or to ask a question. Previous account data didn't seem to be stored anywhere. He tried to remember the predictions and scrawled his recollections on sheets of paper, now covered the desk.

Rachel banged on the study door. "Christian, open up. What's the hell's the matter? You've got Jessica crying in bed and now you've locked yourself in the study."

He stood up, unlocked the door and sat back down as Rachel entered.

"What's the matter? Why have you locked yourself away?"

"It predicted it," he said. "The fencing competition. It said I would lose."

Rachel looked at the swirling colours on the screen.

"A friend wins a duel and Burnham still has challenges. It's part of the same reading."

Rachel stared at the screen, then back at Christian. "It doesn't say anything."

"It doesn't *now*. I lost the account. I've had to reinstall it."

"Well, what does it say now?"

"It says nothing *now*. It's collecting data or something. I don't know. But look, I've written down everything it's said before." He showed Rachel all the paper in the desk.

"Darling, you're frightening me."

"Zach had me convinced for a bit. But the way he taunted me, I know it knows about me. Look, it can't be anything else. Everything it said has come true."

"No! This is obsessive."

"Look at the evidence. First the tree. Then William Thorpe was found to be passing emails to the other side so I had to sack him. It predicted I would lose the sabre contest. How can it know my project is called *Burnham*? How the fuck can it know?"

"It looked a bit like a tree, yes. And then, I knew it was called the Burnham project. I might have told somebody without thinking about it."

"No." Christian shook his head vigorously, his eyes darting left and right across the paper. "You didn't. And *it* knew. Not you. I don't care if you knew or not."

"You're reading too deeply into it. This is how the whole spiritual thing works. Vague predictions that can apply to anybody. It's confirmation bias. You only see it after the event, it's not real. It's not a prediction. Come on, how can Zach make a program to predict the future? It's just a game."

"Don't you see? The app *knows*. How can it know?"

Rachel covered her mouth but soon the giggles took her.

"It's not fucking funny," Christian said.

Rachel laughed more.

"Why are you laughing?"

She pointed to the sheets of incomprehensible scribbling.

Christian looked at the scrawled lines and crumpled bits of paper he'd been interrogating to find hidden meanings. "It's not funny," he repeated, but as he spoke a titter escaped his lips.

Rachel leant forward and drew her finger across his lips until his smile built into a full laugh.

The two of them laughed together until they were howling. Christian's abdomen was sore and his cheeks ached. Every time the laughter ebbed Rachel would look at the papers and start again. Finally the merriment subsided.

"Come here," Rachel said, walking round the desk to hug him. They embraced and between giggles they kissed. Christian relaxed in her arms and his fears were swept away by the comfort and support of his wife. He held her tight around her waist, breathed deeply and allowed the month's stresses to fall from his shoulders.

"You must have been so tense from work this month," Rachel said after the long embrace. "I think you need some time off."

"I do," he sighed. "I'll try and finish earlier this week. We'll go away for the weekend."

12

Christian failed to finish early the next week. Even though he'd promised, he worked longer hours, got in earlier and worked later. Rachel took up the slack with childcare, and he barely saw his family. Although the review had gone well, and only minor changes had been made to the documentation, a tickling doubt remained, born by the app's predictions. The forecast loss of the bout with Zach unnerved him. He widened his enquiries and interviewed the bosses of Beaufort & Soames' clients and staff closely associated with the deal.

He found initial irritation at his requests for time, but considered it to be in the best interests of all parties concerned. He feared his success at rehearsal was a dangerous diversion from what was really going on.

On Thursday night he managed to leave by eight, and he and Rachel went to bed early. But by midnight he dreamed he was on a long run through Bristol's dark, empty streets. He'd been running for hours. His footsteps echoed between the stone buildings on either side of the road. He was lost. He was trying to find his way home.

A fire engine raced past, its sirens splitting the cold air. In that instant he knew it was going to his house. Rachel and Jessica were in danger. He sprinted after it, his feet smacking into the road like hammers on soil. The fire engine raced away from him. He took a left turn to find a shortcut but ended up back at the bottom of Park Street with the steep incline still ahead of him. The harder he ran, the slower he seemed to go, and the steeper Park Street became. It stretched above him like a desert road disappearing to the heavens.

And then suddenly he was in the garden at his house. Flames leapt from the windows and through the collapsed roof. He screamed out for his wife and daughter. He had to get them, he had to get to the door. Tangles of tree roots, giant foxgloves and huge lilies stopped him from progressing through the garden. He could see the front door. An orange glow emanated from the opening and spilled into the garden. The heat of the fire singed his cheeks. He leapt over a giant tree trunk and squeezed beneath a fallen branch.

Suddenly his progress stopped. He couldn't move. He was frozen. Blocked from moving and now lying on his back on the filthy ground, naked.

A familiar voice spoke from above. "I've been missing you," Lilith said. Her face was close to his stomach. He felt her warm breath as she spoke — one hand rested on his waist below his rib-cage. He breathed heavily through his nose.

"Why have you kept away so long? Do you doubt I am in control of you?" she said slowly, blowing the words onto his skin. Her hand hovered over his penis, barely touching it: tickling, tantalising.

He cried to save Rachel from the fire, but he longed for Lilith to take him fully.

"I know what you really want," she said. "You need to pay attention to me, not the house." She lay over him, in absolute control with Christian unable to move.

"Why aren't you helping?" he screamed but, as in his previous dream, no sound came. In an instant everything he cared about disappeared. The flames, the house and the garden were gone.

It was just him in the dark, on his back with Lilith above him. He couldn't see her, but he sensed her, like a stranger's gaze on a bus, or the invisible menace from a group of drunk men. He felt her warmth. Her fragrance excited him. He wanted her. His mouth went dry. He felt her thighs open around his legs as she positioned herself to accept him.

*

122

"Oh my God!" Rachel shouted.

Christian immediately woke up, startled, his heart thumping. He was lying across her, face down with his head in the pillow, bucking his groin into the gap between her body and the mattress.

"What are you doing?" She turned on the bedside lamp. "For Christ's sake, you've come all over me." She threw back the sheets and wiped herself along her swollen waist.

Christian yanked his pyjamas to his waist from their position around his knees and sat up. His searing embarrassment was hidden by the dim lighting. "I'm sorry," he said. He wondered if she could see the dream images written on his face. "I was dreaming."

"Bloody hell." She got out of bed. A damp patch spread out in the centre of the bed. "What were you dreaming of?"

Christian flushed but said nothing. The shame of his dream and the manner of his waking pushed him to silence.

Then Rachel laughed. "That must have been some dream. I hope it was about me." She rubbed her hand along her side. "Can you manage to change the sheets?"

Christian closed his eyes and dwelled on the sickness in his stomach. It had felt so real. His heart still raced at the thought, and yet in his dreams he had forsaken his family to make love with Lilith. It terrified him, not because he thought such a thing was ever possible, but because had enjoyed it.

Rachel came back into the room and threw him a couple of sheets. "So, what did you dream about? Must have been very exciting from the way you were moving around. I've never known you have a wet dream before," she said as she helped him smooth the linen across the mattress.

Christian didn't speak. He felt ashamed, angry and dirty.

"Are you embarrassed about it?" Rachel teased him. "Christian, darling, you don't have to be embarrassed about a wet dream." She laughed. "Come on, let me know the juicy details."

"I don't remember much. Just sex with an anonymous woman on top of me. I don't know who it was."

She studied him. "You didn't know? *Really?*"

He shrugged. "Wish I could remember. It might have been worth the trouble."

They climbed back into bed, but Christian couldn't sleep. His exhaustion demanded that he sleep but his shame at the continuing dreams about Lilith kept him awake. He lay in a sweat for another couple of hours before getting up and quietly walking downstairs. He dug a fresh box of PG Tips from the back of the cupboard and brewed a strong tea. It helped him relax. He pondered about going out for a run but the tea relaxed him, so he fetched his phone from the hall table and sat at the kitchen island with the intention of reading the news. The phone vibrated the moment he sat down. He read the notification.

> *Do you want help planning your day? Why not try a reading? It's been five days since you installed the Algorithm.*

It caught him off-guard, unnerved him. He felt that the bloody thing had been waiting for him to pick it up. Nonetheless, he clicked in the link to be taken to the app and spoke into the phone. "If you know everything about me, have I done enough to save the project?" he asked.

> *You feel like you are under other's control while things move around you. Your challenges will continue for the next two weeks, and then I see resolution. Projects can still fail. A person close to you is under pressure, money is an issue, and beware of the road.*

Well, that's fucking great, Christian thought. It really was like a spiritualist reading: vague, indeterminate and could apply to anybody. Who didn't know somebody under pressure? Especially in a law firm. It was the very definition of pressure. And of course he was going to keep working. And fucking everybody has money issues and should be careful on the road.

He gripped his phone and momentarily thought of throwing

it at the wall.

Except… Except it fucking knew about the project. There it was, no mistaking it this time. No sketchy graphic or indistinct scratching. Text. Plain and unmistakeable. His mouth went dry as he re-read the words: "Projects can still fail." Well, he wouldn't let this one fail.

He opened his browser and found the Pikey Pete conspiracy video in the History folder. He scrolled through the comments until he found Mary Beckett's literary agent and tapped out an email:

> For the Attention of Author Mary Beckett.
> Dear Mary, I'd like to ask you about the psychic app
> you talked about on Pikey Pete's conspiracy video. Is
> there a direct email I could use, or perhaps a telephone
> number?

He crept upstairs so he wouldn't wake Rachel again and slipped into his work clothes. He had to keep pushing to find any errors with his work, and he had another line of enquiry. If he went now, he would join the London-bound traffic but be back by lunchtime.

After an exhausting time with Dave Hinchley at Epoch's headquarters in Swindon and a frustrating drive through heavy M4 traffic, a terse voicemail from Howard waited for him when he arrived at the office: "Come and see me when you get back from lunch."

Christian listened to it twice, disliking the implication. Apart from the fact he had not been at lunch, messages from Howard usually presaged a serious discussion. Christian took the concrete stairs to the executive suites and knocked on Howard's door. No answer, but voices from inside indicated Howard was holding a heated conversation. Christian entered.

Howard stood at the window holding his phone to his ear,

dressed in his usual oversized grey pinstripe. He gestured for Christian to sit at the coffee table.

"It's under control, you have nothing to worry about," Howard said.

Pause.

"Yes, he's with me now."

Pause.

"I'll call you back as soon as I've spoken with him. Yes, everything is moving ahead smoothly."

Howard turned back to the window, nodded, and tucked the phone into his inside breast pocket. "Dave Hinchley has concerns," he said.

"I've just come from Dave. He didn't express any issues to me."

"Is the Burnham deal under control?"

Christian was astounded Howard could ask this. For a moment he wanted to show his hurt at being doubted, but knew Howard was not being personal. It was a simple enquiry requiring a straightforward response. "Everything is on schedule. We've completed another review and we're ready for presentation to the clients."

Howard took off his jacket and hung it over the chair behind the desk. "This other review you've been doing?"

"Yes."

"Why? Is it necessary? What are you worried about?"

Christian hesitated.

"I'll tell you why I ask," Howard said. "Dave smells a rat, and so do some of the team here. He thinks you are anxious about some aspect, and he wants to know what it is. Your persistent worrying of their management team is giving him the jitters, and when I heard what was happening, I must admit I felt a bit nervous myself. I've given you a lot of rope on this deal, Christian. You'd better not hang me with it."

Dave Hinchley has the morals of a pit dog and the style of plank of wood. How dare he go back to Howard with this? Christian clenched his fists and felt his nails dig into his palms. But before he could respond Howard said, "Coffee?"

"Sure. Yes, please."

Howard walked over to the percolator. "As far as Beaufort & Soames is concerned, the questions stop at rehearsal. Anything more is counter-productive. Now is the time to shut up and take the money." He poured coffee into two white china cups on matching saucers. "Milk and sugar?"

"Just milk."

"In the spirit of shutting up and taking the money, I've asked William Thorpe back into the programme. I hope you'll be able to work with him."

"But—"

Howard raised his hand. "We're not going to go into this," he said with a force Christian had only ever seen reserved for juniors. "I'm letting you know that William has the confidence of Dave and what happened before was more complicated than you know. That's all I can say. He'll report directly to me, so there's no reason for you to talk to each other. But I am asking you bluntly, is there is anything else I should know?"

"I can't object more strongly," Christian said. "How can Thorpe be back in after leaking documents?" It wasn't Thorpe being back in that incensed him so much, it was that he would be reporting directly to Howard. He felt betrayed and angry.

"I'm asking you to accept this decision. For now. For the good of the firm. But I'll ask you again, is there anything else I should know?

Christian wanted to throw his arms out in fury and smash the office to fragments. "No, Howard. There's nothing. It's under control from my side."

Howard brought the coffee over. "I get suspicious when an employee uses my first name like that. It usually means they are hiding something."

Christian thought about the prediction: *Burnham fails.* How could he admit why he'd ordered the review, and why he'd been talking to the clients? And all the expense. "After you expressed your confidence in me as future Managing Partner, I was determined to make the Burnham deal a complete, unambiguous success. I have spared no effort in making sure that is the case. If that has meant additional and sometimes uncomfortable questions, well, I'm not sorry. I would do it again." He knew this was a good story; enough to convince Howard. "On this project, there can be no room for error in the analysis, or the prospects for the deal, or third-party side-swipes. Thorpe was only discovered as a result of the thoroughness of the team but when we discovered the leaks we had to redouble our efforts." He sipped his coffee, hoping his calm exterior portrayed confidence. "As it turns out there were only *very* minor — I won't even say mistakes — factual inaccuracies in the programme."

Howard sipped his own coffee but kept his eyes on Christian. "All right, I understand," he said. "But unfortunately your zealousness has prompted Epoch AI to conduct its own review of the deal. You will now have to go along with every request Dave makes, no matter how frivolous it seems. The boot is on the other foot. I don't doubt we will in due course receive notification of a review from IntelliTech lawyers also. Be prepared for their questioning. I don't doubt your conscientiousness, but I think you have shown a degree of naïveté in this review. You know the old adage: once the sale is made, keep quiet. It is a useful saying. I suggest you remember it."

Christian seethed, but looked at Howard straight in the eye. "That seems fair, Howard."

Christian's overloaded emotions meant that he was unable to think clearly for the rest of the day. Emails piled up in his inbox: he let them overflow like a laundry basket filled with unwashed clothes. His head churned with the humiliation. He felt played by the predictions. He turned his phone over and over in his hands while anger washed over him in great waves. He thought of Lilith on top of him in his dream, of corpsing at the crucial moment in the fencing competition, of how Howard insinuated he'd lost control of the project. He'd fucking saved the project by getting rid of Thorpe, who was now back. His mindful breathing exercise couldn't touch the shameful feelings.

He sat in his office chair until eight p.m. He picked up his car, drove to Clifton and, after circling, parked on the street in the only remaining space some distance from Zach's flat. He walked the few hundred yards onto St John's Road, rang the doorbell and waited. No lights came on. He tried the bell once more. Still no answer. He peered between the shutters on the bay window: no lights were on in the lounge, the flat appeared empty.

He walked to the side of the building and climbed back up to ground-level between some trees at the edge of the property. He stalked along the edge of the railway embankment for twenty feet then hopped over a wooden fence and into the back garden. He stopped in the shadows to survey the back of the house. Lights were on in the first floor flat but Zach's flat had just a glow in the kitchen window like an orange night-light.

He walked softly to the French windows that opened into the rear bedroom and heard a recognisable rhythmic thumping from within. His heart raced. He became intensely aware of the volume of his own breathing. He wanted to stop the game, as if he was a five-year-old playing hide-and-seek hidden under a bed. The noises fascinated and dismayed, and then sound abruptly stopped. Leaning in, he inched towards the glass, focused on a narrow crack in the curtains.

A naked male figure moved repeatedly across his vision, from right to left and then back. He pushed his face closer to the glass to see more of the room.

Lilith lay on the bed face down and naked. Her legs were apart, her hips raised on a pillow. Dim orange lighting cast a dark shadow between her legs. Zach stood at the edge of the bed. He leant forward over Lilith and lay on top of her as she lifted her backside clear of the pillow.

Christian gaped at the stolen vision, his conservative-self discarded. Suddenly, like an alarm in the dead of a deep sleep, Lilith turned her head and smiled directly at him. He jumped backwards and gasped. He stumbled and tripped on a flower pot. It broke with a deafening crack that echoed along the garden wall and bounced off houses on the far side of the railway cutting. He bolted for the back fence and the cover of the trees.

As he leapt over the wooden fence, the curtains were thrown back and the garden flooded with bedroom light. He ducked behind a tree, and turned to see Zach retrieve the sabre from the display on the bedroom wall and march to window. Zach stood naked, peering into the garden, while his free hand tried to open the doors. Lilith stood up from the bed and covered herself in a dressing gown, but not before Christian caught a glimpse of her breasts as the white fabric closed around her. He drew in a deep breath. His heart thumped. A trickle of sweat ran down his armpit.

He eased along the embankment twenty feet above the rail tracks, making as little noise as possible. He trod carefully on the slippery, damp soil. He checked both ways to make sure nobody could see him. He hopped over the wall, bending his knees to soften the sound of his shoes on the tarmac.

"Who's there?" Zach shouted from the garden behind.

Christian walked away from the house without looking back and took a long route back to his car. He prayed Zach was not about to sprint after him and take a swipe with that sabre. Or, worse, discover his dark, voyeuristic secret. Lilith couldn't have known who it was at the door, he told himself. With the bedroom lights reflecting off the glass, she'd have seen simply a vague shape, if she'd seen anything at all. It was a coincidence that she turned. Perhaps she'd heard his feet on the step.

He sat in the driver's seat. He took a packet of baby-wipes from the glove box and cleaned his arms carefully. He concentrated on his hands where they had grasped the vegetation and fence posts, and on his cheeks where they'd pressed against the glass. His shame was cooled by the cleansing. He took off his shoes and meticulously wiped the heels and uppers. He felt better. Less dirty. He lay back in the seat trying to come to terms with his own actions. Time passed. He listened to the nine p.m. news bulletin which was taken up almost entirely with a discussion of the coming Brexit vote. He focused on each word and attempted to block out thoughts of his night stalking. The newsreader's voice soothed with a soporific quality. Slowly the shame dissipated. He watched a car full of youths drive by in a souped-up ancient Fiesta. Office workers returned home late after a drink. A gentle breeze shook the tops of the plane trees.

With the shame deeply buried within, Christian returned to Zach's flat. The doorbell had been covered by a plastic bag and a sticky note saying *Do Not Use*.

He knocked.

Zach answered the door immediately as if he'd been waiting just inside. "Hey, mate. Come in."

"Hi, mate." Christian tried to sound normal. "What's with the doorbell?"

"You've missed all the excitement," Zach said.

Christian followed him into the lounge. Zach was clothed in a loose-fitting ensemble of beige cotton tunic and multi-coloured Himalayan trousers, but with bare feet. Christian sat on the dark-blue sofa in front of a low, square table cluttered with magazines, candleholders and small oil bottles, with a large cut-glass ashtray in the centre.

Zach sat down in the leather sofa opposite and grabbed a silver box from the table. "We had to phone the coppers."

Christian put on a puzzled expression. "What happened?"

"A prowler in the garden. Right up to the window. We think he was trying to burgle the place. The bell had gone moments before, but we hadn't answered it. Otherwise engaged." He winked. "Checking to see if we were in before forcing the back door, I suppose. I'm going to have to put a floodlight out there. He was a bit surprised to see me naked at the window. Knocked over one of the big flower pots in his rush to get away." He laughed. "I'd have had him with the sabre if I'd had any clothes on." Zach opened the silver box and took out cigarette papers and a small bag of grass.

Christian forced a laugh. "I'll bet. What did the police say?"

"Useless. I had to convince them to come round and check for fingerprints on the doorbell, by pointing out that catching criminals was their living. I didn't put it quite like that, of course. But of course they can't come round till tomorrow so I've had to cover the bell so nobody gets accused of robbing us. Lucky you didn't push it. You'd have the coppers round." He looked Christian up and down. "You just finished work?"

Christian was still in his suit. "Yes, I came straight round. Finished late again. No Lilith?"

"She's putting some stuff together for work. She loves working late. Overnight. I don't know how she does it."

Christian smiled. "I'm glad about that, actually. I wanted to talk to you about… Well, about Lilith. And that app of yours."

Zach looked at him with his head to one side. He rubbed cannabis leaf between his thumb and forefinger and sprinkled it into the paper. "What about?" He picked up the construction and rolled it into a large joint. He licked along the length to glue the paper into a tube. He didn't appear interested in the conversation.

"What's she *really* like?"

Zach picked up a lighter from the table, put the joint in his mouth and lit it. He puffed a few times before the weed caught, drew a deep breath and held. Finally he blew the smoke upwards into the room. "Why?"

"Remember that night we downloaded the Algorithm?"

"It predicted the tree coming down. Awesome." Zach moved his hand across his body as if the word *Awesome* was in lights on an imaginary billboard. He laughed and took another drag.

This wasn't going the way Christian had hoped. His friend's behaviour was already annoying him, and he'd only just lit the spliff.

"Does Lilith have anything to do with the occult or magic?" Christian thought it best to get the question out in the open.

Zach choked on the smoke as laughter burst out from his lungs and into the air. "Is that what you think?"

"So many things on the app have come true." He pulled out this phone and laid it out on the table. "Unless you've been reading up on the Black Arts it must be Lilith."

Zach leant over and inspected the screen. He looked up at his friend with a comic, shocked expression on his face. "Well," he said, moving his gaze around the room like a mad man, "I did read some of my dad's Dennis Wheatleys when I was a boy." He kept the face for a second before bursting into laughter.

Christian hated dope. He waited for Zach to calm down.

"You're serious!" Zach said.

"It predicted the tree, and it predicted I'd lose the club competition. It predicted the Burnham project would fail, and it's going to fucking custard. What else does it know? It still predicts a car crash, and something about being under pressure and money problems."

Zach, serious now, put the joint down, picked up the phone and held it up. He swiped the screen and inspected the predictions it had made. After some time of silence he put the phone on the table. "It's made up. I can see some of what you're saying, but most of it is stretching the imagination. It doesn't actually say *car crash* does it? It's just a game, man. I admit it sometimes seems uncanny, and, yeah, we want it to be, but it doesn't know shit that it can't find out from the internet." He paused and studied Christian's face. "Are you all right, mate? Seriously, I'm worried about you."

"Me?"

Zach nodded. "Yes you. Are you feeling okay? You're taking this a bit seriously. It's entertainment. Put it away if it's fucking with you."

Christian wasn't getting the answers he wanted. There had to be more to it. It didn't add up that a computer program could predict the future. He picked up his phone and reread what it predicted. "How can it know so much? The cyber guy at work tells me the server it runs on is probing our network, and then I saw this video online about it having some sort of magic embedded in it."

Zach shook his head and raised his hands in mock surrender. "Hands up there. That *is* Lilith. She's been planting stories with bloggers and vloggers. We pay to get those stories out there. They don't come cheap, but they've been fantastic for us. You should come with me to Frankfurt and meet the team. They're an odd bunch of geniuses, but chunks of our budget go on creating these sorts of stories. And honestly, they're believed." He picked up the joint, still smouldering in the ashtray, and took a big draw, held his breath until lack of oxygen forced him to exhale a giant cloud of smoke into the air below the light.

"The video talked about the programmers that burned to death. Is that marketing too? That's fucking distasteful if it is."

Zach stared at his friend then took another toke. He looked sad for a moment, then put it back on the ashtray. "Look, mate. It's not all been a picnic, and we don't write the scripts, we just make suggestions. The accident was real. It was fucking terrible. It messed us up for a bit. But shit, life goes on, right?" He picked up the joint, tapped the ash from the end and relit it. "It *can* seem intuitive. So much so that we added smart filters to make it less direct. People got scared."

"You filter it?"

"To make it more like going to a medium or a gypsy at the fair. They wouldn't tell you really bad stuff even if they saw it. So we make sure the Algorithm doesn't scare the crap out of you. The unfiltered stuff is still there in Dark Mode, but not everybody gets that."

Christian shook his head. "Now you're saying it *does* know. Which is it?"

"The tree was pretty amazing, but it's not so unbelievable, is it? It's what the app is supposed to do. You know, it's fucking clever. I'm proud of it. It trawls everything it can find, all your emails, social media, your browsing history, it finds who your connections are and it listens to conversations. It puts things together in a way humans simply can't imagine. I actually don't know how it works in depth, we just enable a great big neural network in the cloud and let it do its stuff. I can take you through all the technical details about competing algorithms and Bayesian network inference, if you like, but Lilith has wrapped the whole horoscope and prediction thing around it. She's the genius who's making us money, not the tech. There's that old Arthur C. Clarke quote about how advanced technology looks like it's magic. It *is* magic, in a way. You mention the things you care about, and it correlates with your online history. Your calendar has an entry for a fencing event, it looks up the weather forecast and knows there's a storm. It's very clever — but it can only *guess*. And anyway, I've wanted to win that sabre competition for so long it hurts. I made a commitment to winning, about a year ago, and I've trained. The Germans love their fencing and I got a great coach. I admit it, you've always been better than me. But this time I did something about it and put in some extra training. It's thanks to Lilith. She's given me back a sense of self-worth. Like I had before we lost the baby, and before I had my work stolen."

Christian sat back and folded his arms. He wasn't convinced. It could be the drug: Zach got flippant and combative on dope. He watched Zach take another deep draw on the joint then place it back on the ashtray, where it seemed out of place next to the joss-stick holders and purple scented candles.

"What's her family like?" Christian asked. "That was a pretty weird wedding, with all the pagan stuff and maypoles and fertility rights."

Zach rubbed his eyes with his left hand. He sniffed. "Pretty cool. International. They live in Frankfurt most of the year. Her mum pleases herself with art and crafts. She spends time in yoga retreats and spiritual events."

"Spiritual how?"

"Are you still on this witch shit? Lilith as some sort of new Devil-worshipper? Woooo." He laughed. "Don't go crazy on me, mate. She is a beautiful person who I happen to love." He picked up the butt, took a puff then stubbed it out. "It's getting on. I'm tired, I had a busy day. Don't you think you should be getting back to your own family? It's gone eleven."

Christian took the hint. He didn't remember ever being invited *out* of Zach's house before. In fact, it had always been the exact opposite. He felt ashamed as he walked back to his car. Not only had he been prowling around the back of their property, but he'd accused his mate's wife of witchcraft as though he was some sort of latter-day Salem prosecutor. But this smartphone app was coming between them. Christian explored his thoughts, searching for his motivation. Was he jealous? Jealous of Zach's success with the app and his relationship with Lilith? Was his unconscious mind working against him?

13

When Zach returned from nearly five years abroad following the death of the baby, it had been a tough time for everybody. The financial markets had collapsed in the sub-prime loans fiasco and as Christian took up his new role in the Acquisitions department of Beaufort & Soames he knew lay-offs were inevitable. He just hoped he would make enough of an impression to be safe in his position. He reasoned that if he did make it through the year, and out the other side, there'd be less competition for partnerships — so there were grounds for optimism.

Zach remained uncontactable for most of his time away. Christian received an occasional email to his work address and even the odd postcard, but his own messages were never replied to. Zach's invitation to his and Rachel's wedding went into a black hole, so Christian got married without his friend as his best man. He heard that Zach had been taking his ski instructor certification in Queenstown, New Zealand, and the year after spent winter in Japan. Then that he'd been taken on as crew on a yacht, sailing the Pacific. As far as Christian knew that was where he was today. His friend had spent five years attempting to forget the loss of his child, his broken marriage and the wind-up of his business.

Through mutual friends, he and Rachel had patched together the story. After the baby died Lilith abandoned Zach, as if he was the one to blame. She returned to her family and lost contact with him. He pursued her, begging her to return, but he failed to change her mind. No one blamed her. How could they? Eventually Zach just fucked off. He left Germany with a single rucksack and the change in his jeans' pocket. For the first eighteen months Christian had not received so much as a scrawled note on the back of a Juicy Fruit wrapper. Zach had become a long-lost friend.

So it was all the more surprising that in January 2009, on a bitterly cold Friday morning as Christian walked to the office focusing on keeping his shoes dry, he was stopped by a long-haired, bearded backpacker standing at the doors to the office building.

"Christian."

"Excuse me?"

"Christian, it's me."

Christian looked up from his shoes and studied the face in front of him. "Zach? What the fuck? Zach. Jesus." He wrapped his arms around his friend and was enveloped in a stale odour of smoke and mould. He pulled back and held Zach by the shoulders. "It's good to see you. We've been totally worried for five fucking years, you bastard."

Zach grimaced and shrugged. "Sorry, man. You know." He scratched his beard. "Shit to sort out."

"So… why now? What're you doing?"

"I'm back. Surprise, surprise." He stretched his arms out in that megalomaniac gesture of his. "What are you doing today? Fancy skipping school?"

"Erm—"

"Come on. Where's that wild side? I predict you can take a day off."

"Yeah, the mile-wide wild streak I display so often." Christian looked at his watch. Seven-thirty. "Look. Give me an hour and I'll clear my diary. Let's get pissed."

"Now you're talking."

"There's a café on Passage Street just round the back of the block. It's called Extra Extra. By the bridge. Meet you there in an hour. They do a good breakfast."

"Waiting for you, mate."

When Christian detached himself from the office and found Zach an hour later, his friend had made a nest at one of the side tables in the café. His battered rucksack was resting on one chair to his left and a large plastic bag bursting at the seams sat on another to his right. The small white coffee cup on a white saucer before him looked like a buoy in the ocean against the vast black beard Zach had allowed to bloom.

"More coffee?" Christian asked.

"You bet. Any chance of a full English?"

Christian laughed. "Anything you want. You skint?"

"I'm just putting everything I have into something else."

"Even the price of breakfast?"

"Everything."

Everything. Such a simple word, but the way Zach said it, focusing intensely on Christian's face as he spoke, gave it the weight of a mountain. A monolith. A challenge that should not be faced except by the boldest and, perhaps, the most foolish. Serious and uncompromising.

Christian went to the counter and ordered two full English breakfasts and two coffees. When he returned Zach was holding a white device in his hand attached to a small keyboard.

"Looks interesting," Christian said.

"Have you seen one of these?"

"No. What is it?"

"This, my friend, is a world-changer. A smartphone." Zach passed the device over and Christian turned it over in his hands. It was clearly a phone, but with miniature attachments of a computer. A keyboard appeared when you slid it apart, and it revealed a screen a bit bigger than two passport photos side by side.

"Is this like the Apple thing?"

"Like it. Yes. But this is open source."

"Free?"

"Not free. But free to change and adapt. The software, anyway. Unencumbered by patents or copyright."

"Sounds like a hippie wet-dream."

"It's an HTC Android phone. The first on the market in the UK and it's going to be massive. Everybody will have one."

Christian didn't see it. "I have a computer on my desk and a mobile phone. What do I need this for?"

"It's the next evolution in personal computing. The fact anybody can create and distribute software on it means I can reach a worldwide audience. They have a store to publish programs. Apps."

"I thought that's what the internet did. Why is this new?"

"This is the internet on the move. Anywhere. In the toilet, walking home, on the bus. And I mean proper internet, fully functional. Like on your computer but now in your pocket. A friend."

Christian turned it over again. He paid attention to the screen. "It looks like a Windows desktop."

"Yeah. It has a similar metaphor on the user interface. Point. Click. Open. Close. Drag. Stuff like that. But look at that one in the top right."

Icons had been set out on a grid. At the top right-hand side of the grid was a horoscope sign. *Your Future.*

"This is your old website thing?"

"Yep. Online. In your pocket. By your bed." Zach laughed. "You want to know how to approach a problem, this will tell you. Want to know what the future is going to bring, this will tell you. Want to know how your family is going to do—" Zach stopped and took a deep, controlling breath before looking back at Christian with a sad smile. "I needed to get back into this. Understanding your future is part of getting to grips with the past."

"I thought you'd given up on the software. What with, well…"

"So did I. I guess I've healed somewhat. Anyway, I've been working on it. And when this device came out I had to have one."

"It's fascinating." Christian put it on the table between them. "But how are you? I've not seen you for five years and you show up with a mobile phone. I don't care about mobile phones. You look like a fucking mess. You need a bath. Have you got any money? Where are you staying?"

"With you."

14

Christian jolted himself awake with a loud cry and sat up in the bed. For three nights he'd been unable to get the image of Lilith and Zach fucking from his mind. Her naked body beneath Zach's was burnt on his eyes like a camera flash. When he was awake the picture played in his mind and obsessed him; when his heavy eyes closed his mind would play out a 3D virtual-reality version as if he was right in the room with them. It was exhausting.

And although the dreams disgusted him, he woke with an erection or shameful wet patch around his pyjamas. He knew some deep part of his psyche was enjoying it.

Rachel sat up next to him and turned on the bedside lamp. "I can't put up with this much longer."

"What do you mean?" He knew. He couldn't bring himself to admit it.

"Look at you. You're in a sweat. You don't come home from work until late every night. It's been going on for weeks and weeks. I'm exhausted and I need some sleep. You wake me up every night, you're so restless. I'm tired, and I'm worried for us."

"For us?"

"Yes, for us. We're so exhausted it's affecting how we relate to Jessica. It's making her behave badly just to get attention. You're never here to play with her. She's bullying some of the children at playgroup, and she won't listen to me. She needs a father. I'm struggling to do everything around the house and rest enough for the baby. I'm due in ten weeks. I need to be relaxed and secure. You have to be stable for me." Her face screwed up as she started to cry.

"There's nothing to worry about. Work is just taking up more time than I expected. It'll be over soon."

"That's what you promised weeks ago."

"I know. Things keep coming up."

She sobbed. Christian held her close into his chest and kissed the top of her head. He breathed in her scent and it relaxed him. He pulled her tight.

"You keep promising, but you've changed. I don't know where we stand with you anymore. We used to be your top priority, but I can't predict when you're going to come in or stay out. Tell me I'm still important." She forced the words out between her sobs, her shoulders rising and falling in time with her gulps of air.

"Rachel, you are my life. Look at me." He held her head in his hands and stared into her eyes. "You and Jessica mean more to me than food and drink. I love you." He dabbed a tear from her cheek. "Please believe me, darling."

She looked up. Looked right into him. "I do believe you, but you've got to give me more than words. You have to be there for us. Why do you work so late?"

"It's this project. It's taking up my time. It has to be right." He sat back against the headboard. "I'm doing it for the family. It's going to set us up. I can't afford to let this slip — it needs my constant attention."

"Are you trying to convince me or yourself?"

"There's nothing wrong with it," he said. "We've been through every aspect of the project. I've driven the team mad with tiny requests. As far as I can tell it's now perfect. Nothing wrong with it. It can't fail."

"Does that mean you'll come home next week? Finally make good on your promises?" Rachel studied him with tight lips and hard eyes.

Christian was sorry he'd put her through these few weeks of madness. But it had to be done. He had to go through this. Hadn't she always said she'd support him? He looked into her eyes with the intention of calling her to task, but her expression had softened.

She shuffled towards him. She held his face. "You look so tired, love. This project has tied you up day and night for weeks. And now you're keeping us both from sleeping."

He reached to his bedside table and picked up his phone. "It still says the project will fail."

She grabbed the phone and puzzled over it. "This?"

He nodded.

"Have you been working late because of this?" She waved it in the air. "Have you?" She raised her voice, staring at him, "I take it from your sheepish look that you have. Are you fucking stupid? This is a dinner-party game."

"It's not just a game. How can it be?" He grabbed the phone off her. "The tree, then the newspaper reports, and William Thorpe. I had to go over everything again. And I've got to do it again now. Otherwise I'd be negligent."

"No, Christian. You didn't have to, and you don't have to go over it again. It is your choice. You're obsessed. I think you need to see the doctor."

"Listen to me." He grabbed her arm. "Something's going on. It even knows my dreams. It said I would be *Charmed by Lilith.*"

"Charmed by Lilith. What's she to do with anything?"

"Don't you see? It's those dreams I've been having. That wake me up. It's Lilith."

"Lilith?"

Christian looked away, ashamed. He lowered his voice to a whisper. "Yes. It's Lilith in the dreams. I didn't want to tell you. I'm sorry. She's got some power over me."

"Christian, you're scaring me. You've been having fantasy dreams about Lilith? And you didn't tell me because you were embarrassed?" She laughed. Not a kind laugh, a mocking laugh. "I'm sure Lilith will be flattered when you go around there and explain. You fucking turd."

They sat in silence for a moment. An image of Zach laughing over the predictions flashed in Christian's head.

Rachel sighed. "I'm sorry. That was uncalled-for. I'm exhausted and you're in a different world. I think you might need some help. But right now I need support for me and Jessica, and the baby."

Christian couldn't take in her apology. He barely heard her. He knew the project would fail unless he made it work. She had to realise how important it was. The thought of them all laughing at him as he worked his arse off trying to make things right made him angry. What about what he needed? "Right now," he said, mimicking her expression, "I need to give it my undivided attention and *I* need *your* support. That's fair, isn't it?"

She stared at him; eyes narrowed. "If that's how you feel you can give it your attention now." She pushed him. "Get out the fucking bed," she screamed. "If you can't support me, then I can't support your stupid fucking project. Get the fuck out." She pushed him again, trying to roll him out of the bed. "You tosser! You won't make love with me and you dream of sex with other women. Get the fuck out!" Her face turned bright red. "Get out!"

Christian shut the door behind him and found Jessica standing by her bedroom door clutching Everywhere and crying.

He knelt down and put his hands out to cuddle her. "Mummy's tired right now, and she needs to have the bed to herself." He stood up, stopped himself from crying. "Nothing to worry about, sweetheart. Come on, I'll help you back into bed."

As if there wasn't enough to do without being hampered by internal audits. Geoff McMahon, red-haired chief of accounting at Beaufort & Soames, had requested a meeting via a yellow sticky note posted on Christian's desk monitor.

"What is it, Geoff?" he said, as the door opened and McMahon stood before him with an armful of documents. Christian remembered his own time working for Internal Audit and the bleak relationships it inspired. Softening, he corrected his antagonism. "Come in, sit down. How can I help?"

"I hate to bother you like this, but I needed some information regarding your expenses policy on the Burnham project."

"Yes?"

McMahon held the papers to his chest, seeming to size Christian up. He put the papers on the table and began to leaf through them. "What is the policy?"

"Any expense that the team claim is allowed. I trust them to know what is acceptable."

McMahon nodded and stared, waiting for more explanation.

"I like my staff to be efficient and have a high morale, so it's important they get all the support I can give them."

"And what about your personal expenses?"

"What do you mean?"

"How do you control those?"

"The same as everybody else."

McMahon smiled. "I'm sorry to have to press you, but it's your personal expenses claims that are a worry. Not the team's, although they *are* generally high."

Christian tapped his fingers on the desk. "Senior management are allowed every discretion when it comes to expenses. My car, all the petrol, entertaining, meals out. I put everything through the project books. I do not have work time and home time." He smiled. "Like you do, for example. Every waking hour is Beaufort's, and I am entitled to be paid for it."

"Yes, of course. That's covered in your salary." McMahon smiled again. He was beginning to irritate Christian.

"Just what are you getting at? Come to the point."

"Your expenses claims are vastly in excess of the figures the guidelines allow. More than any other manager here at Beaufort's. You are claiming for obviously personal items. Let me see." He picked out more paper records from the manilla folder. "Children's *Balamory* videos, services for tree surgery, a weekend trip to Amsterdam. I have checked this, and the firm has no clients in Amsterdam. Perhaps it was a speculative trip?"

Christian suddenly realised this could be serious. "Wait a minute. No one's bothered about this. Who the fuck creates these guidelines? Isn't it me and my colleagues that run this firm?"

"I think Mr Beaufort runs the firm. Not you."

Not yet, anyway. Christian sat back and tapped the desk again. He sensed politics at work. "Tell me, Geoff, how has this little audit come about?"

McMahon raised his eyebrows. "It's funny, really. The Burnham team have been examining expenses for a thorough review, to ensure the project was squeaky clean. On your instruction, I understand. The only irregularities uncovered were yours. Ironic isn't it?"

Christian stared. The weasel was grinning as if he had uncovered a vast fraud and was being heaped with praise. *Accountants! What a pathetic bunch.*

"Geoff, you know as well as I do that senior management have complete discretion when it comes to expenses. Perhaps I shouldn't say it, but there you are, it's a fact. It's been done like that for years."

"Unfortunately we *do* have strict policy towards this sort of thing, and while it remains minor it's fine — and I don't believe it's policy to obstruct our executives. But once revealed, we have no choice except to act. The Revenue will come down on us like an avalanche in the Alps if we aren't seen to be snow-white."

"Save the ridiculous metaphors." *Stupid little upstart.* Christian had never liked the man. Always wearing a dark pinstripe and red braces with one of those bold blue shirts with the white collar that made him look like an Eighties derivatives dealer.

"Geoff," Christian said, calming down and recognising this would only be solved if he collaborated. "What do we have to do?"

"You will pay the money back and receive a written warning."

"You're joking?"

McMahon shook his head. "I've been through your expenses for the last couple of years. That should satisfy the Revenue, and I've taken out the claims not directly attributed to the project. From my calculations you owe…" He sorted through yet more folders and loose sheets. "A hundred and thirty-six thousand three hundred and twenty-eight pounds."

Christian was staggered. He leant back in the chair. Over a hundred grand. "That can't be right," he said.

McMahon shrugged. "It's all here. Flights and hotels added on are the most. You like business class and five-star hotels, it seems. For you and the family."

"It *can't* be right. That's fucking ridiculous. There's been a mistake."

"I think not. But please check with your own records. And, sorry to rush you, but this needs to be done straight away. I've got Howard breathing down my neck on this, for some reason."

After McMahon gathered his notes, leaving Christian in silence for twenty minutes thinking through the ramifications of the debt, the door opened and Howard walked in. "Well," he said, "this isn't good, but I wouldn't worry unduly. As long as the money is repaid quickly it shouldn't cause too many problems."

Howard sat across the desk in the same position McMahon had vacated, "Inflated expense claims are not something I worry about when we're getting results. So far, you have been exceptional." He smiled. "You do *normally* get results."

Long pause. Christian broke the silence. "You *know* this is ridiculous. I am an exec, and I'm not the only one to use the firm for holidays or for my wife's car. When you sail to Cowes where do you stay? In the company-owned villa. As far as the Revenue is concerned it's a legitimate business expense for the promotion and marketing of the company."

"Christian." Howard's look meant, *You're on dangerous ground here*, but what he said was, "You're right, of course. All the senior management have perks, there's a culture of it. But only you have attracted attention by insisting on a thorough review of budgets and reports. You brought this on yourself. You must give every assistance to Geoff and go through the expenses on the project again. You'll claw it back when the deal goes through. It will be nothing compared to your completion bonus. There's one more thing. IntelliTech confirmed they will be conducting an inquiry into the whole deal as well. I think they are focusing on your role, and they might review our charges and expenses. She was joking, I think, but the CFO asked if our bill was going to wipe out the profits from the sale. Revisit both client accounts for the last three years, and make sure there's nothing else. It could be embarrassing for us. The project is unravelling. You'd better get it under control. And I need the results tomorrow."

"Any other time, Howard, you know, but I have to get back for Rachel. I promised her."

Howard stood up. "It's tough at the top. You'll make the right decision, I know."

*

146

Rachel liked to browse through *Hello* when waiting at the surgery. It was a release from real reading, a regression to childhood and those wonderful pony magazines. She flicked through the photographs searching for somebody she recognised, but after a few pages her eyes closed and her head dropped against her chest. The tiredness was overwhelming. All she wanted to do was lie down.

"Mummy, they're calling you."

She opened her eyes to find Jessica tugging at her sleeve. Her daughter had taken to carrying her teddy bear with her wherever she went, and Everywhere's greying fabric lay limp across her shoulder.

"I'm coming." Rachel pushed herself up against the back of the lime-green chair. "Come with me, Jessica." The five-year-old slipped her hand in her mother's and they walked to the consulting room at the front of the building.

"Just a routine check today, Mrs Jarvik."

The midwife looked up from the desk. Brenda Lassing was unforgettable: her red cheeks and blue eye-shadow were better suited to the cover of a Seventies *Vogue* than on the face of a rotund midwife with a Bristol accent. Rachel smiled. She knew all the staff, and sometimes she felt comfortable with it, but today she would have rather had a stranger. She didn't feel well.

"You sit on the chair and be quiet, darling," Rachel picked up her daughter and plonked her beneath the eye chart.

Jessica immediately started to read the letters she could see in the mirror opposite. "E, F, P, T…"

"Shush!" Rachel put her finger to her lips and Jessica began to mouth the letters rather than speak them out loud.

"How are you getting on?" Brenda asked from behind a mound of paperwork.

"I'm exhausted," Rachel said. "My husband hasn't been sleeping and it's keeping me awake. I want to lie down all the time, as if I have a heavy weight on my shoulders."

"Yes." Brenda nodded. "We'll take your pressure and check your bloods."

"I've had a headache for three days as well."

Brenda readied the blood-pressure cuff then dropped into a

seat next to Rachel. "Have you taken anything?" she asked as she rolled Rachel's sleeve up and fastened the cuff tight. She put the stethoscope on without listening to the reply.

Rachel smiled and cupped her bump. "No, not with the baby."

Brenda pumped the cuff as if working out at the gym; an exaggerated fist-clenching and intense expression. Rachel watched the needle climb on the pressure gauge and saw the midwife's concerned expression. Brenda tapped the gauge, let the cuff down and took the pressure again, taking extra care placing stethoscope. "Your blood pressure is on the high side, pet. Can you lie on the couch? I have to check the baby."

Rachel exposed her midriff and Brenda felt for the baby. She gelled the doppler and lay it on Rachel's abdomen. The baby's heart beat came through strong and clear. She seemed satisfied.

"I need you to pee for me, pet." She handed Rachel a small transparent cup and helped her down from the couch. "The toilet's on the left."

Rachel waddled out the door.

When she returned, Brenda waved a small plastic stick in the sample and inspected the coloured pad at the end against a chart. "Hop back on the couch and relax, pet. I won't be long."

"There's nothing wrong, is there?"

Brenda put her hand on Rachel's arm. "No, pet. Just relax." She swayed out the door.

Rachel was concerned the midwife called her "pet" so often in an overly very friendly way. *Probably nothing.*

Five minutes later Dr Hanson appeared with Brenda right behind.

"Hello, Rachel," he said. Dr Hanson rechecked her blood pressure, took her temperature and her pulse. "Had any aches and pains?"

"My neck and lower back, and I told Brenda about the headaches."

"How are your joints?" He picked up her hands and inspected them, pushing the skin down at the knuckles.

"Well, they're swollen a bit. I put that down to the pregnancy."

"Rachel," Dr Hanson said, "I want you to stay here on the

couch while we get you an ambulance. I can see your hands are a bit swollen and your blood pressure is on the high side. Just to make sure nothing bad is going on, we need to investigate, do some more blood tests. We can only do that at the hospital. It's nothing to worry about, it's all routine, but I want you to have the best care we can give you. It's your job to stay relaxed and not to worry."

Rachel tried to sit up.

"Stay lying down, Rachel." He put his arm on her shoulder and applied a gentle pressure.

She put her head back on the pillow. "John, my pressure's only up because I haven't been sleeping and I'm worried about my husband's work."

"That might be, but I don't want to take any undue risks."

"Nothing's going to happen to the baby, is it?"

"No. Right now we want to make you completely rested and quiet. It's just a precaution. Indications are that you have a condition called pre-eclampsia. It occurs in about ten per cent of pregnancies and is easy to control. The hospital will run a series of tests and monitor you for a while, just to be safe." He took a pencil and pad from the desk. "Give me your husband's number and I'll make sure he gets called. He'll be able to pick up Jessica?"

"Can you call my mother instead?"

Jessica was still sitting in the corner of the room, her legs hanging halfway to the floor and Everywhere tucked up to her cheek while she sucked her thumb. She was frowning.

"It will be an adventure for you, to go with Grandma?"

Jessica nodded.

Dr Hanson scribbled the numbers down. "Brenda will be right back," he said. "I'll give your family a call. Lie down and don't worry." He turned to Jessica. "You look after Mummy for five minutes."

Jessica nodded, climbed down from the chair and stood by the couch holding her mother's hand.

15

The message that Rachel was in hospital reached Christian mid-afternoon, four hours after Rachel had been admitted.

Jo knocked at the door, entered and didn't wait for him to speak. "Sorry, Christian, but it's your wife, she's been admitted to hospital. I've had a message from switchboard."

He looked up from his screen. He stared. He said nothing. He had been focused on sorting out the expenses fiasco. His eyes were blurring from lack of sleep and the argument with Rachel still burned his heart.

"She's been taken to the antenatal ward at St Michael's. Your mother-in-law has been calling," Jo said.

It took several moments for the information to sink in. "What about my daughter?"

"She's at home with her grandmother."

"Is Rachel okay?"

"I don't know the details. The message said she was in for observation."

"Okay. Okay." He stood up from his chair. "I have to go."

"Of course. Don't worry about anything here. I'll take care of it."

Christian walked out of the office partially dazed at the news. As he digested the information he sped up, and by the time he was down a level from his floor his heels clicked as he leapt two steps at a time toward the car park. He flew through the emergency exit into the basement.

Within fifteen minutes he was touring the hospital environs searching for a place to park. *Fuck it, a public hospital with no parking. How did they manage to plan it like that?* He squeezed his car along the terrace above the rear entrance. Every space was taken, if not by a car then by double yellow lines. Panicking, he pulled up on a grass verge straddling yellow lines. Parking tickets would have to wait. He dashed back along the terrace to the doorway.

Crashing through a series of rubber and Perspex doors he found the lifts. He repeatedly bashed the buttons and stared at the level indicators above the metal doors. *Come on!*

He ran onto the antenatal ward to find it unattended. He banged on the reception desk. "Hello?" Nobody answered. A series of open-plan rooms with half a dozen women in each opened onto the corridor. He paced along the ward checking each room. He couldn't see Rachel.

He ran back to reception. "Hello?" he called. He heard talking behind the door at the end of the desk. "Hello?" he shouted.

A nurse poked her head around the door, "Be with you in one moment," she said, and disappeared. Christian raced around the desk and opened the door. "Where's Rachel Jarvik?"

"Do you mind?" the nurse said. "We'll be out in a minute."

"Look, my wife is in here, I don't know where. I want to know where she is and I can't wait for you to finish your box of Quality Street."

The nurse stared at him, seemed to think better of a confrontation and put her tea down. "When did she come in?"

"This morning."

"Yarvick with a Y?"

"J. As in jam jar."

"She's in Room Four, at the end. I'll take you down."

Rachel was surrounded by curtains; a chrome drip-hanger stood by the bed.

Christian sat in the chair and grabbed her hand. "I'm here, darling," he whispered into her ear. Her eyes were closed: dark rings made them look hollow and her lips were the same grey as the hospital walls.

He held her hand. Her eyes opened slightly. "Christian," she said, and half-smiled before her eyes closed again.

"She's been sedated, Mr Jarvik. So she can sleep."

"What's happening? Is the baby all right? We had an argument. Oh God!"

"Everything is fine. She's doing well. Don't worry." The nurse picked up the chart from the foot of the bed. "She's been stable since she came in. It may be a while until I can get a doctor to talk to you, I'm afraid, but there's a ward round at six when you can talk to the registrar."

"Is it okay to use a phone?" He pulled his mobile phone out from his inside jacket pocket.

"That's fine. Just keep your voice down. I'll be back as soon as I have some news." She backed through the curtains and drew them closed.

Christian was about to phone Rachel's mother when he saw a notification from the Algorithm. He flicked the app open:

Someone is under pressure and money is an issue.

He stared at the words as a chill crept up his back. He looked over at Rachel. Had it really predicted this? And his expenses problems? He was being watched — or worse, played for a fool. He started to sweat. What if he had been warned but had done nothing about it? That would make him guilty of causing Rachel's illness by doing nothing.

He put his phone in his pocket, rubbed his eyes, then put his hands back over hers. He stroked her hair and told her he loved her and everything would be fine. He would find a way to help her, to fix things.

Sometime later, while the thoughts of how he could have foreseen what was coming churned in his mind, the curtain was pulled aside and a doctor in theatre greens appeared with a clipboard. "Your wife has pre-eclampsia, Mr Jar-Vik. It's a serious condition of late pregnancy but easily treated, and we've caught it nice and early. We're bringing her blood pressure down with methyl dopa and a magnesium sulphate infusion. But there's a chance we will have to deliver early if things don't improve. Can I please have your consent for a caesarean, in case it's required." The registrar handed over the clipboard and a pen. He pointed to where Christian should sign.

Christian hesitated. He'd been waiting for hours and now it was over before it had begun.

"We want to keep her under close observation," said the doctor. "Just in case her or the baby start to get into trouble. A high blood pressure can cause organ failure. It may be best to deliver the baby quickly. It's not ideal, the baby is ten weeks away from full term, but we might have to make that decision. We'll only do it if it's *absolutely* necessary, we'd much rather the baby went to term."

Christian read through the form and signed. "What happens now?"

"She's stable at present, and she's resting. I suggest you get some sleep yourself, Mr Jar-Vik. The nurses will call you if anything changes, but I expect it will be a quiet night."

"What causes it?"

"How pre-eclampsia develops is not well known. An incorrectly formed or small placenta are theoretical causes, but the condition can't be predicted. There are some indications: if the mother is small-framed or has a history of hyper-tension, but we don't know for sure." The doctor stood up, tucked the consent form under the spring clasp of the clip-board and hung it from the end of the bed. "We see lots of women with this condition Mr Jar-Vik, and we're very experienced at treating it. Magnesium sulphate has been a game-changer for pre-eclampsia. She'll be fine. There's nothing to worry about."

Christian wanted to shout, *It's pronounced Yar-vick not like a fucking jam jar — it's fucking Danish,* but all he did was nod. He wanted to help his wife, but all he could do was stroke her hair and keep the seat warm.

That fucking app had foreseen all this. He pulled out his phone. It was unbelievable. He angrily scrolled through its Help screens.

The app had its origins in the six months when Zach stayed with them after returning from his round-the-world, self-seeking adventures. If Christian resented the intrusion on his newly married life, he kept the thoughts so deeply hidden in his limbic system they rarely surfaced, even when Zach insisted on watching sport or came back from town stoned. Rachel was less inclined to let Zach soak up her husband's generosity, but she complained only to Christian. If it had occurred to Zach that his host was less than pleased by his attendance as a third person in a traditional two-person relationship, he didn't show it. Rachel thought Zach could be thick-skinned and insensitive; Christian thought he was cool and laid-back. Christian loved having his mate around; Rachel loved Christian.

Yet the moments of tension had been few. Zach spent many hours locked in his room working on his app. He achieved some success with thousands of downloads. He wrote a blog and managed the PR himself. Yet he never seemed to have money, and after a while the Jarviks stopped asking how it was going. Despite his worries, Christian survived the financial meltdown of 2008 and Rachel had defended some high-profile local criminals. Together, 2009 saw their earnings double.

Zach arranged his room like a Moroccan tent. He draped rich tapestries from the walls, covered the knee-height futon with red-and-gold cushions and burnt tiny cones of incense each evening. In the rest of the flat, the Jarviks painted the walls block-pastel shades and hung nondescript Habitat pictures in grids across the walls. Work was everything for them: the decorating, incense, coloured existence of freedom that Zach represented appeared frivolous, eccentric, immature.

But the huge benefit for both Christian and Zach was their return to fencing twice a week. Christian had been only a casual member of the club in recent years, but when Zach returned the two of them thrust themselves back into fighting like Tom and Jerry and trained for the competitions. After one late-July training session, they returned to the flat and plonked themselves in the lounge with cold beers, both still in fencing jackets and breeches, sweaty from exertion.

"I don't know how you got a hit on me this evening." Zach said, taking a gulp of the beer and slouching back into the sofa. "I was on fire."

"Do I need to remind you who actually won the bout?"

"Winning is not all. There's style, tactics, strategy,

entertainment. It's not just about the score. Come on, how many times have we had this conversation?" Zach grinned. "If there were points awarded for performance, I'd have the world fucking championship by now."

"But why have style, tactics and strategy if it's not to win?"

"Art for art's sake. Would you ask Banksy to take part in a mural contest? Or would Leonardo da Vinci care that he won a ceiling-painting competition? I don't think so. I am the artist here. You, my friend, are the pedestrian voyeur."

"That's fucking nice. I'd put it somewhat differently. I'd say simply that you lost. Zach is a loser. The method of losing was by imagining that somehow style and entertainment counted in a sword fight. People who shared your genetics are strewn across the ancient battlefields of England, dismembered and forgotten. But the pedestrian voyeurs live on to fight another day and are now the powerful elite of society."

"Attractive pallor, boys," Rachel said from the door. Snuggled in a pink dressing-gown, she carried a glass of water, a copy of *Red* magazine and had tied her hair back in a bun.

Zach studied her. "No wine tonight?"

Rachel smiled. She sat down in the armchair and tucked her legs beneath her.

Christian put his bottle down with a click on the table. "We, um, we want to have a chat, actually, Zach."

"Okay. Well I wanted to say something too, since we're all gathered together."

Christian looked at Rachel. Rachel looked at Christian.

"Why don't you go first, Zach," Rachel said.

"Sure. Look, I don't want to seem ungrateful. You guys have been the best since I got back, and I can't be easy to live with. But I've decided I should move out."

Christian and Rachel stayed silent. They had been planning this conversation for a couple of weeks and had been dreading it. Now Zach had pre-empted their words.

"I'm going to make a couple of changes. The smart-phone app I'm working on is getting some attention, but it's not going to make me rich without some serious work and I don't have the capital. I don't have the money to pay you guys any rent. But my news is, I've got a job."

"A real job?" Rachel said. It was blurted out in a moment of disbelief and happiness, but Christian realised the true nature of her comment. She wouldn't believe it until it happened.

"It's with this firm called Rational IT, or Rationality. Cute, huh? They're into great things with machine-learning and I can help them. I'm way ahead, even with my own little app, so we thought we'd join forces. I met the CIO at last month's OpenAICon. You've been a fantastic support for me, but I've got to get on with life." He trailed off for a moment, his head bowed. "With a paid job I can set myself up again. It's time."

Rachel moved over beside him and put her arm around him. "It's the right thing," she said.

"And not only am I starting a new job, I got a long letter from Lilith." Zach smiled. "Typical of her to write a letter rather than email. A bit pre-industrial."

Christian was uncertain this was good news.

Zach caught the mood. "It's okay, guys. I'm not about to run off after her. Well, not yet. I'm going to play it cool. Take my time."

"How is she?" Rachel asked.

"She's back in Frankfurt, at her parent's place. Like all of us, she's maturing. We got married a bit early. In hindsight."

"Impetuous and creative as always," Christian said.

"She's still focused on having a family, but…" Zach trailed off and picked up his beer.

It had been seven years since they'd split up and Zach must have hurt every day. Lilith surprised Zach with the occasional message, but was otherwise absent. As Christian understood it, she was no longer able to get pregnant and the loss of the baby had eaten into her like woodworm.

Zach sighed. "You guys. You really are the best." He hugged Rachel and kissed her on the cheek. "Now. You're going to tell me you're pregnant, aren't you?"

Rachel turned to Christian with comic daggers in her look, as if she was angry. As if to say, *you told him*.

Christian shrugged. *I don't know how he knows*.

16

With Rachel in hospital and Jessica with her grandparents, Christian found the house cold and lonely. He put on the central heating and was about to pour a drink when his mother-in-law rang. "I was about to call," he said. "How's Jessica?"

"She's sleeping fine," Diane said. "We've pushed our armchairs together for her so she thinks she's got a little camp. We've told her she'll be able to see her mum tomorrow. Is that right?"

"Yes, I think so. I'll be with Rachel when she wakes up, and then I'll come over to you." He poured a good helping of whisky and downed it while Diane gabbled on. She was naturally worried. "Everything's going to be fine. Try not to worry. Rachel's stable and sleeping. She's in good hands. Is Ray okay?" He poured another whisky.

"He's on good form tonight. We'll be fine. You focus on Rachel and we'll look after Jessica. I've asked Ray's nurse if she wouldn't mind helping out for a few days. She's going to come in for some extra hours."

Christian sat down without turning on any lights in the lounge and sipped his drink. He thought about Zach. Did his friend know what Lilith was really like? *Love.* That was a fucking laugh. Christian could see she was no good, that she was subverting their friendship using her occult games and the app. He pulled out his phone and opened the app. What had Zach said about Dark Mode? He went to the menu and scrolled down. There it was. *Dark Mode–Premium.* He clicked:

Dark Mode uses the latest predictive technology mixed with the magic of intuition. It delves deep into your

past to bring you your future. You must be over
eighteen and of sound mind to enjoy all your possible
tomorrows. May your gods be with you.

He ticked a small black box in agreement and spent fifteen minutes confirming his credit-card details and entering more personal information. It wanted all sorts of things like passport and NHS number. Whenever he hesitated it popped up a message saying that the more it knew about his past, the more accurate the predictions would be.

Finally, there was a black screen with a single blood-red button in the middle labelled *The Algorithm presents Dark Mode*. He clicked. The button dissolved into a circle of rotating tarot cards. *The algorithm is working. Wait for your future.*

He watched the screen for five minutes before filling his glass to the brim. He took a swig. Then another. He stared at the moving cards until the screen-saver kicked in and the phone went blank.

As Christian continued to drink, his fury grew. He forgot the app and his thoughts turned back to Zach and Lilith. What were they doing? *Why don't I just fucking ask her? I'll just ring her up and see what she has to say. Zach obviously doesn't know what's going on.*

He picked up his phone and called Zach's house. "Zaaaach, it's Christian. How's the magic going?"

"Christian. Hey, you okay?" Loud music blared out behind Zach. People were shouting and singing. Christian could hardly hear what was going on. "Hang on, I'll take you into the hall."

"What's going on? Sounds like you're 'aving a party?" Christian slurred. He tried to focus on saying each word perfectly. He took another slug.

"A few friends round is all."

Zach was clearly embarrassed. Christian hadn't been invited. Of course Zach would be embarrassed, now Christian had found out. The music continued to thump in the background. A door slammed and the music level dropped.

"It's an impromptu thing. Christian, I've got some great news. We just decided to celebrate."

"She pregnant?"

"Lilith?" Zach laughed. "No. You've had few drinks, haven't you? Why don't you come round? Have a few more over here." He continued laughing as if it was some private joke. "We secured a huge contract today with a firm here in Bristol. It's going to put the company on the map. It's fantastic."

Christian heard Lilith's voice in the background: "Who is it?"

"Christian."

Lilith came on the call. "Hello, Christian." Her voice was loaded with promise.

"Lilith, I'm on my way. I hope you're not tied up."

"Are you feeling okay?"

At that moment the phone vibrated in his hand. Christian pulled it from his ear. A notification from the Algorithm. He opened the app and began reading. In the background, the tinny sound of Lilith and then Zach asking him if he was okay softened into oblivion.

Rachel woke up with a pummelling ache in the top of her head only an hour after the night shift had come on at the hospital. The day had been punctuated with checks on her blood pressure, and she felt as if the weight of a thousand hammers bore down on her. The pain, the heat of the hospital and the lights shining through thin curtains stopped her going back to sleep. She kept her head motionless on the pillow and her eyes closed, listening to the evening's activities around her. Her mind wandered from Jessica to Christian and back. She worried about them, worried whether Jessica would behave herself for her grandmother, worried whether Christian would be able to fix himself dinner. She felt guilty for calling him a turd and hoped he'd forgive her.

She heard movement around her bed as the curtains were drawn back. Metal rings scraped along the rail. She followed the progress of the fabric in her mind. At least two people were in the cubicle with her. She didn't open her eyes.

She felt her shoulder being touched. "Mrs Jar-Vick?"

She opened her eyes but the bright lights burst in. She quickly closed them to shut out the pain. "Where's my husband?"

"He was here earlier." It was the nurse's voice. "He'll be back in the morning."

Rachel slowly opened her eyes again to see a blurred human shape in front of her dressed in theatre greens. She pushed herself over, and the nurse raised the bed a couple of inches. She had a feeling of déjà vu — had this happened earlier? She felt as if she had endured weeks of blood-pressure tests.

The doctor flicked the notes over. He took Rachel's blood pressure again. "I met you yesterday when you came in, if you remember, Mrs Jar-Vick. I'm Doctor Fitch."

"It's Yarvick," Rachel said. "As if spelt with a Y."

"I'm sorry. Jarvik, then."

Two other doctors stood behind him with arms folded. The nurse stood on his right. "We might have to deliver the baby, Mrs Jarvik. I'm going to keep a close eye on your condition for the next few hours, but if your blood pressure doesn't drop by morning we'll have to perform a caesarean." He turned and spoke to a doctor behind him. "Jane, can you book the theatre for tomorrow late morning? It seems likely we'll need it. And has the patient been consented?"

Rachel didn't hear the reply.

"It's best if you sleep, Mrs Jarvik. We're going to give you some more sedative and you're not to get out of bed again tonight. Is there anything you want to ask?"

"Is the baby all right?"

"At the moment, the baby is fine. If he shows any signs of distress, we'll be whipping him out." He turned to the juniors. "Was there a scan on admission?"

"It's with the notes."

Fitch studied the scan. He nodded. "You get some rest, Mrs Jarvik, and I'll see you later."

Rachel closed her eyes.

*

Christian strangled the steering wheel while reversing out of his drive. He gripped so hard the foam indented beneath his fists. After reading the *Dark Mode* prediction he'd got up from the chair, picked up his keys and gone to his car. He threw his phone on the passenger seat, pushed the Start button and slammed the car into reverse. His mind churned with thoughts of Zach and Lilith. Hadn't Zach introduced the app, and then defended it? Hadn't Lilith encouraged his participation and then befriended Rachel to get in with her, while taunting Christian in his dreams? Everything stemmed from the Algorithm and that first night when the tree collapsed. And now they had some great deal going while Christian's business project failed. Zach had been evasive and changed the subject when they last talked, said the Algorithm was just a game. But it couldn't be. It knew too much. *They must know more than they were letting on. Because now it was terrifying:*

> This is your first Dark Mode prediction, Christian, I am working on more. Someone close to you is in grave peril, while you are tied up and have business matters that will not go the way you hoped. You must be strong to avoid loneliness. A confrontation is near and a legal matter must be contained.

Christian felt like smashing into the cars parked at the side of the road as he rounded the corner. He kept his car skimming within an inch of their wing mirrors.

He double-parked in the railway station alongside a burnt-out wreck and stumbled over St John's Road to Zach's property. Music was audible from the flat, but not as loud as he'd imagined from the telephone, and the raucous guests he'd expected to see loitering outside were not there. He staggered down the steps to the front door and pushed it open into a man and a woman standing inside, putting their coats on. "Hey, be careful," the man said.

Christian thought he knew them. He couldn't be sure, but he wasn't here for them. "Where's Zach?" he asked.

"What are you doing here, Christian?"

He turned at the mention of his name. He tried to focus on the person's face. Slowly the picture came into view.

"No hard feelings, I hope?" the man said. He offered to shake hands.

"Dave?" Christian showed his confusion by nearly falling. Unable to take Dave's hand, he held himself up with a stretched-out arm propped against the wall. "Wha' you talkin' 'bout?"

"You've had a few, mate. We'll catch up next week."

Christian's thoughts cleared momentarily. "Have you got something going with Zach I should know about?" He might be drunk, but he knew Dave Hinchley never mixed business with pleasure. And Dave didn't do pleasure. It was all business.

"We'll talk next week. You need to sober up." Dave and his wife left and the door closed behind them.

Christian stared at the door, attempting to make sense of the encounter.

"Christian, is that you?" Zach appeared from the kitchen carrying a bottle of wine. "I thought we'd been cut off, I didn't expect you to come round. Nearly everybody's left. It was just a little thing." He held up the bottle. "Nightcap?"

"You bashtard," Christian slurred. He fell towards Zach, holding himself up again on the wall of the hallway.

"What?"

"You fucking bashtard." He lunged and grabbed Zach around the middle, knocking the bottle to the floor and pushing him backwards. The bottle smashed on the terracotta tiles, spraying glass fragments and red wine over both of them. They barged through the bedroom door until both men collapsed against the wall. Christian tried to punch but Zach was too close. Instead he flailed against the flax carpet, taking the skin off his knuckles. Suddenly he was pinned to the floor by his shoulders. Christian struggled against a large man kneeling on his back.

Zach stood up and helped constrain his friend. They picked him up from the floor and held him upright.

"You've fuckin' gone behind my back!" Christian said.

"You're drunk, mate. What are you talking about?"

"What was Dave doing here? You've fucked me over, haven't

you? You and that fucking witch harlot of yours. You're ruining my life, you fucking cunts."

"I think you'd better leave."

"What're you doing to me?"

Lilith appeared in the doorway. "Oh my god! Zach, what's happening?"

"Christian's drunk and accusing us of something."

Christian stared at her, unable to speak. His body was being supported by the people around him, and he couldn't focus. She wore a long white dress that fell open at her cleavage. *She could be naked under it.* He shook his head. The hint of sex angered him. The thought that he wanted her made him furious; the thought of her intruding on his dreams and his marriage raged within him.

"You know what you're doing, you witch!" he shouted. "You're slowly taking it from me. My success, my job, my money, my wife. Everything you're jealous of. That algorithm's told me."

"Christian, don't be fucking stupid," Zach said. "Let's get him onto the bed. He needs to calm down. Lilith, can you ring Rachel?"

Lilith went back into the kitchen.

Zach and the last guest helped manhandle Christian towards the door. "She's in hospital. You can't call her." His words were so slurred Zach didn't understand. Christian got his arm free and took a swing at the other man holding him.

"Christian, fucking stop it!" Zach shouted.

The anger and the alcohol made Christian demented with fury. "You fucking did it! I don't fucking know you!"

Zach and the male guest held Christian tight around the top of his arms as he bucked his head back and forward. "Stop it! You've said enough," Zach said.

Somebody said something about the police.

"No need for the coppers," Zach said. "Let's get him into the bedroom. We'll lock him in until he calms down and Rachel comes for him. He can't even speak properly."

Christian swayed his head around to look. "You're a bunch of cunts. You need the fucking pigs to do your work for you. She's in fucking hospital." He hung in their arms like a bag of garden waste. They carried him to the bedroom and put him on the bed, holding him down as he struggled.

"Calm down, calm down," Zach said. "We'll talk in the morning. It's obviously upsetting, whatever it is."

On the bed where he'd seen Lilith and Zach making love a few days earlier Christian did calm down. He stopped struggling and thought of Rachel. He loved her. He hated Lilith, but her scent lingered on the sheets and on the pillow. He cried.

Lilith stood by the door, holding a mobile to her ear. They watched him, they were talking, whispering to each other and then, in the gloom, he was sure they laughed.

Zach appeared over him. "Sleep it off, mate. I'll get a blanket."

The door closed. He heard more voices. More laughing.

Time passed. He continued crying. It could have been a minute or an hour later. He didn't know. He didn't care. His head was spinning and thumping like a drum on a merry-go-round. In the background, gentle voices continued in murmured whispers interrupted by brief laughter.

He took a deep breath, rolled off the bed and staggered to his feet. He wobbled, reached out to support himself on the bed, then turned and ran at the doors. He crashed through the French windows, which flung open into the garden and swung hard against the walls. He ran to the low fence at the back of the property and made his way onto the road.

He fumbled in his pockets, looking for his phone. Rachel! What if something had happened? He needed to get home and clear his head. A cool breeze wrapped around his neck and for a moment he could think straight. He swayed over the road to his car, trying to walk as straight as possible. He tried the handle three times before remembering to click the key fob to unlock the doors.

The car moved fast around the corners with a mind of its own. He put his foot down hard and watched the speedometer shoot up — he'd never noticed it so clearly before, he could put his foot on the accelerator and the dial responded instantly. He turned left at the end of St John's Road. Lines of parked vehicles on both sides narrowed the road, but he knew the way was straight. He just had to keep the wheel still as he drove. He glanced in his rear-view mirror and saw Lilith's eyes staring back at him, merging with headlights from the car following.

"Fuck off!" he screamed. He turned to check the back seat and in his fury took his hands off the wheel. She wasn't there. What the fuck was happening? At that moment his front wing caught the edge of a parked car. His BMW twisted in the road, jumped up the opposite kerb and smashed into a bath-stone wall, knocking the iron balustrade from the top and bending it to the ground beneath the car's chassis. The car came to a rest suspended in the air with its wheels spinning. He slammed the gear stick into reverse, and gunned the engine into a motionless piercing roar.

"Fucking hell!" He opened the door and fell a foot from the top of the smashed wall onto the footpath. He swayed around the car, inspecting the damage. A light went on in the porch of the house.

He looked toward the blackness of the Downs. His house was a short walk over the top, beyond the lights. He set off across the dewy grass between stands of dark-green foliage.

17

When she woke, Rachel knew her daughter was next to her. Jessica's warm little hand was in hers, and the soft-earth smell of Everywhere was next to her.

She thought about her body and its position on the mattress. She was lying facing up, her hands alongside her torso. A white sheet covered her from chest to toe. When she moved her feet, a breeze rushed down her body as the cover behaved like a giant lung and pulled air in from around her neck. The pounding headache persisted.

"Everywhere says he will look after you," she heard, and the soft toy was placed on her shoulder in the same position that Jessica carried it.

She knew her daughter was there, but drowsiness and pain behind her eyes meant she found it difficult to push her eyelids open. She smiled gently, enjoying the tiny hand in hers and the knowledge that Jessica loved her.

"Everywhere says you're going to get better in time for tea."

Rachel was aware of many people coming and going: her mother, Jessica, Zach and Lilith. They hadn't said much, just sat quietly. Lilith whispered to her. A prayer, maybe. Lilith helped her to drink from a straw.

Painfully bright lights burned through her eyelids to intrude on where she slumbered. She watched the occasional thought and listened to the subdued movements going on around. For fleeting moments the heaviness lifted, and she was able to talk. "Where's Christian?" she asked.

"We don't know." It was Zach's voice. "I'm sure he'll be here soon." He didn't sound sure.

"Can you tell him I love him?"

"You can tell him yourself, when he gets here."

Christian woke in a cream-walled police cell lying on a built-in platform with a stainless-steel toilet in the corner opposite. He felt nauseous, as if his stomach was going to erupt. The back of his neck ached and his head throbbed. He wrestled himself up from the bench and crawled on his hands, allowing a grey blanket to fall to the floor.

A jail-cell toilet. What human animals had used it?

His bare feet kicked a metal tray and sent a cold cup of tea scuttling across the floor. He pulled himself to his knees and retched into the pan. Nothing came up but a spit of yellow bile in a dry heave. He spat it out, scraping it off his tongue with his teeth then coughing the residue away.

The exertion made his head thump, as if his skull was being pulled apart by rhythmic pulses in time with his heart beat.

He hung his head over the pan, grasping the side of the bowl. The strong smell of disinfectant caused the retching to build, his stomach muscles began to contract, and he felt a wave of cramp build from his belly to his throat. The pain in his head was unbelievable, a huge pressure from the back of his neck around to his temples beating with a strong throb. He heaved from deep in his stomach releasing a gob of yellow fluid. He coughed out strings of bile. The nausea passed, and he collapsed around the base of the toilet.

For a few moments he remained motionless. He breathed erratically, hoping the pain would subside. He needed to get to the hospital, see Rachel. The throbbing lessened. He pulled himself over the toilet and hung his head across the bowl. This time the coolness of the air near the toilet water calmed him. He draped himself around the bowl like a necklace.

He had a misty recollection of fighting at Zach's house and then driving in his car on top of a wall. He knew how drunk he'd been. And he knew he was paying for it now.

A key turned in a metal lock and the door opened. "Christian Jarvik. I think you're sober enough now to answer some questions." It was a police officer in a short-sleeved white shirt.

"Officer," Christian said, pushing himself up, "I need to speak to my wife."

"After you've spoken to us, we might let you use a telephone."

"You don't understand, she's in hospital."

"I think *you* don't understand. The minute you drove your car when you were four times over the legal limit was the moment you gave away the freedom to act as you choose." The officer pushed in a bucket and mop. "You have some cleaning up to do. After that we'll listen."

Christian stared at the bucket. A metal cylinder straight from the set of *The Shawshank Redemption* and a string mop.

"Don't just stare at it. Get cleaning."

"Do you have any gloves?"

"Get cleaning, Mr Jarvik."

The officer watched as Christian wiped the floor around the toilet and where he'd spilt the cup of tea. "Best not forget the bench and wall."

A huge splatter of vomit lay in the corner of the room at the end of the bed where Christian's head had been lying. It spread from the plastic mattress to the wall and onto the floor, coating the vinyl with a deep red stain. He put his hand up to his face and felt the dry stomach contents on his cheek. He wiped the wall and mattress, then mopped the floor until the officer was satisfied. Then he followed him along the corridor of cells and up a flight of concrete steps to an interview room. A set of four plastic bucket chairs and table were set out in the middle of the room. He looked at the white clock on the wall.

9.30 a.m.

Christian supported his head in his palm, his elbow resting on the desk. The throbbing was quiet until he moved, then it galloped inside his head as if he'd woken a herd of wildebeest.

9.35 a.m.

The cop entered with a cup of tea and a couple of Paracetamol tablets.

"I didn't know the police offered such a service," Christian said.

"Sometimes people get lucky." The cop put the delivery on the table and walked out.

The tea was welcome, but as Christian drank it, nausea rose within him. He breathed deeply and irregularly. He put his head down on his hands and stayed as still as he could.

9.45 a.m.

He made it through the bout of nausea. He lifted his head. He wondered why he was still in the interview room on his own, and how much longer he would have to wait. He desperately wanted his phone for news of Rachel.

He took two steps to the door, risking the galloping throb associated with movement, and tried the handle. It was locked. He peered through the small fire-glass window, rippled with wire, to the distorted empty passage. He pushed his cheek against the glass in an attempt to look along the walkway, and caught some movement. The lock turned, and he stood back.

"Sit down, Mr Jarvik."

In front of Christian was a short round man. Ginger hair swept over his crown and his white-and-pink complexion was peppered with freckles.

Christian sat down. "I need to call my wife," he said. "She's in hospital and may be having an operation right now. Please let me use the telephone."

"This won't take long, Mr Jarvik. We've got better things to do than keep you hanging around the station."

The man sat down opposite and laid out a few forms and reports on the table. He stared at Christian but didn't speak. He looked down at the notes, looked up, looked back down and turned a few pages. He put a pencil in his mouth while he read some scribbled notes. He removed the pencil and put it down between them. The red paint had been chewed off, and beige wood showed through.

He saw Christian looking at the pencil. "I used to smoke," he said.

Christian nodded, surprised at the candour. *Get on with it.*

"You've been a bit of a prat," the man said.

Christian shifted uncomfortably on the plastic seat. "Look, get me a date with the magistrate and let me go. I need to see my wife. Take my driving licence if you want. She's in danger. I need to be with her."

"All in good time. The hospital tells us she's doing okay." He put the pencil back between his teeth, then twiddled it round with his fingers before removing it. "It's not just the driving under the influence, you see. Lucky for you, no one wanted to make a complaint from before the crash." He smiled. "Or you might have had GBH to add to your collection."

"What are you talking about? Collection?"

"Well, let's see." He read from the notes. "Drunk in charge of an automobile, reckless driving, abandoning the scene of an accident, damage to property, and attempted burglary. Or perhaps it was prowling. Or stalking?"

"What?"

"What were you doing at 22a St John's Road on the night of the twentieth of May?"

"That's a friend's house."

"The same *friend* you assaulted last night?"

Christian closed his eyes. "Officer, whatever your name is—"

"Worthing."

"Worthing, yes—"

"Detective Inspector."

"Detective Inspector Worthing—"

"That's right."

Christian put his hand up to his head and, before he knew what was happening, started to cry. The tears fought through his thumping head and ran down his cheeks, each sob bringing fresh pain. *What is happening to me?*

He swallowed, took a deep breath. "Detective Inspector Worthing. You're married?"

Worthing nodded.

"Please let me call my wife. I have to know how she is. Please."

"She's doing okay." Worthing seemed to be considering the request. His tongue swept along his bottom lip as if seeking blemishes in the skin. "A touching display, Mr Jarvik. But let's get this statement out of the way, shall we?"

"Statement? What fucking statement?" Christian shouted. "I haven't done anything except drive my car into a fucking wall."

"One more outburst like this and you will be back in the cell

170

for an hour, then another, then another, until you behave sensibly."

Christian shut up.

"At least you remember the accident." Worthing tapped his pencil on the table and looked down at the notes.

Is he reading the notes or just using silence to get to me? Trying to break me like in some American movie?

"Where's the nice cop?"

Worthing ignored the comment. "In your own words, Mr Jarvik. What were you doing at 22a St John's Road on the night of the twentieth of May?"

"Last week? I was visiting Zach and Lilith. Nobody at home. I mean, I thought nobody was home. But they couldn't hear the bell, apparently. I went around the back to check." He remembered the naked figures, the low lights and the orange glow from the bedside lamp. "They were making love in the bedroom and I was embarrassed, so I decided to call back later. As I left, I tripped over a flower pot and ran."

"This is a friend, you said?"

"Yes."

"The one you assaulted last night."

"Yes. I mean, no. I didn't assault him. I was angry. He's—" Christian decided it wasn't time to go into details. "It's complicated."

"Some friend."

"Our relationship has deteriorated."

"Why?"

Christian immediately thought of Lilith in the white dress and the plunging neckline. His dreams of her as his mistress and then of Dave Hinchley blithely asking if there were any hard feelings. It was all tied together with the app. "They've got this app," he said.

"An app?"

"They're using this app to control me."

"An app on a phone? To control you?"

"It predicts the future. It should be illegal."

Worthing scratched his neck and looked over at the door. "How does it control you, exactly?"

"Everything it says has come true. I don't know how. It's some sort of black magic." With the alcohol dissipating and in the formal setting, Christian was aware of how crazy he sounded.

"What was that last bit, Mr Jarvik? Did you say 'black magic'?"

Christian wiped his forehead. "Look, I don't understand it. They've published this app that gives you a reading for the future. It can predict what's going to happen. It said I'd have trouble at work and that a tree would fall down and it said Rachel was in danger — under pressure. Her blood pressure is dangerously high. It's all come true. I don't know how it does it."

"Like a horoscope?" Worthing picked up his pencil and twiddled it in his fingers. "Are you a Libra, Mr Jarvik?"

Christian realised this line of thought was not going to go anywhere. All Worthing needed was an explanation, a commitment to behave, and he'd be allowed out. "No. I'm not a Libra."

"I'm a Sagittarius myself. My wife says it makes me sensitive. I don't know. What do you think?"

Christian wondered if Detective Inspector Worthing was taking the piss. He said nothing.

"I'm sure she'd love an app like that," Worthing said. "She spends all her life having her palm read or going to sensitives. Nonsense, I say." He smiled. "You're a successful lawyer, Mr Jarvik. I'm sure your business isn't run by the recollections of Nostradamus."

Christian shook his head. "I am a happily married man. My wife is expecting and is now in hospital. I want to go and see her. What do I have to say to get out of here?"

"Just the truth, Mr Jarvik. The simple truth." Worthing smiled thinly. "Are you having an affair with Lilith Hunter?"

"No!"

"Are you stalking her?"

"No! I am not a stalker."

Worthing raised his eyebrows. "I would be inclined to believe your story, if we didn't have a witness who watched you at their bedroom window for ten minutes. Some show, I imagine."

Ten minutes? It couldn't have been anything like that. Thirty seconds at most. "No, that's not true. I left as soon as I realised what was going on. I was ashamed."

"So it's your habit to go around the back of properties when the owners are not at home?"

"No. Maybe. It depends. I might. I rang the bell. I thought—"

Worthing sat back and folded his arms. "What did you think? What were you going to do? Round the back, I mean? If they hadn't been in?"

10.03 a.m.

Worthing seemed intent on detaining Christian as a personal vendetta against lawyers. After Christian's statement had been written down, checked and signed, and he had sat waiting for another hour, the custody officer gave back his phone, shoes, belt and jacket, a note about where the car had been towed to and how much it cost to get it out.

"As I understand it, you won't be driving for a while," the custody officer said.

Christian dashed from the police station. He strode up the hill to St Michael's, as fast as his hangover would allow, and found his mother-in-law sitting in the reception area, outside the antenatal ward.

"Diane." He walked straight over and hugged her.

She shied from his embrace and turned her head from his kiss. "Where have you been? You don't need to tell me. I can smell the alcohol on your breath."

Christian looked down at himself. His shirt was stained with vomit; he hadn't showered.

"I'm sorry, Diane. I'll explain later. Is Rachel okay?"

"They're going to take her to theatre and deliver the baby by caesarean."

He sat down. "Oh Jesus." The woman he loved and had been with for twelve years was about to be cut open, and he hadn't been able to get to her. He grasped his wedding ring and rotated it around his finger as he thought of her laughing eyes and sparkle. How she didn't let him get away with anything and laughed at him when he was arranging ornaments in perfect symmetry. He wiped his face with his hand and felt the scabbing vomit on his cheek.

"Is Jessica okay?"

"She's with Ray's nurse. She's fine."

"Have you spoken to the doctor?"

"They're getting her ready for surgery."

"Is she still on the ward?"

"Yes. In the same place."

He stood up. He paced the twenty metres to Rachel's room and felt as if he stayed motionless while the hospital moved around him. A white and green dreamscape, in which only he was aware of the oppressive reality, drifted past him and faded into a blur.

A nurse stood on the far side of the bed preparing a theatre trolley. Rachel's eyes opened as he approached the bed. "Christian," she said. She raised a hand.

He cupped it as he might a fragile butterfly. "Hello."

She smiled.

"I'm here now," he said. "Don't worry about anything. It's all being taken care of. You concentrate on getting well."

Her eyes beat open and closed in a slow rhythm. "Lilith said a prayer for me."

"What, darling?"

"She's heavily sedated, Mr Jarvik," the nurse said. "She might not make much sense."

Christian nodded and cupped Rachel's hand more firmly.

Rachel's lips, the colour of the grey walls, moved like a ripple. Christian put his ear close to hers. "What did you say, darling?"

"Lilith said a beautiful prayer."

"Lilith was here?" Anger rose in him. He suppressed it. He stroked her head while imagining Lilith and Zach at his wife's bed; all concerned and putting on loving faces, ingratiating themselves with his in-laws. Then he arrives reeking of alcohol and covered in vomit. They appeared respectable and worthy, while he was reduced to shit on a shoe.

"Mr Jarvik." The registrar Christian had seen the day earlier slipped through the curtains. "Can we have a quick chat?" Christian followed the doctor back past reception and into a small room. A filing cabinet stood in the corner with a box of tissues and a collection of toys on top. The floor was carpeted with plain ochre tiles and several chairs were backed against a deep-ribbed radiator under the window, like an iron skeleton beneath the light.

"Take a seat, Mr Jarvik." The doctor sat down on the edge of a chair and clasped his palms together between his knees. "I'm afraid your wife's condition has not improved. We have to deliver the baby."

"Will she be all right?"

"The operation is routine, but your wife is weak, so it's not without risks. However, if we were to do nothing, and your wife's blood pressure remained the same, we could be faced with a more serious situation. A caesarean is the best option. Once the baby is delivered, we can expect a gradual normalisation of her blood pressure." He leant forward. "I cannot say there is no risk, but the baby is thirty weeks and currently strong."

The warmth sapped out of Christian, leaving him cold and shivering. He wrapped his arms around his body and stared at a join in the carpet tiles. The dirt from a thousand pairs of shoes had been rubbed between the squares, slowly separating them and producing a checkered pattern of despair.

"How long will she be in theatre?" It wasn't the only question that entered his head. The real questions were driven by fear. Fear of loss. He wanted to know how he might cope without her, how his daughter would grow up motherless.

"The delivery takes a few minutes, and then she'll be kept under anaesthetic while we sew her up. All together she should be out within half an hour. Now, because the baby is only thirty weeks it will have to be incubated. You understand that means the baby will need to stay in hospital until it is forty weeks old."

"Yes."

"If you'd like to wait here until the operation is over, I'm sure the nurse will fetch you some tea."

"Thank you. I'll wait with Rachel's mother."

"And Mr Jarvik. There's a bathroom along the corridor near the lifts. You'll be able to get cleaned up there."

Christian took the doctor's advice and sought out the bathroom. In the tiny hand basin he pumped a dispenser to gain a smidgeon of liquid soap. He washed his arms, face and neck and looked for a towel. There was none. He used toilet paper to dry himself: tiny bits of tissue rubbed onto his stubble and stuck to the back of his hands. He picked some it off in the mirror then returned to the relatives' room.

They waited.

Diane used her tea cup as a crutch. Christian watched her lift the cup and tip it just enough to damp her lips without reducing the level of liquid. She wet her lips and stared out the window.

Then she said, "How's Jessica getting on at pre-school?"

"Very well."

She nodded. "Does she enjoy it?"

"She seems to."

"That's good." She took another pretend-sip of tea and put the cup down. "She'll be going to junior school soon."

"In September."

She nodded, her eyes watering. She sniffed.

Christian moved next to her. "She'll be fine, Diane. She's tough."

Diane smiled and patted Christian's hand. "They're taking so long?"

Christian looked at his watch. Forty minutes. "They'll be out soon. Don't worry." He wished the doctor hadn't given him an expectation.

Ten more minutes passed with neither of them able to speak without tears. Something must have happened. Christian felt fear in the depths of his bowels, a stirring not unlike sickness or a bubbling spastic gut. The feeling spread into his throat.

He went to find the nurse. She was at the reception desk tidying and moving forms from one pile to another. A whiteboard behind her head recalled admissions and departures. Rachel's name was still against her bed number.

"Any news?" he said.

"Nothing yet," the nurse said, her voice chirping in false hope. "I'm sure Doctor will be with you shortly. Would you like more tea?"

He nodded, but when he tried to say "Yes please" his throat failed to make a sound.

When the doctor entered the waiting room he sat down and looked from Christian to Diane and back. "First, congratulations. You have a beautiful baby boy." He smiled. "He's doing very well and doesn't seem to be overly concerned about coming out early."

Christian sucked in a mouthful of air and swallowed the tears. "Rachel is doing well."

Christian clasped Diane's hand hard in her lap.

"There were some complications which is why we took so long. She had a fit during the procedure, but she's calm now. We've placed her in a darkened recovery room to prevent any more seizures. She needs complete quiet with no stimulation." He smiled. A worried smile this time, like the smile you see when somebody is reminded of fun times they had with a recently departed friend or relative.

Diane put her head on Christian's shoulder and began to sob. Her presence, holding onto Christian's arm, helped suppress his own tears. "Is she in danger, Doctor?" he asked.

"I see no reason to worry unduly. We're doing absolutely everything we can and she's in the best place." That smile again. "With the baby delivered it's taken some pressure off her system, and we're following the guideline treatments."

Christian felt, at that instance, as if a hole opened up in the back of his neck and the air was sucked into his mouth and out the back without passing into his lungs. An empty, unnourished feeling that left him gasping.

With Diane crying gently on his arm, he followed Doctor Fitch to paediatrics and the incubating baby.

Diane gasped. "He's so small."

A tiny creature smaller than Christian's hand lay wrinkled in a Perspex cot upon white fabric. Plastic tubes emanated from the baby's mouth and arms and a white nappy was wrapped around his bottom. The head, oversized, with eyes clamped shut, rested on its side and his tiny thumb was in his mouth next to the tube. A white wool cap covered his head.

"Can we hold him, Doctor?" Diane was right up against the transparent covering on the cot and peering at the shrivelled child.

"No. I'm sorry. He's extremely vulnerable right now, and we have to be careful of infection. When his strength builds, you can hold him. A few weeks, probably."

The baby's hand opened and closed, enough to grasp a crease in the blanket.

Christian's thoughts raced with despair. What if Rachel didn't get to see her son? "Can we see my wife?"

"Not right now. We'll fetch you when you can spend a few minutes with her."

Christian nodded.

The doctor's bleep sounded. He turned it over on his belt and inspected the number on the display. "Excuse me," he said. "The nurse will fetch you when she's ready." That smile again. He left Christian and Diane to make their way back to the waiting room. Few words passed between them; the silence was interrupted only by the occasional cup of tea being brought in by a nurse. The china cups clattered as they were placed on the table or collected on a tray. All the nurses seemed to have practised the same smile as the doctor — concerned.

Later in the afternoon when the traffic outside was beginning to build for rush hour they could hear vehicles on the main road and the occasional whine of ambulances arriving at A&E. Christian tried to make sense of the noises by separating the cars from the lorries and, when he tired of that, cars from cars, imagining different makes and models at different speeds, all passing the hospital in the same way they passed the bank or the bus depot, unaware of the dramas playing out inside the walls.

The nurse popped her head round the door. "You can see her now."

"Is she improving?" Christian asked.

"Yes, she's stable." Pause. "But you have to be quiet. No talking. She's sedated, but she can hear you and we don't want to risk another fit. Please don't touch her. She's sensitive to stimulation."

They followed the nurse to a small dark room, lit only by a dim night-light in one corner. Christian's eyes adjusted slowly. A bed formed in the darkness, then a shape on the bed, and finally Rachel's head, attached to ribbed tubes much as the baby had been.

He approached carefully, aware of the slightest squeak his shoes made on the vinyl floor. He stared. Rachel's chest rose and fell, pushing the hospital blankets up and down, accompanied by a gentle gurgle. The weight of plastic tubes pulling on the side of her mouth distorted the beautiful lines of her cheeks. Christian longed to see her smiling.

He and Diane stood silently, unmoving, for a few minutes, until the nurse tapped them both on the shoulder and gestured they should leave.

Diane left to take care of her husband and Jessica. Christian promised a regular call. He walked back to the waiting room. Six hours later, nearing midnight, the nurse shook him gently by the shoulder. She had been reporting every hour and Christian had stayed awake by reading the crumpled magazines, but tiredness had eventually got to him.

"She's responding to the treatment, Mr Jarvik. It's been a worrying time, hasn't it."

He nodded. He felt he was still asleep, but gradually the words sank in. "She's better?"

The nurse smiled, a normal smile this time. "She's stable and her blood pressure has fallen."

Thank God.

"You might be better off sleeping at home, Mr Jarvik. Get cleaned up and have something nourishing to eat. Those vending machines aren't for a balanced diet." She smiled. "We'll call if we need you."

Back at the house Christian showered and collapsed into bed. The sheets enveloped him, stroking him with soft cleanliness and Rachel's perfume. He fell asleep nestled into her pillow.

Rachel called along the hallway to where Christian stood letting more guests flood into the house. "Melissa wants more wine and Howard is waiting for you in the lounge."

The house had filled with people, so many people over the last hour that Christian wondered how they had managed to fit in. They stood shoulder to shoulder like pilchards in a tin. Christian could barely move through them.

"In the lounge, Christian," he heard Rachel call.

He made his way slowly through the crowd. Every person he passed wanted to shake his hand or exchange a kiss. They congratulated him, hugged him, expressed their happiness for him. He felt great. In control and loved.

A chant began. "Christian! Christian! Christian!" It echoed through the house as every person joined in. He felt fantastic, as if he had won a gold medal at fencing or run a record marathon.

He made it into the lounge. It was packed with people clapping and cheering. Colleagues, university alumni, old friends, relatives. Howard was giving a speech on Christian's giant contribution to Beaufort & Soames. Partners and managers from the firm clapped at the words. Everybody he knew was in the room, it seemed. As he entered a space cleared in front of him.

"Christian! Christian! Christian!"

He stood in the middle of the space taking the applause and cheers. The crowd stopped cheering and fell silent. A magical stillness settled on them, and they all held a gentle, expectant smile. His nerves along his spine fizzed.

Then he looked down as something stroked his thighs.

Lilith was kneeling in front of him in her black evening dress. From his position he could see in the gap between the dress and her breasts.

"Lilith, what are you doing?" Christian tried to say, but his mouth closed and the words remained unsaid. He tried to move but he was locked in place as if he was tied down. Panic rose even as his groin registered arousal. He stared at the audience who began to clap again, slow, gentle claps.

Lilith looked up at him. She smiled. She stroked her shoulders and then her hands lowered to stroke her breasts. Her smile broadened.

"Lilith, stop." He tried screaming the words, but none came out. The clapping increased its tempo, getting louder and faster.

"Stop! For God's sake, stop!"

Lilith put her hands between his legs. She stroked him through his trousers.

The clapping increased.

She released his belt, unzipped him and once more looked up. She smiled mischievously and licked her lips.

"No, Lilith. No!" he attempted to say, but this time his words were quiet and suppressed. He knew he wanted her to continue.

She pulled his trousers down. They fell to the floor, revealing his erection. The crowd cheered. She leaned forward, took him in her mouth and bit down hard. Blood sprayed upwards and outward splattering her face and chest. She bit down harder, as a shark might tear chunks from a fish, and severed his penis at the base. She held it briefly in her mouth then spat it out before the shrieking, crazed audience.

Christian awoke screaming and panting. His hand went to his genitals in panic and relief spread through him when he realised he was still intact. He lay motionless recovering for some minutes, attempting to cast the dream from his memory. Lilith created these nightmares deliberately to humiliate him, to destroy him. He had to end it.

He climbed from the bed, rolled his soiled pyjamas into a ball and threw them in the wicker basket behind the door. In his dressing-gown he went downstairs to the study and took out his smartphone. The veteran spiritualist Mary Beckett had replied with a phone number and address: he had forgotten he'd contacted her. But then his eyes rested on a notification from the Algorithm's Dark Mode as it flashed slowly in the top left border of the screen. He clicked.

> *Your own morality has driven your work to failure, and your obsessions have endangered your family. But the end of your torture is close. Death is always near us, but for some it is nearer than for others.*

Christian read the words and started crying. Was there nothing he could do to stop it from tormenting him? Was this his punishment for putting money before friendship? Is that what it meant by "morality"? Did it know the shame he felt that one of the best deals he'd ever constructed for Beaufort & Soames was the sale of Rational IT while shitting on his friend?

Christian had buried the memory as deeply as he could. Not spoken about it to anyone. Not admitted it to Rachel. No one knew his connection between the deal and Zach. They could never know he had been instrumental in suggesting the sale, finding a buyer, negotiating the price and revealing the potential of Zach's work to Rational IT's leadership.

He had known the sale would result in restructuring, that most of the team would be unlikely to survive the transfer. That was business. Couldn't be helped. It was Christian's job to get the best deal available for the shareholders and leadership, including parachutes, golden hellos and severance pay where appropriate. Zach had been working at Rational IT for two years when it was sold. Those employed at the start had a few shares, but Zach was in the second wave of recruits. He was never going to get anything more than a P45 unemployment slip.

Christian hadn't told his friend what was happening. He'd churned about it, thought about it endlessly, but in the end lawyer's privilege meant he had no choice. He had to keep his mouth closed. He thought it likely Zach would not understand and though he'd dropped hints that maybe Zach should move on, he'd avoided the bluntness that would have been needed.

Zach, as always, had been in his own world. Oblivious to the goings-on around him and focused, to the exclusion of everything else, on solving the technical challenges his work presented. Zach was giving everything he had to the company: his brains, his ideas, his innovation, his time. When the news broke, he finally made the connection to Christian and Beaufort & Soames.

"Did you know about the sale?" Zach made a rare phone call instead of texting, so Christian knew before his friend spoke what the call was about. Christian was standing on a balcony at Colston Hall with glass of champagne, making small talk with the new owners and congratulating the former directors, all of whom had made a tidy fortune.

"Hang on, Zach, I'm still in the office. I'll just take you outside." He covered the phone, made his apologies to the Rational IT CEO and walked outside to the paving slabs on

Trenchard Street. "Yes, mate. What sale? What do you mean? You okay?"

"No, I'm *not* fucking okay."

"Slow down, mate. What is it?"

"Your fucking firm have just sold my job out."

Christian had known the conversation was coming and had prepared his ground. He had no intention of letting this business matter come between him and his old friend. That wasn't done. But it required a few white lies. "What do you mean? What's happened?"

"I've been let go. Effective immediately. This afternoon they've walked us all out and closed the doors. A few numbskulls are left, and most of the management. But me, I'm out."

"Shit!"

"Yeah! Didn't you know?"

"You sure it was Beauforts? We're a big firm, I don't know everything that goes on. What was the name of the buyer?"

"Epoch AI."

"Fuck! Yeah, I knew something was going on there, from the London office. But it's not my account."

Zach was furious, and not just because he had lost his job with only a month's salary in hand. "Most of that stuff is my work. How dare they just sell it like that? It's not theirs to sell."

Christian didn't say anything. At that moment the CEO of the new company walked through the rotating doors with his trophy wife on his arm, nodded his goodbyes and stepped into what must have been one of the first Teslas in Bristol. He was twenty-eight. It was the kind of car, he knew, Zach thought he would have when he sold all his ideas, or made it rich on the back of them. Zach had the technical savvy when he focused, but had not one ounce of business nous.

"I'm going to fucking kill them," Zach said.

Christian listened while Zach vented his fury. Zach *really* did want to kill them. He had dedicated two years of his life to the company on the promise of seeing his ideas get to market and, hopefully, take that market by storm. They would all have got rich. But no, those fuckers betrayed everybody to take a quick profit — still a fuck-load of money, but Zach thought they'd sold out. He doubted they knew what they had. "They've not got a fucking clue without me. It's all encrypted, obfuscated. Most of the code's not on their servers but sat in the cloud. I doubt they know what the fucking cloud is. Twats."

Christian nodded while watching guests leaving the hall and file to the road to pick up cabs parked in the lay-by. "Yeah," he said. But he knew Zach's version wasn't true because Christian had made sure they had everything Zach had worked on. It was part of the deal. Christian may not have been supremely technical, but he had carefully listened to everything Zach talked about for the last six months and relayed it to the team. The rehearsal for this deal had counted on securing all the IP across the company and making certain it couldn't walk out on the day of the takeover. And it hadn't. The staff had not been allowed to log on; all the company smartphones had been wiped remotely. Christian didn't like that he had used his friend like this — but it was, and it remained, business.

Zach could never find out. So how could this app torment him with secret knowledge?

18

By 8.30 a.m. Christian was in Rachel's car and racing along the M5 to Weston-super-Mare. He drove at ninety miles an hour and swept by in the overtaking lane for the thirty-minute journey. He thanked God he wasn't caught in commuter traffic heading north. Dawn had started bright but thick clouds were gathering to the west and when he pulled off the motorway the windscreen spotted with rain and the wipers squealed across the semi-dry glass.

Before setting out, he had called the hospital. Rachel was stable and her blood pressure had continued to fall during the night. He would go and see her as soon as the hospital opened for visitors.

Mary Beckett lived in an unremarkable Fifties terrace house and as he cruised the street staring at the house numbers the rain began to tip from the skies. He parked outside and ran for the gate, holding the collar of his green-wax jacket high up his neck and leaping over a foot-wide puddle of standing water at the kerb. The door opened as he stepped onto the garden path, and a suspicious woman of about eighty held the door in front of her short body and peered through the gap. Her white hair stood several inches off her cracked forehead as a row of snowy hills might stand above a tundra. The door-chain hung tight, under her throat.

"Yes, dear?" she said, as he approached the step.

"I'm Christian Jarvik. I called earlier. You sent me an email."

She stared and the chain swayed like a thick gold necklace.

"Please, Mrs Beckett. I saw you on YouTube. It was Pikey Pete's channel or something like that. I need to talk." He could feel the rain soaking into the back of his trousers.

The door closed, he heard the chain detach and then she appeared again. "Yes, of course," she said warmly. "Come in and close the door." Her normal voice surprised him — he had expected a sound like gravel in a mixer. They must have made it deeper for the video.

The odour of an open fire beckoned them through the house, and he followed Mrs Beckett across a worn, bare wooden floor to the lounge. The fire burnt in a narrow grate, one or two chunks of wood holding the flame and a trail of smoke snaking up the flue. She sat on a blanket-covered sofa wrapped in a crocheted throw of primary-coloured squares.

"It's cold for June," she said. "Sit down, Mr Jarvik." She nodded to a seat on the other side of an onyx-topped table with gold metal trim. Her arms rested on her lap, still, as if part of the sofa, and when she spoke she moved her head gently in rhythm with the words, the movement continuing for a moment after the words ceased, as if she was still speaking from within. Christian found it disconcerting.

"This may sound crazy, but I think I've been cursed," he said. "Everything is going wrong. My career, my finances, and now my wife is in hospital. It all started with the app you spoke about on the video."

Her head began swaying without her saying anything. She rubbed her thighs through the crocheted blanket.

"A number of weeks ago," Christian said, "I had my future predicted. On the app." He put his phone on the table. "We had our palm read and then I got it to give me predictions. I thought it was a joke."

Mrs Beckett stroked her legs in a consistent rhythm.

"Then things started to come true. A tree fell down, my work starting going wrong, I lost a fencing tournament, and now my wife's in hospital. I'm worried. It's predicted that she'll die."

"Turn the phone to me."

Christian took the phone from the table and offered it to her.

"No," she said abruptly. "Just turn it towards me. I won't touch it."

He did as she asked.

"Since the first prediction, everything has gone wrong?"

He sat back in the chair. "Yes."

Her eyes darted towards the phone, "All that's happened was predicted? And everything has gone right for your friend and his wife?"

"Yes!" He knew he'd been right. Mrs Beckett understood.

She leant back in the sofa; her eyes unblinking.

"I can't believe I'm here," he said. "I feel like I'm losing my marbles. Please tell me I'm not crazy. I want to stop it. It's not just the app, it's the dreams and the feeling I'm being pursued."

She stared into his eyes and appeared to sniff him. She moved her hand off her leg, held it above the phone and closed her eyes.

"There's something hidden, too," she said. Her hand hovered over the phone, moving in small, rapid circles. "It's found a place to create trouble. It's enjoying it." She pulled her hand back and opened her eyes. "It's not the app, dear," she said, as if it was as obvious as daylight. "The app's just a computer program, after all. But there's something else, something sensitive and intuitive in you. Something less than benign. I think it's giving you instructions to follow. These are powerful suggestions speaking right to your soul, Mr Jarvik."

"Not predictions?"

"It seems your own actions have caused them to come true, don't you think? I'm surprised it has been so powerful. It would need a very personal connection to bind you."

"Close friends?"

"Maybe something from the physical world that ties you to the spiritual planes. It could be a photograph or an effigy. It all seems a bit old-fashioned these days, don't you think?"

She smiled but Christian's mind raced: "Could it be some hair?"

"That could be it."

Christian stood up, alarmed. "We each had a lock of hair taken when we were first introduced to the app. How do I stop it? How is it making my wife ill?"

"Relax, if you can. It can't make you or your wife ill without belief. It's got you believing. It will take a strong challenge of your will to remove it, but the most powerful weapon it has is *your* mind. If you believe it is harmless, then it *will* be harmless.

The power over you is only what you believe. It will help if you can find how it is connected to you. Do you have the lock of hair?" She looked toward the fire. "The predictions on this phone are only words. It needs faith to make them real."

"Faith?"

"Release your mind from the prison of conviction. Stop believing and it will pass."

Christian's phone vibrated on the table. The hospital. "Excuse me." He picked it up and listened. Rachel was not improving. He had to go back to the hospital.

"I have to go." He started toward the door.

"My gift, Mr Jarvik."

"Yes, of course." He stood in the door and rifled through his wallet picking out a selection of twenty-pound notes. "We said eighty pounds didn't we?"

"That's right, dear."

He put the money on the sideboard. "One more thing, Mrs Beckett. The video you made with Pikey Pete. Was that real or were you paid?"

"I've not seen it, dear. But I don't make money from videos."

Christian ran through the pelting rain to the car.

19

The nurse had said, "She's deteriorating. You'd better come as soon as you can."

It was medical code. Christion knew Rachel was in grave danger. Yet he held onto a strength of resolve that he would be there for her, hold her and bring her through. Each time the fear rose, he pressed on the accelerator. He gripped the wheel and fought every bump and sideways gust of wind. The car swept through the weather, wiping a path in the pooling rain and leaving two water-depleted tracks on the tarmac.

He took the A4 into the city and at the hospital he parked on yellow cross-hatching and ran into the building. He raced past trolleys and patients in dressing-gowns and made for the stairs. He passed the empty reception desk and found Diane sitting alone in one of the family cubicles. She looked up and whispered, "Christian." She looked like a charcoal portrait: the lines on her face had deepened overnight and her cheeks had lost their colour. She burst into tears.

He sat down and pulled her toward him. He didn't know what to say. He wanted to comfort her, but he wanted to be comforted himself. He wanted her to make it go away, and she wanted the same of him.

A nurse moved behind a frosted glass window on the far side of reception.

"Do they know you're here?" Diane asked.

Christian walked to the desk and knocked. The nurse put her head around the door, disappeared and then reappeared with a jug. "How is she?" he said. "Rachel Jarvik."

The nurse smiled as if to say, "I'll be right with you," and began to water a vase of flowers beneath the whiteboard. The world stopped for a bunch of daffodils.

"What's your name?" she said when the water jug was empty and the vase full. She put the jug down next to a keyboard.

"Christian Jarvik. My wife is here. Rachel Jarvik."

She tapped the name into the computer. "Perhaps you'd like to go into the relatives' room."

"How is my wife?"

She smiled. "The doctor will be along shortly. Please, the relatives' room."

He stared at her. "Tell me."

"Cup of tea?"

Incredible. "I don't want a fucking cup of tea. How is my wife?"

The nurse's smile disappeared. "We don't tolerate abuse, Mr Jarvik. Your wife is critical. She's been transferred to intensive care. The doctor will be along as soon as he can."

"Mr Jarvik?" Christian turned to see a young doctor clad in green with a stethoscope hung around his neck like a loose tie. Christian led the way to the relatives' room and took the chair next to Diane.

"I'm sorry. Rachel is very ill," the doctor said. "Earlier this morning her blood pressure climbed suddenly, and she had some convulsions. Her kidneys are failing and she's very weak. She's been moved to intensive care."

"Where's Doctor Fitch?" Diane asked. "He was looking after Rachel."

"Yes." The doctor looked into a corner of the room. "He's with another patient right now. Would you like to see her?" He looked up. *That smile again.*

They followed the doctor through the hospital. Christian imagined his beautiful wife being wheeled along the stark corridors by a green-team of doctors and nurses while she bucked and fitted on the chrome trolley.

In contrast to the dark room of the previous evening she was in a glowing white ward crammed with machinery and chrome drip stands; a windowless bunker in the heart of the hospital with an odour of hot sweat, honey and disinfectant.

Rachel was unrecognisable beneath the tubes and patches. Her swept-back hair was slick with perspiration. She breathed once for every five breaths that Christian took. As her lungs filled, the pipe in her mouth rocked at the corner of her lips. A patch of raw skin had developed beneath the plastic tube.

"Is she aware of us?" Diane asked.

The doctor shook his head.

Christian reached forward, touched Rachel's cheek and drew his fingers across her face. Her eyes remained shut, her body unmoving. Just the occasional lurch of her lungs and the rapid bleep of a monitor signalled she was alive. He stroked her face, noticing the etched lines around her eyes and her ghost-like complexion that merged with the bed linen. He moved a strand of hair that stuck stubbornly to her forehead and smoothed it back. "Rachel," he whispered.

A sudden and rapid bleeping startled him and he leapt backwards. The doctor pushed him aside and jammed his fingers into Rachel's neck to find her pulse. He smacked a red button at the side of the bed.

"What's happening?"

The doctor pushed him back. "Stand clear."

Diane grabbed Christian's arm. "What's going on?" She shook with panic. "Rachel!" she called.

Christian froze. He could only watch as the doctor checked the heart monitor.

Two nurses rushed in. "Cardiac arrest!" the doctor shouted.

A nurse stood between them and Rachel, guarding the scene with outstretched arms. "Please, sir, follow me. We need the room to work."

"What's happening?"

"Please, sir." She put an arm around them both and marched them out of the ward. They turned the corner and a team of doctors raced past pushing a machine-laden trolley.

They were ushered into a small room with metal-tube furniture, a ragged and stained carpet, a pile of magazines and a single-pane window splashed with rain. On the windowsill stood a simple arrangement of flowers in a tiny glass vase and a few children's toys. On a low table, a leather-bound Bible bisected a coffee-stain in the shape of a ring from a long-gone mug.

Diane's eyes were red and puffed like cotton-wool balls. Tears streamed down her face. He held her. He had no words. He couldn't comprehend a world without Rachel. He wept.

Rachel died at 10.26 a.m.

Christian collapsed at the news.

Diane cradled her head in her hands and cried.

They had done everything they could, the doctor said. Rachel's system had shut down. First her kidneys, then her lungs. Her heart failed. He said he was sorry.

Sorry. The doctor was sorry! Christian stared out of the window.

Rain hit the glass and flowed onto the sill. It dripped and tumbled onto the pavement outside. Water from a thousand sills collected on the footpath. It slid in sheets to the gutter at the side of the road and then rushed down St Michael's hill and disappeared into an iron grate.

"I want to see her," he said. The doctor nodded.

She lay as before but now with no tubes or wires attached. No breath escaped her lips and no blood raced through her veins. One side of her mouth was red where the tube had been. Her grey face sported a soft sheen dully reflecting the strip lights. Christian touched her cheek again and felt a slight resistance but no warmth; no life.

"They can't get away with this," he said softly. Each word measured and exact.

Diane put her arm around him. "The hospital did everything they could."

He snapped his head around to look at her. "Not the fucking hospital!"

She stared at him, shocked at the violence in his voice, as if it was a double betrayal.

He looked once more at Rachel's body. He turned and strode out.

"Christian!" Diane called after him.

He ignored her.

20

Christian left the hospital and ignored his clamped car at the entrance. He tossed the keys in the gutter and walked up St Michael's hill and into Redland. Maybe he intended to go home, maybe not, but his route took him across the sodden downs and past his house. He didn't go in. He continued to the Sea Walls at the edge of the gorge and peered across Leigh Woods and beyond to the grey Bristol Channel while the westerly wind punished his face and drove water into his eyes. There he turned and, with the wind barking at his heels and parting the hair on his head, walked to Pembroke Road. The rain smashed into the back of his jacket, but he hardly felt it. He paced the streets looking neither left nor right but walking in a straight line until he could go no farther. Only then did he turn to continue his relentless pacing.

Eventually he found himself sitting on a wall on St John's Road drinking from a bottle of vodka. He didn't remember buying the vodka, but it warmed him and numbed his thinking to one simple repeating idea burned into his alcohol-soaked brain: one person could explain everything that had happened. The predictions, the contract and Rachel's death were all tied together by Lilith. She and Zach were probably laughing now. She had questions to answer. *Zach* had questions to answer. Their house must hold the proof.

Holding the bottle by its open neck he walked to Zach's flat. The gravel path crunched under his feet, as if he was biting into caramel peanuts, and he swigged from the bottle before pushing and holding the doorbell.

"Open the fucking door!" he shouted through the letter box. He took another drink.

He pushed out a tune on the doorbell, a rhythmic taunt, and then used his body weight on his arm to keep the bell ringing.

"They're not in."

A woman in a black polar-neck peered down at him from the top of the steps to the next-door property. Her arms were folded, her head held to one side beneath a small umbrella.

"Where are they?"

"Who are you?"

"I'm a friend." He took a few steps toward the boundary and blinked as the rain hit his face when he looked up.

She stepped back a couple of paces and shook her head. "I don't know where they are." She turned, trotted to the building's main entrance and stared at him while searching her pockets for a key. He took a drink to her health. The door slammed behind her.

Christian walked to their garage door with the intention of waiting in the dry and then confronting them when they returned. The door opened and scraped across the paving slab on reluctant hinges. Inside was full of boxes from the move, a lawnmower hung from the rafters, and on a wooden bench lay a chainsaw beside a rusty oilcan. Christian stared. He remembered Zach had a chainsaw when he moved in. Hadn't they had a conversation about it? Why would he need it? Yet another piece fell into place in Christian's mind. Zach had cut the tree in half when he knew the storm was coming, and fed the information into his app so it predicted the tree falling. What else might Zach have done to make the other predictions come true? Christian felt as if he was being watched, as if an unseen presence was now inspecting him from behind. He thought how Dave Hinchley had been at the house the night he'd come over drunk. Was Zach's involvement with Dave the reason Burnham got into so much trouble? Nothing to do with the fucking app? The thought sickened him.

He turned suddenly to inspect the empty garage. He stared into the dark corners, imagining Lilith standing in the shadows directing him. "Fuck off!" he shouted. "Get out of my fucking head!" His heart pulsed in his chest, sending pressure beats up the arteries in his neck. Sweat poured from his armpits and forehead.

Following the route from the railway embankment to the back garden, he stole through the trees, hopped over the fence and walked across the garden to the rear of Zach's flat, slipping on the grass and mud where feet had worn a narrow path to the rotary washing line. He butted his head up against the French windows and peered into the bedroom. Nobody was home this time. He smashed a square pane of glass out with the end of the vodka bottle, put his hand inside and turned the key. He pulled the door but it was still bolted at the top and bottom. He smashed the top and bottom panes nearest to the bolts and slid the brass mechanisms back. The door opened and he stepped inside.

Little light crept in from the grey day outside and the maroon bedroom soaked up light like the inside of a black box. Crumpled sheets lay discarded on the end of the bed. Clothing lay on the floor; cast off haphazardly. Christian stooped to pick up a shirt that lay at his feet. He smelt it, and the image of Lilith flashed into his head. Her perfume. He closed his eyes and breathed in her scent.

He pulled the doors shut behind him and took a few steps into the room, broken glass crunching under his feet. He made his way into the lounge, flicking on the light switches as he went. He took another swig of vodka, savouring the bitter taste as it slid down his throat and burnt the back of his mouth.

The bookshelf was in the alcove next to the chimney breast. Two shelves had been cleared to display small ornaments and bric-a-brac. Metal figures, a bowl of crystals, small sculptures of heavily pregnant women, a brass incense burner and a small wooden box inlaid with mother-of-pearl. He pushed the ornaments on the floor and scanned the titles.

He read the titles aloud then threw them across the room one by one. He trod on them, putting all his weight on the spines to break their backs. He yanked down another shelf of books and did the same thing. He scattered books across the lounge and laughed as they rotated toward the window like miniature helicopters. Then behind a number of tall wine glasses that had the look of ritual about them — thick crystal with a dark-blue rim in the style of a goblet — he found the books he knew had to be there. A simple wooden bookend held them upright against the side of the bookcase; several titles on the same subject. Christian pulled the books out in one go and stacked them on the coffee table.

He picked up the first title in the pile, *In Search of the Real Wicca*, and discarded it. A collection of photographs of saggy old women in a front room in suburbia. He took another drink and opened up a volume of *The Devil and All His Works*. He browsed the images of Satan, Behemoth and the Green Man, all apparently versions of the same incarnation of man's evil towards man.

A piece of card sticking out from the side of one of the volumes caught his eye. He turned to the page, titled "Connecting with the spirit world to guide your future", and found a small square envelope. His gut told him what was in the envelope before he looked. *My fucking hair.* He tucked it in his pocket and opened a book of herbs, also with a piece of card sticking from the top. He read the page:

> *Examples of herbal supplements that can affect blood pressure or blood pressure medications: Arnica (Arnica montana), Bitter orange (Citrus aurantium), Ephedra (ma-huang), Ginseng (Panax quinquefolius and Panax ginseng), Guarana (Paullinia cupana), Liquorice (Glycyrrhiza glabra), St. John's wort (Hypericum perforatum)*

He walked to the kitchen and rummaged through the cupboards until he found a brown paper bag of herbs similar to the tea Rachel had been using. On the side of the bag was written "Fusion of St John's Wort, Ginseng and Liquorice".

He picked up the vodka bottle, tipped it into his upturned mouth. The biting liquid poured down his throat after running down his chin and shirt. He threw the bottle across the room. He swept the plates and cups from the bench, tipped the kitchen table on its end, kicked the underneath of it to smash through the wooden slats. He screamed.

He rampaged through the house smashing and kicking. He

tipped up the furniture and ripped open the fabric with broken glass. White padding oozed from the rips. He yanked it out and spread it round the room in a snowstorm of rage.

For a few minutes Christian lost himself in fury. He heard nothing of the sound of smashing or the breaking glass. The ornaments and furniture weighed nothing, and he lifted them with ease. Using his body as a demolition ball he threw himself into the cupboards and shelves, flailing his arms and legs, sending everything in his path upwards and outwards in a mêlée of destruction. It was a trance, almost a dance without music, without rhythm and without a tune.

He stopped suddenly in front of a photograph of himself and Rachel. Their wedding day. He picked it from the wall and had to support himself with one hand. *Rachel! What have they done to Rachel?* He stared at the photograph and traced his finger around the line of her face to the spot where the intubation tube had rubbed her skin. Holding the photo to his heart, he collapsed. He wept.

Minutes passed as Christian remained in silent paralysis clutching Rachel's photo. But then the distant wail of police sirens alerted him. The volume rapidly built. Blue and red flashing lights filtered through the blue glass stars of the front door.

He ran out through the bedroom, slipped across the garden and leapt the fence at the edge of the railway embankment. Grabbing handfuls of foliage and digging his heels into the soft mud, he slid down the bank and landed on his feet at the edge of the railway tracks. He staggered along the line and up onto the deserted platform at Clifton station. And then he ran. He zipped up his green jacket against the water and turned up the collar. He ran from Clifton, up and over Redland and down Zetland Road. Rain tipped his wax jacket and dripped onto his trousers and shoes until they squelched with each footfall and hung sodden around his legs. He ran down Gloucester Road towards St Paul's. Rain smacked into his face, ran down his neck.

Low black cloud forced drivers to turn on their headlights, and the combination of spray and bright lights blurred Christian's vision. But he kept running. Water flooded the gutters and formed streams along the side of the roads. He headed toward the city centre. He passed stores of second-hand goods from furniture to stamps, clothing to cars. He ran between cars to cross roads and dodged pedestrians. He ran to a rhythm playing in his head driven by his pounding feet.

He stopped running at the top of Christmas Steps. He sat in the stone alms-chairs and tucked into the shadows. Water dripped down the ancient stairs pooling in the foot-worn hollows of the limestone as a dribble of pedestrians picked along the narrow pathway on their way home or to a place out of the rain. They ignored him as he knew they would.

Traffic passed above on Park Row with an extended sloshing. Orange street lamps illuminated the rain on its way to the tarmac. Christian waited until it was quiet.

The store opposite was Jessica's favourite. A trashy joke shop she loved. He could see her face pressed up against the glass display counter. "Look, Daddy, it's a dog poo. Yuck!" But while she loved the joke shop, he always managed to spend a few minutes in the junk shop next door.

He walked over the pelican crossing and past the joke shop. Continuing up the slope, he turned right to find a loaded skip taking up a parking space. He picked up a brick from the rubble. His hands gripped the rough surface and the edges cut into his fingers as though biting him with reality. He weighed it in his hand. He walked back around the corner to the junk shop and threw the brick as hard as he could at the window.

The glass shattered and sprayed him with tiny shards. Instantly a blue alarm flashed followed by a piercing siren. Christian ducked his head through the smashed window and grabbed the military sabre displayed at the edge of the bay. He yanked it from the hooks, pulled it out of the window, tucked it under his coat and paced up the hill to Park Row.

21

Christian stood behind the soaking trunk of a plane tree and watched the police officer standing ten yards from Zach's house on the bridge over the railway cutting. The officer's head moved from side to side as he surveyed first north and then south toward Christian's position. Christian waited until the officer looked up the hill, then jogged to the next road junction, rolling his feet — heel-toe, heel-toe — to keep silent, and ducked behind trees to remain out of sight. He took the left turn and settled to a casual walking pace. The railway that ran behind Zach's building continued along the back of the row. It seemed unlikely any officers would be watching along the embankment. And if they were? Christian grasped the sword hilt. One unarmed policeman would have a shock up against a sabre.

The cutting disappeared into the Clifton Downs tunnel beneath Duchess Road. Christian jumped onto a low wall and scaled a wire fence. He dropped into overgrown shrubs and sodden weeds. Brambles tore into his trousers and tangled in his hair. Disturbed vegetation released rivulets of water. He slid down the steep slope on his back, grasping grass and roots to slow the slide, then dropped the last ten feet onto the hard-core bedding at the entrance to the tunnel. His feet slapped noisily onto the stones. He leant into the greenery. The officer didn't stir.

The embankment was steep, unlit, and ran well below the properties like a dark river valley. He crept along the edge of the vegetation, keeping a careful eye on the police officer. Beneath Zach's building he attempted to scale the embankment. The rain-soaked leaves and bushes afforded little purchase. Lying with his stomach flat against the slope, he grasped handfuls of roots and pulled himself up while scrabbling with his feet to gain footholds in the soft earth. Leaves slid between his fingers or pulled roots from the soil leaving him back where he started.

Each time he progressed a few feet up the bank his hands lost their purchase and he slid back to the tracks. Attempting to find an easier climb, he stalked toward the officer until he was below a stand of trees bound in place by large twisted roots.

Grabbing handfuls of nettle stems, he hauled himself a few feet by his arms and slid upwards on his belly. The sword hilt dug into his stomach, the blade rubbing on his flesh. Reaching softer earth he dug his toes into dirt and climbed seven or so feet above the railway line, his weight supported by bramble root in his right hand and a precarious knot of wood under his right foot. He breathed heavily to recover from the exertion and with each breath the knot moved gently beneath him.

Tree roots rising from the dirt a few feet away to his left offered a firm handhold and a route to the top. He prepared to leap just as a train's rhythmic drumming burst from the tunnel. He gripped the brambles, forcing thorns deep into his flesh, and pressed his cheek into the bank. He flattened himself against the dirt. He held his breath as the train rumbled through the cutting and the ground shook beneath him. His fingers strained, and just the tenacity of a few weak muscles, like taut rubber bands, held him to the muddy slope.

And then the train was gone. The officers turned from the railway and faced along the road. In one swift movement Christian twisted and leapt across the mud patch, launching himself from the stump of wood under his right foot. He slid across the dirt reaching for the tree roots and grabbed with both hands. His body slammed into the bank, forcing the sword hilt into his ribs and punching the air from his lungs.

His grip held. Slowly breath returned. Grasping roots, saplings and low branches he clambered to the top of the embankment. Leaning into a red-stone wall he traversed along the top of the cutting to Zach's back garden and the decrepit wooden fence that served as a boundary. He hopped over the fence and walked silently to the building.

He stood in shadow beside the French windows at the back of

Zach's flat and listened. No sound came from inside. The broken panels had been covered with corrugated cardboard stuck in place with wide silver tape. He tried the handle. The mechanism clicked and the door offered no resistance, swinging outwards. The heavy bedroom curtains billowed and swayed in the light breeze, creating a triangle of bedroom light on the patio. Christian stood in the entrance. His nostrils dilated to pull in the air. Lilith's perfume lingered. No longer seductive, now an odour that spilt into the night like tobacco from a public bar. He slipped his coat from his shoulders and let it drop to the floor. He stood in a sodden white shirt open at the neck and untucked. His shirt sleeves hung open at the cuffs and his forearms, scratched and muddy from the climb, shone naked in the bedroom light. In his right hand he gripped the sabre, the point forward, raised and teasing the curtains as they plumed towards him.

"Come in," Zach said from inside.

Christian threw back the curtain and stepped into the bedroom. Zach stood at the internal door to the room, sabre in hand and chin high, wearing a black loose-fitting shirt.

"You knew I was coming?" Christian said, nodding toward the sword.

"I heard you in the garden. Diane said you've been missing. You need help, mate. Put the weapon down and come and have a chat. Your kids need you."

Christian shook his head. "Lamentable. Are you really pulling the nice-friend card out?"

"You're in shock, mate. You've got to get a grip."

"In shock?" Christian sliced the air in front of him. "You arrogant tosser. In shock? You fucking think so? Yes, I'm in shock."

Zach tensed and raised the sword to an on-guard position. "Whatever you think I've done, we need to talk about it. You've got it wrong."

"I want to talk to Lilith. I don't think you understand how she's manipulated you. How she's got to me through the app and how she's killed Rachel. And if it wasn't manipulation, *you* are complicit in Rachel's murder."

"That's crazy talk. Come off it, mate. She loved Rachel."

"Don't give me that fucking shit. She fed her the drugs. In her tea. She cut down the tree, or you did. And — I don't know how — she's in my *fucking* dreams, Zach. In my *fucking* head. And that Algorithm knows what I'm doing. How do you do that? I want to talk to her."

"You can't, Christian. You need to calm down first. Put the sword down."

"I want you to hear her confess. Then you'll believe me. Otherwise I have to conclude you're as guilty. Are you?" Christian lunged at Zach with the sabre point and Zach parried the tip by sweeping Christian's blade to his right. The swords clashed and Christian's struck the architrave around the door. A great chunk of wood catapulted into the room.

"I'm not guilty of anything. Try and listen to what you're saying. It's not rational. You've got it wrong. Lilith tried to help. You know you've been here before. The paranoia. When we were students."

"How fucking dare you? That was different. That was all about my results. And my dad. Why have you got a chainsaw, eh?"

"What? It's a fucking chainsaw. Everybody's got one these days."

"I don't have one. But *somebody* cut through the tree. Who do you think that was? She's played me like a puppet and taken everything away. I have nothing left." He lunged again, holding the sword high to cut into Zach's head. The blades clashed again and Zach swivelled around, knocking Christian onto the bed. Christian held his point high expecting a counter-attack but none came.

Zach kept his sabre low. He stood by the curtains and looked down. "You've your children to think of. They need you. Jessica and the new baby."

"Tell me you didn't know. Tell me!"

"Know what?"

"Your fucking Algorithm. It's targeted me, hasn't it? Tell me that was her. Not you."

"It can't target anyone."

"How did it know?" He swiped his sabre across in front of Zach. "How?"

Zach backed into the door frame. "It doesn't know anything. It just guesses. I've told you. It's a *game*."

"Then you're just as bad. You've taken away their mother. Those herbs Lilith's been feeding her. They all affect blood pressure. It's in that fucking book." He sliced at the air and tried to get up to his feet. Zach parried and knocked him back onto the bed with the power in his blow.

"That's ridiculous. They're to help you relax."

Christian backed against the headboard, pushed himself to his feet. "Witchcraft. Magic. That fucking witch of yours. She engineered the whole thing, stealing everything I had and gave it to you."

"You're just finding evidence for what you've already decided. You're in an echo chamber. It's not true."

Christian launched himself across the bed but Zach slipped past him and out into the black garden. Christian raced after him. His eyes took a moment to adjust. Zach's blade flashed in the dull light from the upstairs windows, then the garden suddenly flooded with light from the powerful lamp above the door. Christian ran at him.

They exchanged blows, the sabres rattling off each other, Christian desperate to break his adversary's block. He rained blows onto Zach's guard, smashing his blade down with all his strength but was unable to get through. Then he saw an opening. He feinted to Zach's right shoulder, avoided the parry, then cut across his abdomen. The tip of the blade slid across Zach's skin. He screamed with pain. "Fucking hell! Fucking stop it! You'll kill me. Look what you've done." Zach put his hand to his stomach and looked at the blood transferred to his palm.

For the first time, Christian saw fear in Zach's eyes. "I want to talk to her," he said calmly. "Admit what you've done. I don't care if I win or lose this fucking fight. I've nothing left to lose. Why are you in Bristol, Zach? Why? Are you after everything that I have?" He lunged. Zach parried. He attacked again with a high cut to Zach's shoulder.

Zach retreated. He jumped over the wooden fence onto the top of the embankment and stood using a tree as a shield with his sabre sticking out in front. "No, Christian. This is mad."

"You wanted what I had. You know I sold you out and you wanted revenge."

"Bollocks. What are you talking about?"

Christian clambered over the fence and circled the tree. He wanted a good slice, a hard attack to Zach's head. "And how many others does she show it to? The tart. Flirting like that to get me hooked. Make me interested enough to believe in it."

"She's not flirting with you." Zach was incredulous. "Why would you say that?"

Christian thrust toward his opponent. His blade passed next to the tree and nicked Zach's sleeve. Zach leapt from the other side of the trunk and thrust back at Christian. The sword missed but Christian pushed out with his shoulder and body-checked Zach onto the ground. As he fell, Zach let go of his sword. It flew into the air and span down the embankment, flashing with reflected house lights as it rotated.

"You were my best friend," Christian said. He moved forward and directed the point of his sabre at Zach's throat.

Zach scrambled backwards away from the blade. "I *am* your friend, Christian. You've got it wrong."

"Fuck off." He lifted the sword above his head ready to strike.

"I'm here to sell my company. That's all."

"What?"

"I'm selling my tech. That's why I'm here. To Dave Hinchley. Didn't you realise? I tried to keep it under wraps because of where you work. Your firm handled it. It nearly went belly-up when you fired William Thornton. But he was just doing his job.

Zach's revelation resounded in Christian's head like a gunshot. Sickness rose in him. From the depth of his stomach to his throat, a great burning lump grew and squatted. Now he fully understood. This *was* revenge. Revenge for selling Zach out all those years ago. He'd been a target of the app, of Zach, of Lilith's occult power. Now he had no doubt.

"What the fuck? You cut me out. That was my deal." He raised his sword high, ready to kill his oldest friend.

"CJ. None of it's like that. Dave wanted the best tech. He didn't get everything they promised when he bought Rational IT. Of course he didn't. Rational never understood my work. You knew that."

"Really. Then what about this? Why does Lilith need my

fucking hair?" Christian held the sabre high while in his right hand while he pulled out the envelope with his left. "It fucking *is* witchcraft." He opened the envelope and turned it upside down.

A waft of tiny seeds fell out. Christian watched stunned as they dissipated in the darkness.

"Christian Jarvik! Armed police! Throw down your weapon." The police officer stood legs apart in Zach's back garden aiming a pistol straight at Christian. Behind him stood Lilith, terror on her face. The bright floodlight above the French doors lit through her dress revealing her legs.

Christian suddenly realised where he was. What he was doing. His rage had led him here. He stared at the officer and at the gun pointing at his chest then suddenly, as if nothing now mattered in the world, with Rachel gone and his life in tatters, he stepped backwards over the edge of the embankment and into the fresh air.

A flash lit the trees, flared off his sword, and a gunshot ripped into the night. Christian plunged into blindness. Shrubs and weeds blurred past as he grasped at the sodden vegetation and skidded head-first thirty feet down the almost vertical embankment on his back.

He smacked into the ground with a choking pain in his spine and ribs. He stared upwards. Trees formed a black canopy of encroaching darkness, and blood leached into his mouth. He took a desperate gasp for air. It spluttered between his teeth like dregs through a straw. A wet quivering blade stuck out from his chest. His own sword had impaled him.

Rustling vegetation and urgent voices drifted to him from above.

The dark progressed. It crept from the shadows and, one by one, swallowed the pinpoints of light in the sky. Windows darkened in the houses; street lights dimmed. Voices faded into silence.

Epilogue

"Do we have to let the children go back? Can't we keep them?" Lilith tipped boiling water into two clay mugs and stirred vigorously. She looked over to Zach who had just come off the telephone to Diane.

"Not yet. Diane will be right over. They *are* the grandparents."

"But they're trying to stop us seeing them."

Zach shrugged. "They think it's for the best. It will play out. Don't worry. They're worried too."

"They'll try and get Jessica to say bad things about us so they can put it in their submissions to the court."

Zach shook his head. "Jessica won't say anything bad. She loves us. And I don't think Diane is like that."

Lilith smiled, carried the mugs over to Zach and sat down. "You think they might want to keep them, though, don't you. I can see it in your eyes."

"Maybe." He took a sip. "But Ray's too ill for them to bring up the children. They'll see that soon enough. And Diane has her hands full looking after him. I think they're doing this out of grief. Once they realise we can give the children a loving home, they'll come round. I'm sure of it."

"But if they don't?"

Zach shrugged.

Lilith frowned. "Perhaps we could try another tack."

Jessica burst into the kitchen and skipped across the terracotta flooring to the edge of the table. "Can I have a drink?"

"What would you like, darling?" Lilith said.

"Juice and honey."

"Juice *and* honey. What, together?"

"No, silly. Juice in a cup and honey in a sandwich."

"You've only just had your lunch. You'll turn into a Teletubby if you're not careful." She leant down and tickled Jessica under the ribs, eliciting a squeal of delight. "I will fix you a honey sandwich if you go and fetch me your photograph album."

"The one with Mummy and Daddy in?"

"That's the one."

Jessica raced from the room and thumped up the stairs to her bedroom. Lilith prepared the snack and Zach finished his drink before she came running back in carrying an oversize photograph album. "It was under the bed," she said.

"Let me have a look," Lilith said, putting the album on the table and lifting Jessica onto a stool in front of the sandwich. She turned the pages, commenting on each picture while the little girl munched on the food swinging her legs.

"Do you know what?" Lilith said. "We don't have a nice picture of your grandma or granddad. I think you need one to go with this picture of Mummy and Daddy." She pointed to a close-up of Christian and Rachel with their heads together. Sellotaped over the photo were two small envelopes labelled in a child's handwriting, *Daddy's hair* and *Mummy's hair*. "And if you ask nicely, I'm sure grandma will give you a clipping of her hair to go with these."

A car horn sounded from outside the house. "There she is now," Lilith said. "Off you go."

Jessica crammed the last bite into her mouth and dropped from the stool.

"Don't forget the album, to show grandma what you want," Lilith said.

THE END

Join my newsletter

Go to this link to sign up for my occasional, no spam, newsletter so I can tell you what's happening and send you occasional updates. And while you're at the website, take a look at my other titles.

https://www.williamknight.info

Consider a review

If you enjoyed *The Algorithm* please consider leaving a review.

Reviews help readers find books they might otherwise miss and they give me feedback so I keep writing! I love to read what people say about my work.

You can leave a review on amazon, or on Goodreads, or at the retailer you got this copy.

Warm regards and thank you

William Knight

XYZ: Updating Jack Cooper

by William Knight

"If you are into satire, cynicism and dry humor, then this one is for you." readinggirlreviews.com

Generation X technical whizz Jack Cooper would rather seal his eyes with sticky notes than work in an office full of Gen Y and Z hipsters harping on about dancing-baby gifs.

So when he gets a job with a uber-cool tech start-up, can he break free of his angry 1980s nostalgia and halt his slide into drunken, divorced loneliness? How will he remain sane while bombarded by Instant Messages, smiley-faced poos, and the constant celebration of mediocrity?

The Donated

by William Knight

"Powerfully written and thought-provoking. Highly recommended." The Wishing Shelf Book Awards

When combat veteran turned journalist Hendrix Harrison links bodies stolen from a forensic research enclosure to a powerful pharmaceutical company, he suspects fraudulent manipulation of clinical trials.

With Doctor Sarah Wallace, a determined forensic entomologist, he delves into a world of grisly drug tests, misguided scientists and desperate patients pursuing miraculous promises.

But with murderous interests arrayed against him, Harrison must use his old training, and battle his fear of technology, to expose the macabre price of donating your body to science.

About the Author

William Knight is a British born writer and technologist currently living and working in Wellington, New Zealand. A graduate engineer, he chased a portfolio career starting in acting, progressed to music, enjoyed a brief flirtation with handbag design, before being wired into technology.

As a freelance feature writer, he has written about the many successes and failings of technology for Computing, the Guardian, the Financial Times and the BBC.

The Donated, his first novel, was conceived from a New Scientist article in 2001 and was ten years in development. *XYZ* took a lot less time to finish, but far more time to start. And *The Algorithm* told William when it would be complete.

He's hoping to finish a follow-up to *The Donated*, in the next couple of years.

He continues to write, while maintaining a lively IT consultancy.

http://www.williamknight.info
https://www.facebook.com/WilliamKnightAuthor
william@williamknight.info

Printed in Great Britain
by Amazon